CW01499866

"From the beginning of her career to the end, she was never ashamed to enthral the reader's imagination." That wonderful sentence from literary scholar Edward Wagenknecht describes an even more wonderful writer, the astonishingly imaginative Marjorie Bowen (1885–1952). Who else would open a novella, *Julia Roseingrave*, with the Devil—or so it seems—ringing the bell on a lonely country house and demanding a room for the night? You'd need a will of iron to stop reading at that point. The story that follows duly blends terror, wonder and pity, while also being suffused with intense eroticism.

Such a combination is typical of Bowen: you will experience it again, even more powerfully, in *The Haunted Vintage*, initially published in 1921 and almost unfindable prior to this handsome new edition in the British Library's acclaimed series, Tales of the Weird. It's nonetheless among the finest works by a prolific, multi-talented author who has never quite received the acclaim she deserves.

For most of her adult life, Margaret Gabrielle Vere Long (née Campbell)—the neglected, largely self-educated daughter of a vaguely bohemian and theatrical family—was the very model of a professional writer. She scribbled her first book, the Renaissance swashbuckler, *The Viper of Milan,* when she was still a teenager. Published in 1906 under the penname Marjorie Bowen, it proved a surprising success and won the admiration of, among others, Mark Twain, who invited its then 21-year-old author to lunch. Years later, in his celebrated essay "The Lost Childhood", Graham Greene credited Bowen's zest in depicting an amoral anti-hero as the inspiration for his own career as a novelist.

7

For nearly five decades, until her death after a fall at age 67 in 1952, Bowen wrote indefatigably, six or seven hours a day, in part because she was the main support of a feckless second husband and three sons. She grew so productive that she began to employ a second pseudonym, George R. Preedy, mainly for works set in the 18th century, such as *The Courtly Charlatan,* a novelised account of the alchemist and adventurer, the Comte de Saint-Germain. But she also used the Preedy name for the intense psycho-drama, *The Devil Snar'd*, a short novel about an ancient crime and its malign influence on a troubled modern-day marriage—it's a hallucinatory work that might have emerged from the typewriter of Shirley Jackson. Long hard to find, it can now be read in an anthology, *The Devil Snar'd: Novels, Appreciations, Appendices* compiled by John C. Tibbetts, author of the book-length study, *The Furies of Marjorie Bowen.*

Still another pseudonym, Joseph Shearing, was mainly reserved for fictionalisations of historical crimes of passion, several of them, such as *Moss Rose* and *Blanche Fury*, translated into films. In all, Bowen produced—take a breath—approximately 150 novels and as many as 200 short stories. Few of them have wholly happy endings. As Bowen once wrote, "the men taste the brittleness of success, the women the limits of beauty". A lucky few achieve transcendence or even a kind of redemption.

Today, the best-known works in Bowen's vast output are her terror tales and *contes cruels*, several of them reprinted in British Library anthologies, including the Christmastime classic, "The Crown Derby Plate" (in *Sunless Solstice*), "They Found My Grave" (in *The Night Wire*), and "Kecksies" (in *Mortal Echoes*). Other reader favourites are the horrific and heartbreaking "Scoured Silk", and the very strange revenge tales, "Florence Flannery" and "The Avenging of Ann Leete". Unfortunately, several excellent collections of Bowen's short fiction are

THE HAUNTED
VINTAGE

THE HAUNTED
VINTAGE

MARJORIE BOWEN

With an introduction by
MICHAEL DIRDA

This edition first published in 2024 by
The British Library
96 Euston Road
London NW1 2DB

The Haunted Vintage was first published in 1921 by Odhams, London.

Introduction © 2024 Michael Dirda
Volume copyright © 2024 The British Library Board

Cataloguing in Publication Data
A catalogue record for this publication is available from the British Library

ISBN 978 0 7123 5586 5
e-ISBN 978 0 7123 6848 3

Cover and frontispiece design by Mauricio Villamayor
with illustration by Mag Ruhig
Text design and typesetting by Tetragon, London
Printed in England by CPI Group (UK) Ltd, Croydon, CR0 4YY

MIX
Paper | Supporting
responsible forestry
FSC
www.fsc.org   FSC® C171272

CONTENTS

now only available second-hand, the most important being *Twilight and Other Supernatural Romances,* opening with a substantial introduction by Jessica Amanda Salmonson and concluding with *Julia Roseingrave.* However, *The Bishop of Hell and Other Stories,* its contents selected by Bowen herself, has recently been reprinted in an inexpensive paperback and contains her most memorable tales of the strange and terrible. To supplement it, look for *The Grey Chamber: Stories and Essays,* edited by John C. Tibbetts. It reprints, among much else, a story that Bowen was especially fond of, the mind-boggling, surrealistic "The Sign-Painter and the Crystal Fishes". Nobody knows what it means but everyone agrees it's unforgettable.

Of Bowen's dozen or so supernaturally-inflected historical novels, only *Black Magic* (1909) retains some currency, partly because it was chosen by Dennis Wheatley, the author of *The Devil Rides Out,* for his Library of the Occult. Subtitled "A Tale of the Rise and Fall of Antichrist", this epic thriller, set during the Middle Ages, focuses on a student of the dark arts who rises to power in the Catholic Church. It consistently undermines the reader's expectations. Schemers become saints, murderers turn out to be self-sacrificing, and a diabolically wicked overreacher gradually earns our sympathy and even our admiration: "If I be a devil, I go whence I came... I have known Love, conquered it and by it have been vanquished. Whatsoever I am, I perish on the heights, but I do not descend from them."

The Haunted Vintage belongs in the same class as *Black Magic.* In a preface to a 1926 reissue Bowen wrote that it was "an attempt to gather, within one structure, the fantastic figures that still people (if shyly and furtively) neglected ruins, deep forests, and lonely rivers. Where man has been, and is no more, is the favourite haunt of such as these—old gods, old fiends, and creatures neither ghost nor fairy, but living in the borderland of dreams."

Set during what is probably the late 18th, or early 19th, century, the novel opens when Lally Duchene, once a close companion to the young Duke of Nassau, arrives at Eberbach Cloister, a former monastery that bears an evil reputation. Legend has it that Saint Bernard was tricked by the Devil—in the shape of a boar—into building on unholy ground. More recently, Eberbach has been repurposed as a prison, mainly for peasants who have violated the duke's strict forest laws, and as a madhouse for the insane. For ages beyond recall, the region—part of the German Rheingau—has also been known for its wine, though strange rumours surround its annual vintage or grape harvest. Secluded in a deep valley, Eberbach is bounded on all sides by hills and a dense, dark forest in which it is easy to get lost.

Love, whether forbidden, hopeless or rejected, nearly always forms a major theme in Bowen's fiction, and this novel is no exception. It turns out that Lally has been appointed commandant of this godforsaken outpost as punishment for an apparent attempt to seduce the Duke's intended bride, Pauline. Only Pauline, Lally and one other know that it wasn't merely an attempt—the two had been actual lovers. Still, Pauline's greatest ambition is to become Duchess of Nassau and nothing is going to stand in her way.

Despite Lally's roguish past, Bowen means for us to like her intelligent, self-aware protagonist—and we do: "He possessed... a whimsical humour which caused him to smile even at his own disasters; he had the cast of mind that sees the world as very small after all, and mankind as very insignificant." Nonetheless, Eberbach will test Lally to the utmost and then a little more than that.

To start, he finds Luy, the soldier assigned as his body-servant, inexplicably repellent. During his first tour of the prison, he then pauses, almost involuntarily, at the cell of a young girl "whose countenance seemed to him lovely with gentleness and innocence". She is in solitary confinement for "dissolute conduct"—but also rumoured to be a witch. When Lally later asks this Gertruda, whom he takes to be a peasant, if she used to labour in the fields at a nearby village, the girl answers that she knows nothing of such work. Lally quickly adds, "Yet men employed you at Kiedrich." To which she drily replies, "Yes, men employed me." The young man blushes.

In the dark evenings, Lally occasionally glimpses or thinks he glimpses a shadowy creature, doubtless a boar, nosing around the building where he sleeps. Sometimes, it is accompanied by a more upright shape, "dimly white" and wearing what looks to be a bright coronet. One day, just outside Gertruda's cell, Lally happens upon a strange gold chaplet of ancient workmanship. How it came to be there is unknown.

Throughout these pages, Bowen gradually intensifies her initial atmosphere of the forlorn and desolate, of both menace and enchantment. More and more, the looming, tangled forest beckons seductively, like similar forests in the pantheistic weird tales of Bowen's contemporaries, Arthur Machen and Algernon Blackwood. Yet inside Eberbach everything is kept almost fanatically spotless and clean. What's more, the cloister buildings apparently induce a kind of mental languor, sapping one's willpower. And its inhabitants are unsettling. The Lutheran pastor, Herr Sandemann, both ministers to the inmates and passes his evenings studying alchemy and ancient German superstitions. At one point, the unnervingly serene, imperturbable Gertruda even exclaims, "Who do you think I am?" There is no answer, but Lally, in her thrall, struggles against the allure of this enigmatic femme fatale. When she runs through the woods, Gertruda's "colouring seemed to blend with the colouring of the forest, so that she seemed part of every leaf and flower".

Rich in elaborate descriptions of both Nature and certain experiments in distilling rare essences, Bowen can also paint an arresting scene with just a few brush strokes. At one point, Lally observes some peasants at work one late summer afternoon: "Where the corn had been gathered and bound into sheaves and stacked, seven leaning together and a large one turned over all to form a thatch against possible rain, babies, watched by elder children, had been placed on some bright, clean, worn garment to sleep in the shade." It might be a tableau by Brueghel, shimmering with a haze of heat and sunlight.

Halfway through the book, the Duke of Nassau—incognito—arrives at Eberbach, eventually followed by Pauline. In what way, will this prince, as Luy mysteriously complains, "spoil everything"? At Eberbach the duke, a somewhat pale aesthete to begin with, grows noticeably wan and mystical, especially after an ancient temple is unexpectedly discovered, one apparently devoted to the worship of Mithras, a god of light and fire and human sacrifice.

Ford Madox Ford once argued that a novel should accelerate and intensify as it nears its end. In *The Haunted Vintage* Bowen practises just such a *progression d'effet*. As the long-anticipated vintage nears, she enhances the novel's already heavy, hothouse atmosphere, increasing the sensation of cloying over-ripeness, like that of a grape about to burst its skin or a hot day before the storm breaks. Episodes of ecstasy and phantasmagoria mix with allusions to nixies and kobolds; there is talk of strange "foreigners" who help harvest the grapes. Are pagan forces covertly gathering for an assault on this decayed citadel of Christianity? By the time the vintage finally arrives, Bowen has screwed the tension to an almost unbearable degree: what will happen to Lally and the Duke, Pauline and Gertruda? One can hardly turn the pages too quickly, as the natural and the supernatural blur, then dazzle, then overwhelm.

One bit of advice: readers used to fast-moving modern fiction will need to take their time with *The Haunted Vintage*. It's a slow burn. Instead, savour the sumptuous language and shivery innuendos, pause to wonder and worry about the various characters. As Bowen once said, "the intellect rejects what cannot be proved" and yet, beneath the surface of rationality, "the emotions accept what cannot be explained". Perhaps *The Haunted Vintage* can be best summed up in the Latin phrase so beloved by Arthur Machen: *Omnia exeunt in mysterium*—Everything ends in mystery.

MICHAEL DIRDA
2024

MICHAEL DIRDA is a Pulitzer Prize-winning critic and longtime book columnist for *The Washington Post*. He is the author of the memoir, *An Open Book*, several collections of essays, and the Edgar Award-winning, *On Conan Doyle*. His current research focuses on classic mysteries, weird tales, and adventure fiction.

A NOTE FROM THE PUBLISHER

PREFACE

From the 1926 edition of The Haunted Vintage *published by Thomas Nelson & Sons, London.*

The short extract at the beginning of this book is taken from a queer little book picked up in a dusty byway in London. It was apparently printed and published in English at Frankfort in 1837, under the title of *Bubbles from the Brunnen of Nassau*, by "And Old Man," whom I have recently discovered to be Sir Charles Bond Head, Bt. It is a refreshing and charming piece of writing, and from a very pleasing account of the Monastery of Eberbach on the Rhine, I have conceived the following romance.

The story is an attempt to gather, within one structure, the fantastic figures that still people (if shyly and furtively) neglected ruins, deep forests, and lonely rivers.

Where man has been, and is no more, is the favourite haunt of such as these—old gods, old fiends, and creatures neither ghost nor fairy, but living in the borderland of dreams.

While they are undisturbed, who is to know of them?

They have the wilderness to themselves, and flee at the sound of the trespasser's footsteps, though he may catch the echo of their sighs and of their laughter in the trees.

But sometimes some human comes to inhabit the very heart of such a fastness, and then he finds himself drawn in, enmeshed and captured by a phantasmagoria which will cause the human passions to droop drowsily, and the material world to become remote as shadows over distant fields.

The new Commandant of Eberbach, Captain Lally Duchene, came to the old and ancient monastery in the Rhinegau, fairest of all the haunted lands.

These Rhinelands were dedicated to Bacchus. Mithras, the oldest god in the world and he whose worship was most universal, had his altars there! Here the old Kobolds that haunt the silver-mines watched the Boar lead St. Bernard of Clairvaux through the dense forests to the place where Eberbach Cloister was to be raised, *on who knows what unholy ground*.

This tale tells of two men who came to Eberbach long after the monks were dead, when the altars were dismantled, when sweet grain, hay and harvested roots were heaped and stored over the old tombs of the princely bishops and knights—when the wild forest, encroaching on holy ground, had grown close to the edge of the vineyards where once the grapes grew for the sacramental wine. Of these two (who both loved the same woman, and for her had fallen into hatred of each other) only one returned to the world in human fashion. *But who shall say if he was the happier?*

MARJORIE BOWEN.
Sandhurst, Kent,
June 1925.

I suddenly saw close before me, at the bottom of a most sequestered valley, the object of my journey, namely, the very ancient monastery of Eberbach.

The sylvan loveliness and the peaceful retirement of this spot I strongly feel that it is quite impossible to describe. Almost surrounded by hills, or, rather, mountains, clothed with forest trees, one does not expect to find at the bottom of such a valley an immense solitary building, which in size and magnificence not only corresponds with the bold features of the country, but seems worthy of a place in any of the largest capitals of Europe... Three or four of the monks of this once wealthy establishment are all that now remain in existence, and their abode has ever since been used partly as a government prison and partly as a public asylum for lunatics, the whole of which was admirably kept in complete subjection by a garrison of eight soldiers.

Bubbles from the Brunnen of Nassau, by an Old Man published in English at Frankfort O.M., 1837

CHAPTER I

The new commandant of the prison and lunatic asylum of Eberbach took up the lamp and went to his door and listened.

It was his first night in the old monastery, and he could not rid himself of an intolerable sensation of strangeness. He had arrived when it was dark, after a ride of hours through the solitary forest, and he had no clear impression of his new place of abode; his mind retained but a confused picture of a huge building and vineyard and cathedral in the moonlit valley and an interior of great corridors, rambling rooms, dark stairs, Gothic windows, and great statues in unexpected places. He had not yet inspected the building, and he had given but a glance at the eight soldiers who formed his garrison. On his table lay the keys and a list of the prisoners and lunatics now under his charge.

He stood at the door, listening. He was certain that the utter silence had been broken by a distant wailing. He knew that he would have many strange sounds to hear while in his present employment, but to-night his senses were so alert and his nerves so taut, that he must listen to this cry and trace it to its origin.

It was not repeated.

The beams of the old-fashioned horn lamp cast long rays down the rough stone corridor, showed dimly one or two doors, then faded into utter darkness. Though it was full summer the air was damp, and yet not fresh.

The commandant felt a slight chill touch his flesh. He returned to his room and set the lamp on the high stone mantelpiece.

It was an extraordinary room—perhaps that which had belonged to the prior when Eberbach had been one of the most flourishing and magnificent monasteries in Germany. Two large, splendid mullioned windows had been curtained across by a length of coarse green cloth; the tessellated pavement, in worn shades of blue and red, was partly covered by a square of rough dark carpet; the walls, which had the hooks for tapestry, were rough and newly whitewashed; in one corner the shadows filled a hole which the commandant guessed had been once occupied by a holy statue. The chimney-piece was very finely carved in stone, with deep cut figures of beasts and fruit, and above was a picture set into the wall, and so smoke blackened that it was impossible to discern the subject. A soldier's bed with coarse blankets, a camp chair and table, a shelf with a common ewer and basin, and a few pegs, were the sole furnishings of the room.

"The Duke is economical," sneered the commandant.

His own handsome and numerous luggage, still strapped, was piled about the room and looked out of place in the grim chamber, as did the young officer himself, with his elegance and powder and spotless Nassau uniform. He seemed a strange choice for such a post, and as if he was conscious of this, and scornful both with those who had sent him to such a spot and himself for coming.

He sat on the one chair, absorbed in the pool of shadow that the high-placed lamp left untouched, with one hand to his chin and the other hanging down.

The silence was absolute. He was surprised not to hear the rustling of leaves; he had thought that the forest sloped down to the very doors of the old monastery; that had been the impression of the darkling ride. He was anxious for daylight, that he might explore this curious place; the novelty of it exhilarated him, despite his contempt of the whole affair, for he was used to a city and a court.

With a gentle movement his half-open door was pushed wide. Luy, the soldier who was to act as his body-servant, looked into the shadowed chamber.

"You are very soft footed," said the commandant, without moving, "and I thought that you were in bed."

"It is not as late as it seems, Herr Captain," replied the man respectfully. "And I thought your Excellency wanted the valises unstrapped."

The commandant was eyeing the man with a kind of deep curiosity.

"Were you servant to my predecessor?" he asked.

"Yes, Herr Captain."

"What kind of a man was he? Like me?"

"Oh, no!" the fellow grinned, looking up from the straps he was undoing. "Like the Herr Sergeant."

"The right type for such a place," observed the commandant. "What do you think of me?" he added abruptly.

The soldier shut his lips. He was a small, lean type, with a shrewd, ugly, and remarkable face.

"Well?" urged the commandant, who still never moved from his careless, tired attitude.

"I have lived in Wiesbaden, Herr Captain," replied the man quietly and slowly. "I have been here only a few months."

"Yes?"

The fellow looked up, half impertinently. "I *heard* of your Excellency when I was in Wiesbaden."

"I suppose so. What do you know of me, eh?"

"I know—that you are Lally Duchene, Herr Graf."

The tone in which the man spoke—that of a strange cringing insolence—was new to the commandant; it interested him.

He looked through the shadows at the kneeling figure of the man who had also lived in Wiesbaden when that town had been his residence.

It was curious that they should come together with this intimacy. How often might not this man have watched his coach roll through the streets of Wiesbaden; how often had he not turned over his tongue fabulous, scandalous, wild stories of Lally Duchene, the foreigner, the Duke's friend?

"You never thought to see me here," remarked the commandant.

"Nor myself, Herr Graf," returned the soldier; then, with an underlining of his former touch of impertinence, "We are both of us *unfortunate*, Herr Graf."

The young captain laughed. "The fellow thinks of me as a fallen favourite," he thought. "He and his companions mouth over strange versions of my story; the dark heart of it they never guess."

Still in his lounging attitude, and with no change in voice or look, he yet put the other very decidedly in his place of inferior and servant.

"I think that your name is Luy. I shall call you that as you are to be my body-servant and it is the custom of this simple place. Perhaps you are used to the larger licence of a town; here, among the few of you, with such a responsibility, there must be a strict discipline and obedience."

"It has always been strict, Herr Graf," answered the soldier, now without that insolent inflexion.

"I was told that your sergeant had you well in hand."

The man opened the valises; curiosity showed in his handling of the clothes, few but fine—mantles of rich cloth, belts and boots of expensive leather, cravats and falls, ruffles and handkerchiefs of elaborate needlework, exquisite linen.

"You need not take all those things out," said Lally. "There is nowhere to put them."

"There are plenty of cupboards I could bring in to-morrow, Herr Graf."

"To-morrow we will see. Eberbach must be curious by daylight."

"Curious, indeed!" Luy was animated, eager, "It was a queer place to put criminals and lunatics, Herr Graf."

"Why, very proper," answered Lally Duchene, "since isolated in this great forest, they can have no hope of escape. To break away from Eberbach would be but to perish in the wood."

"Maybe, Herr Graf, but Eberbach is no fit dwelling, even for a madman."

"Too lonely, eh?"

"Haunted, Herr Graf, haunted!"

The commandant smiled; he had expected this. He knew the easy credulity of the vulgar, their gaping appetite for the marvellous, their fear of nature and their instant attribution to the supernatural of her unknown aspects.

"The wood frightens you," he said.

"It was a wild beast chose the spot, Herr Graf," replied Luy. "A little boar, who appeared to Saint Bernard and bid him build his monastery in this valley. You may see the grinning pig's face carved all over the building."

"That is a stupid, unromantical tale," remarked the commandant. "Are any of the monks yet in existence?"

"A few at Kiedrich, they say, Herr Graf, but I have never been so far. They must be old men, as it is twenty-two years since the bishop inherited the monastery—ten since it came to the Duke."

"Give me that paper I put aside with the keys," said Lally, "that I may be a little prepared for this inspection to-morrow."

When this was put into his hand he bade Luy bring the lamp nearer, and, as the man held it, scanned the list of those unfortunates over whose existence he was now absolute master.

He found that he was in charge of two hundred and fifty prisoners and a hundred lunatics.

The paper, which had been prepared by the former commandant, very neatly showed the classes into which these were divided and sub-divided.

On the ground floor the men and women undergoing first sentences were separated in groups of various trades, such as weaving, tailoring, and carpentering, and worked under the direction of an overseer. These numbered about two hundred, the majority being men.

Above were the old offenders, or those convicted twice, in solitary confinement—forty-five men and five women.

In another and older part of the monastery were the lunatics, about sixty of whom were paupers and supported by the Nassau Government, the others being persons of means, whose superior maintenance was paid for by their families. These lived together in groups of eight or nine, an iron cage being provided in the corner of the room for any who might prove refractory, the more desperate cases being confined upstairs in solitary cells, and the most dangerous of all being isolated in a kind of summer-house in the orchard.

There followed many details of the plan and management of the prison that was almost entirely self-supporting, and but rarely visited save by some curiosity-impelled traveller.

There was also a list of the names of all the prisoners, with their crimes and trades attached, and one of the lunatics, with an account of the violence and duration of their terrible disorder.

There was no doctor in the asylum save among the madmen, but the list stated that one might be procured at Kiedrich, distant half a day's ride through the forest.

Lally Duchene read no more. His mind wearied of all this dry detail, and shrank from the thought of the conscientious labours of his predecessor, who had toiled in Eberbach for seventeen years without recognition or change.

"Shall I be here seventeen years?" he wondered as he bade Luy set back the lamp.

The speculation was whimsical. He rose and looked with distaste at the camp bed. He noticed that Luy was eyeing him covertly, and curtly dismissed the fellow.

It did not please him to find this man from Wiesbaden in this solitude, where he had thought to be unknown and unnoticed.

Now, of course, everyone, even the prisoners, would talk over Lally Duchene.

What strange tales would they not mouth round between them; what wild reports and crazy surmises; what desperate imaginings would twine about his rise and his downfall! They would look upon him as no better than themselves, condemned to exile, imprisonment, shorn of his splendour in a disgrace only gilded by the clemency of the Duke.

Lally Duchene thought of all the curious eyes he would have to face on the morrow. He was used to curiosity, to envy, to dislike, to being marked out and pointed at, the butt of veiled malice and cowardly scorn; here he had looked for peace—forgetfulness, perhaps. He wondered if he could get this Luy changed. But the mischief was done; the man had certainly already spread the gossip of Wiesbaden through Eberbach.

He stood irresolute, tired, wishful of the oblivion of sleep, yet reluctant to stretch himself on the hard, strange bed and face perhaps frightful dreams, longings, and remorses.

After all, what did it matter if all of them knew all that Wiesbaden knew of him? No one was aware of the reality save the Duke and one other.

And they were his underlings, bound to obey and use a respectful demeanour; he had complete power over all—soldiers, prisoners, and lunatics.

The early summer night was chilly in this thick-walled room. He walked up and down with an instinct to keep himself warm, then stopped abruptly, for the pacing gave him an impression that he, too, was a prisoner.

He went to the window and looked out into the fresh pure darkness. As he leant against the wide stone ledge he felt his heart beating strongly against the hand that gripped the sill.

CHAPTER II

When Lally Duchene drew the rough curtains aside from his deep-set windows next morning it was with a large sense of change and freedom.

He did not feel like a man suddenly thrust into hopeless exile, but more as one swiftly liberated from a tiresome bondage, as if all that old splendid life in Wiesbaden had been a gorgeous captivity.

He wondered if all men violently and unceremoniously hurled from their high positions felt this sense of relief.

Yet how he had enjoyed that other life; striven for it, exulted in it, exploited to the full every minute of it!

No one could have ever relished success with more appetite than he, made a more magnificent use of power and opportunities. Looking back over the years in Wiesbaden, he could not blame himself for a single chance lost or misused.

And yet he felt, for the moment at least, neither regret nor repining. Perhaps it was the reaction after long strain, keen anxiety, deep agitation, and the shock of the final crash of all his fortunes.

He possessed, too, a whimsical humour which caused him to smile even at his own disasters; he had the cast of mind that sees the world as very small after all, and mankind as very insignificant.

He could visualise himself at Wiesbaden, a gay, eager, triumphant figure, climbing, climbing, then suddenly cast down; he could visualise the Duke, his friend, the keystone of his fortunes and then his bitter enemy, unchanging, omnipotent, worshipped in this small territory that was his, seemingly placed, in his steady radiance and his cool power, above any stroke of fate, yet, after all, in the final issue more smitten than Lally Duchene; he could visualise the woman, desirable and fatal, yet somehow featureless in the recollection—and smile at all three.

With his elbows on the window-ledge and his face in his hands, he looked out on the early morning.

His room was higher than he had thought it to be; he was amazed at the height of the building, at its size and magnificence.

The valley lay green beneath him, almost filled with orchards and a huge vineyard, and opposite began the outlying trees of the great forest that spread from the Mainz to the Rhine.

The isolation was complete; the nearest human dwellings were at Kiedrich, the other side of the forest, and impossible to find without a guide. Beyond this was the former residence of the bishops of Mainz, the Tower of Sharfenstein, now the property of the Baron von Ritter, a nobleman who was nearly always at Wiesbaden. Beyond this, several hours journeying brought one to the valley of Schlangenbad, one of the watering-places, tiny and remote, that served to swell the revenues of the Duke. On the other side the Rhinegau stretched to the river's edge, and was only inhabited by peasants absorbed in their daily toil.

Lally Duchene knew this; the position of Eberbach had been drily pointed out to him on the map of Nassau when the Duke had given those curt orders for him to take up this strange post; but the solitude that he now felt was not the solitude that he had imagined when in Wiesbaden.

There was a softness in the air, a radiance in the sky, a majesty and wonder in the fringes of the great wood, a strangeness and freshness in everything that forbade depression, at least to one of Lally Duchene's temperament.

He came from an Irish-French family. His great-grandfather had followed Patrick Sarsfield to France nearly a hundred years before; a Parisian heiress had given a foreign name to the exile; and the family—adventurers by disposition, need and necessity scattered all over Europe. Lally's father had settled in Nassau, buying property there with the proceeds of his early adventures in Canada, but he brought a French wife with him, and there was no drop of German blood in Lally, though he was a subject of the Duke and an officer in his army.

The father and mother had wandered away from Nassau and died in Paris, but Lally had founded his fortunes in Wiesbaden and on the deep friendship of the Duke, who was of the same age, though of so different a disposition. As Lally Duchene—count by a French, and marquis by a papal, patent, known as "Graf" in the Duchy where both titles were considered doubtful—surveyed the valley of Eberbach and the forest slopes opposite, he wondered if he had been wise to stay at the court of Wiesbaden; he was of a race and a tradition to have succeeded in larger fields. Well, there was time yet; he was only twenty-five.

He turned from the window and took up the list and keys from where Luy had put them last night beside the lamp.

Strange that he, in his downfall, should have complete power over these hundreds of human beings—outcast wretches no doubt, but still human beings. Standing in the generous sunshine that poured into the old chamber like a rush of sparkling wine cast into a stone cup, he glanced down the list of the prisoners' offences. Nearly all offences against the Duke—killing his game, cutting down his trees, carting away grass and leaves, breaking in some way his minute forest laws. There were no murderers, and but a few thieves. Those women who had not robbed the ducal preserves were marked with the one word, "*dissolute*."

"They are none of them criminals," thought Lally Duchene.

He had but little sense of discipline or law; had he been the Duke, Eberbach would have been empty.

But he had his ideas of soldierly honour, conventional enough—as long as he was in the Duke's service he would obey him; he might be trusted to rule Eberbach even though his heart would never be in the work.

It was possible, he thought, that the Duke had chosen Eberbach as his place of punishment that he might realise the power of the ruler of Nassau and how rigorously their petty offences against him were punished.

The Duke was but a German princeling, yet as absolute within the narrow limits of his territory as any sultan or shah. Lally thought him capable of wishing to remind the man he now hated of his despotic power. Lally, at least, reflected on this aspect of the matter.

As he studied the list he remembered that the Duke, if he wished, could put "Lally Duchene, self-styled count and marquis, and sometime captain in our armies," thereon for any offence he chose to invent.

The foreigner, whose family had never taken root in the Duchy, whose sole hold on any position had been the personal favour of the Duke, who had been envied and hated for his good luck, might safely be degraded, despoiled, and imprisoned without fear of a protest from anyone.

Lally thought over his relations and connections, numerous and loyal, but scattered and poor—soldiers of fortune, free lances or frank adventurers. None of them could help him. He saw his own position as entirely perilous; he was as much at the Duke's mercy as an insect held between a finger and thumb, unharmed as yet but unable to escape.

Since he held himself as the Duke's equal in everything, save the accident of position, this was a sore thought for his pride, but one that would not be lightly dismissed.

It accompanied him as, with his list and keys, the sergeant, and Luy, he went round his new domain. In Eberbach, at least, he was as absolute as the Duke of Nassau.

His first impression was of the cleanliness and freshness of the building. All the windows were open, the walls whitewashed, the woodwork scrubbed, and the air as fragrant as that of the valley without. He remarked on this to the sergeant, who replied that it was the greater part of the prisoners' punishment to be forced to this cleanliness, foreign enough to their nature and habits.

"Are they all, then, such low wretches?" asked Lally.

"They are criminals, Herr Graf, or they would not be here in Eberbach," replied the sergeant.

"One can take a handful of grass or a pile of leaves from a forest without being a criminal," remarked Lally. "Do you think it is so easy to remember when alone in a wilderness of trees that it belongs to the Duke?"

"It is not difficult to remember, Herr Graf," said the man stubbornly, "for everything in Nassau belongs to the Duke."

Lally saw a smile on the impudent face of Luy, and wondered if the words had been spoken with any meaning. The sergeant was a solid fellow, but there was no doubt that he had heard Luy's flamboyant tales.

Lally disliked the little red-eyed soldier more than ever. He was sorry that choice had fallen on so disagreeable a person to be his body-servant.

They descended the white stairs to the ground floor and proceeded down a long whitewashed passage, Luy, who carried the keys, unlocking every door as they came to it and stepping aside for the commandant to see his prisoners.

The partitions between the monks' cells had been taken down, so that four or five cubicles made one large room. In these chambers the prisoners, in groups of eight, worked under the direction of an overseer elected from among their number.

The first room accommodated the weavers, who were making rough cloth for the use of the establishment; the second carpenters, who were turning rude chairs; the third shoemakers, sitting crouched over their work; the fourth tailors, who were cutting and sewing the materials that their companions had made. They were all clean, sober, dull, and silent; very few of them even looked up as the door was opened. Besides these there were, the sergeant explained to Lally, a number employed in forestry and agriculture, besides the cleaning and repairing of the building, so that Eberbach was entirely self-supporting. It did not seem such an ill life to Lally. He had to admit to himself that, if the crimes were slight, so was the punishment.

"These people have no need to greatly dread a visit to Eberbach," he said.

"They dislike to leave their homes, Herr Graf," replied the sergeant.

Lally Duchene was silent; he had never had a home.

On the other side of the building he visited the women, passing first through some splendid cloisters which framed a fine herb garden and a beautiful stone well.

On the walls here hung four and twenty dark and stiff oil-paintings of monks, all exactly alike.

"Why do they keep them here?" asked the commandant.

The sergeant believed that it was because no one had troubled to give orders for their removal.

The women were found to be as soberly employed as the men in washing, sewing, basket-making, and knitting woollen garments. They sat close together, talking in whispers, and fell into an abashed silence when their new master looked in on them.

Women were also employed, said the sergeant, in the kitchens, and sometimes in the orchards or gardens.

Lally next visited the old refectory, which was now used as a school for the youngest offenders. He there found among the new benches a person whose humble existence had been hardly mentioned to him—the pastor.

A dull, colourless-looking individual, he was employed in imparting religious instruction and an elementary knowledge of arithmetic, reading, writing, singing, and weaving.

Lally exchanged a few words with this pastor, who said that he held a service here three times every Sunday.

"Why not in the cathedral?" asked Lally.

The Lutheran replied that that was too large, and used as a store-house for grain and hay.

Lally went his way with the artless singing of the imprisoned children in his ears. He inspected the kitchens, the stores, the stables; everywhere blanched floors, whitewashed boards, spotlessly clean people moving quietly about their appointed tasks.

"The Duke's arrangements are admirable," said Lally, with a hint of a sneer.

He entered the great cathedral attached to the monastery, and saw bundles of sticks and grass and chaff lying on the rich tombs of bishops and priors, some windows bright with painted glass, some plastered up with mud, parts filled with a rude wooden structure that served for a granary, parts open and bare to the now strong sunshine.

He would have visited the summer-house where the fiercest lunatics were confined, but the sergeant warned him that it was best not to disturb these; so he passed on to the other madmen, who seemed cheerful enough in their little groups, and only different from the other inhabitants of Eberbach by reason of their idleness. The review of those in solitary confinement was not so pleasant to Lally.

The melancholy, the ferocity, the gloomy laughter, and hideous aspect of these unfortunates were such as to make the young commandant glad when the last cell was locked again.

Nor was the visit to those criminals placed in solitary confinement much more relishable by a man like Lally Duchene. Deprived of the great solace of work, entirely cut off from all knowledge of the world, these wretches often spent three or even five years in these tiny cells.

The one privilege ever accorded them, as the result of persistent good behaviour, was the allotment of some task with which to occupy their gloomy leisure.

Thus the first cell that the sergeant opened showed a man at work on a coffin for a maniac who had just died, and in the second cell the occupant, with a kind of ferocious zest, was mending a pair of boots.

The others sat idle and listless in a corner in attitudes of absolute dejection, altered by an upward glance of peculiar anxiety when the door was opened.

The cells were clean, and each of the small windows was open on the fine air of the forest, while the prisoners all seemed in good health, but their expression was such as to make Lally Duchene wish that he did not have to look at them nor to catch the glance of bitter despondency with which they beheld the doors of their dungeon close.

The sergeant told him that the two last cells contained women, and Lally inwardly winced.

When the first of these was opened the prisoner sprang up with hysterical violence and hurried towards the door with such impetuosity that the sergeant slammed it forcibly in her face.

"She is the mother of little children," he said, as if in apology for her lack of fortitude, and proceeded to unlock the last cell. There stood before Lally in the full light of the little window a young girl whose countenance seemed to him lovely with gentleness and innocence.

She was the first of those in solitary confinement who did not raise desperate eyes; she stood looking down, her features convulsed with an expression of grief, as if she with difficulty refrained from bursting into tears. Her slight figure was leaning against the wall for support, her dark head pressed against the whitewashed surface.

Her misery was so evident that Lally stepped back, and they locked the door.

"What is her crime?" asked the commandant.

The sergeant pointed to the board outside the entrance to the cell, on which was written the name and offence of the occupant.

Lally Duchene looked up and read: *Gertruda Gerhardt*, and underneath, in larger letters, the one word, *Dissolute*.

CHAPTER III

That afternoon Lally Duchene left the monastery and went out alone into the woods. His new post did not seem as yet very onerous. The establishment ran smoothly in its familiar grooves without any interference from him; both soldiers and prisoners were perfectly disciplined, and the daily life went on with uninterrupted monotony.

The new commandant could find nothing to alter, nothing to suggest; he looked on the strange little world about him more as a spectator than as a master. Presently, perhaps, he would find his place; now his office seemed a sinecure.

He was acutely conscious that his little garrison was aware of his story—the public version of it—and all faintly hostile, perhaps faintly contemptuous.

He was sure that both these feelings were more than faint in the mind of the Lutheran pastor, whose manner had been frigid and unfriendly.

A wonder whether, after all, he would find the life bearable, a reaction from last night's sense of relief and freedom, was checked by the exceeding loneliness of the scene through which he moved.

The sergeant had directed him to a spot from which a fine view of the river could be obtained, and to this he made his way, already filled with a dim desire to see a glimpse of the world from which he had been so rudely severed. It was a cloudless afternoon of bright sunshine which, filtering through innumerable leaves, made a pattern of radiant light and transparent shade in the grove of oaks through which Lally ascended the mountain-side.

The foliage, the grass, the flowers, had yet all the freshness of spring while expanding in the luxuriance of summer; the late violet, primrose, and cyclamen yet lingered in the thick damp mosses, and in the undergrowth that separated the far-apart trees were the white petals of the first wild roses and the tiny stars of the strawberry plant.

It was an enchanting period of the year, and Lally Duchene, who knew little of nature save in the autumn hunting season, was startled by the sheer loveliness of his surroundings.

The minute objects along his path attracted him by brilliant and persistent beauty—a cobweb in the shadow, which had saved it from destruction, the pearls of dew hanging on the almost invisible threads; the small, vivid cups of the mosses; the strong, moist blooms of the little curled away flowers, the purity, colour, and sheen of these, so different to any court bouquet; the young golden-red shoots round the boles of the giant oaks—all these things fascinated him with a deep delight as he slowly made his way up the hillside, guided by notches cut by the woodmen on every third tree.

Without this help he would certainly never have found the track, so twisting and tortuous was the unpathed ascent to the top of the mountain that on this side shut in the valley of Eberbach. Presently the oaks, the undergrowth, the grass, moss, and flowers, gave way to a plantation of firs; between the straight red trunks was nothing save a thick carpet of needles and a few bright hardy plants vivid in the auburn shadows.

Lally found himself at the top of the hill.

His eyes, which had become accustomed to a close range and intimate objects, were startled by a sudden large and distant view of seemingly boundless extent, which instantly impressed him as the most marvellous prospect which he had ever beheld.

The view which thus flashed on him in the full dazzle of summer light was that of the Rhinegau blooming with vineyards, rice and corn-fields, hop gardens, and orchards of plum, almond, and apples which had in some instances not wholly lost their blossoms. Beyond the river curved from Johannesburg to Mainz, the water one golden glitter, and again, beyond the farther bank, an immense fertile and lovely country faded into the soft blue of the distance.

There was no boat on the river, no dwelling-house in sight, but here and there might be discerned the figure of a peasant—the brown garb of a man or the white kerchief of a woman—bent low amid the crops or vines, the brilliant, fresh green of which showed already a few feet above the rich earth.

To Lally's quick mind this wide and gorgeous scene depicted the abundance and splendour of the world. The vineyards, the fruit-trees, the corn, the river, the women, the unbounded horizon and the dimly sensed cities just visible through the sun mists of the distance—was it not a vision of life, of all life could hope to contain? At least it symbolised all that Lally Duchene had ever endeavoured to achieve.

He sat down by one of the fir-trunks and took off his hat, and gazed deeply at the opulent prospect as one might drink strongly of heady wine.

In his youth and grace and ease of pose, in his air of eager vitality, he was no unfitting figure for the foreground of the picture at which he looked.

The Nassau uniform and buff belt set off a figure tall and strong; the dark hair, that showed reddish in a powerful light, was turned back, too thick, too stiffly curling, from a face characteristic of Latin blood in the dark complexion, short, high, arched nose, full lips, wide golden eyes, heavy sweeping brows, and the vivid expression of animation and keenness indicating senses alert and perfect and a disposition passionately amorous of life.

Combed and powdered, subdued and correct in Wiesbaden, he had not looked more notable than many another gentleman; here in the fir-grove, bathed in sunlight, he seemed both unusual and splendid.

It was not natural for him to remain long in a contemplative mood, and he soon rose and gave a last half-defiant glance at the entrancing prospect.

"Had I not been a fool," he said to himself, "I should not be outside all that."

After he had taken a few return steps through the belt of firs he saw beneath him what he might have seen during his ascent had he thought to give a backward glance—the valley of Eberbach, with the cathedral and monastery in the midst.

The view from which he had just turned away might be taken as symbolical of life's fullest fruition; this scene as surely represented seclusion from the world, negation of human instincts, and a complete loneliness; yet the view was, though in so wholly a different manner, of equal loveliness. Magnificent, large, and stately as a king's palace, the monastery, with colonnades, towers, and spires, orchards, gardens, fir plantations, and vineyard, showed as strangely in the empty valley as if it had been created by the stroke of an enchanter's wand.

So completely enclosed was the monastery, on one side by the hills, on the other by the forest; so lonely was the valley, untraced by any path or road, that no picture of more utter retirement from the world could well be imagined. The monks of St. Bernard who had wished to say farewell to life could not have better chosen the spot in which to pass their monotonous lives; here indeed, forgotten by all, they themselves might forget. Lally wondered if any of them had ever climbed to the brow of the hill and looked at the vineyards, with the women working among them; at the river and the distant towers of Mainz; or if they had for ever remained in the valley, without regret or longing.

So splendid, regal, and stately did this church and palace, which was fit to adorn a large city, look, that it seemed a sour irony that it should be used for confining criminals and lunatics.

Lally, descending through the oak-groves, could imagine himself one of the knight heroes of the wild old Rhine legends coming suddenly upon an enchanted castle where some beautiful woman was imprisoned.

He thought, not for the first time that day, of the girl: in solitary confinement. No fairy princess this, but a poor, degraded creature, shamed and punished; and he was the jailer.

Certainly he had misjudged her character from her face; she had seemed to him of a childlike innocence. Dissolute! What did they mean by dissolute?

Lally paused, leaning against one of the oak-trees, and stared down at the noble building in the valley.

Dissolute—a word associated with cities, with a different type of woman, with women such as—

He checked his thoughts with a certain violence. If they meant what he thought they might mean by this ugly word, there was a certain lady might be, in other circumstances, placed beside this wretched girl—an amazing, a horrible, an unendurable reflection.

This Gertruda (he recalled that the name meant a witch) looked as if she was a peasant. He associated her with the great forest or with a little hidden village like Kiedrich, but it might be that she came from some town, and was indeed rooted and grown in ugly vices. He would like to have asked her history, but to show any interest in the one prisoner with charm and youth would, with his history, have been to too surely provoke a blaze of comment, a grin of meaning, in his watchful little garrison, in the dull pastor, in the sharp-eyed prisoners themselves. News of it would surely even reach the Duke—and that other woman in Wiesbaden.

He was not at all sure of Luy—by no means certain that he was not a spy—some creature of the Duke's sent to pry and note, report and sneak information of his doings into Wiesbaden. The Duke affected loftiness, a cold generosity, but Lally did not believe in this; he had no great credulity as to the virtues of mankind.

Slowly he descended towards Eberbach. The valley was in warm shadow, but the spires of the cathedral caught the golden light of heaven, which was refulgent with the deepening hue of the late afternoon.

The loneliness of the place suddenly smote Lally as with a physical pain. Was he to endure months, years, of this? Never seeing more of the world than might be glimpsed from the pine-grove at the top of the hill? Never to have any company but that of lunatics and prisoners?

He hastened through the fir plantations that surrounded the monastery, and turned into the great gate surmounted by colossal figures of St. John, the Virgin, and St. Bernard, mutilated but still bearing traces of their original brilliant colouring. As he paused to glance up at their majestic figures he was accosted by a man who rode rapidly up on a small donkey.

"Eh, Herr Captain, I have been waiting to make your acquaintance."

Lally looked at him with a leap of hope, followed by instant disappointment, for the fellow was commonplace, not young, shabby—no kindred spirit here.

"I am the doctor," he explained, rather disconcerted by Lally's patrician air—a little grandiloquent, a little sneering—which was neither understood nor liked in Nassau, and also stamped him at once as a foreigner.

"You live here?" asked the new commandant drily.

The little man explained that he came from Kiedrich, and unless specially sent for rode over once a week. Monday was his day. This was a particular visit to make the acquaintance of the new governor of Eberbach.

"The place is very much understaffed," replied Lally indifferently. "There should be resident doctors, a secretary, a larger garrison."

The doctor protested.

"Eberbach is extraordinarily healthy, Herr Captain; it is surprising how little illness there is."

"Do any of your maniacs ever recover, Herr doctor?"

"Not often. On the other hand, they seldom die."

"A great blessing, doubtless," observed Lally drily.

He looked up at the great figure of the Madonna in her faded blue robe, standing, with her attendant saints, in clear light and shade against the background of the sun-flushed woods.

He knew that the doctor lingered in the expectation of an invitation to supper, yet could not bring himself to give it. He was not used to troubling about those who were indifferent to him, nor did he find it easy to assume the manners of perfunctory civility. He was also perfectly aware that this man disliked him, and he thought it foolish that they should inflict each other with their company.

But the doctor did not go; his small, fair eyes were full of curiosity; all the details of the young man's person would soon be spread through the village of Kiedrich, where everyone had already heard the story of Lally Duchene.

"You will find the method of governing Eberbach admirable, Herr Graf. The last commandant devoted his life to the work."

"It is admirable, within limits," replied Lally. "Once it is permitted to herd and confine together people for picking leaves and grass not their own—why, it could not be done better."

"Why, you would not complain of the game laws?" cried the startled doctor. "That would be to exclaim against His Serene Highness!"

"And that would never do," smiled Lally. He saw that the doctor, like most of the Duke's subjects, regarded their sovereign with almost superstitious awe and reverence, and this both irritated and amused his cynical mood.

"I daresay," pursued the doctor, "that the most forlorn wretch under your charge, Herr Captain, is happier than the miserable Popish monks who once enclosed themselves here."

"I believe these monks were happy enough," replied Lally. "Miserable men could not have built this magnificence."

The doctor glanced at the monastery buildings. It was obvious that it had never occurred to him that they were splendid; to him Eberbach was just a Government building with which he was proud to be connected.

"There are some bad cases here," he said, bringing the conversation to his own level.

"Of lunacy? I have observed them."

"Among the criminals also, Herr Captain."

"I observed no serious offences on my list."

"Theft, Herr Captain, drunkenness, dissoluteness."

"Ah," said Lally. "I saw that word above the cell of a young girl."

"Gertruda Gerhardt?"

"Yes."

"She is in solitary confinement for five years."

"Is her crime so serious?" frowned Lally.

"You are interested, Herr Graf," said the doctor, with an instant leer. He disliked Lally the more the longer he studied him; his vivid face, his rich hair, his arrogant figure, his cold manners, his flamboyant history, all were so many causes of offence to the quiet provincial.

"She is very young," said Lally steadily, hating him.

"And very wicked. They say she is, as her name denotes, a *witch*."

"These rustic superstitions," smiled Lally, and turned away with his hand on his hip.

CHAPTER IV

Lally Duchene soon became acquainted with his duties, which were indeed monotonously simple.

In the morning the sergeant came to him with a list of the occurrences of the previous day—a mere formality; afterwards he drilled the soldiers, first in the ancient, then in the modern manner, and gave them their orders for the day—another formality, for one day went by exactly like another, with such slight differences as might be occasioned by the arrival or departure of a convict, a death, a funeral, or some change in the daily routine caused by the different seasons.

But these matters and other details, such as the management of the stores, the orders in the kitchen, and to the outside labourers, were managed by the sergeant.

The commandant had to every day inspect the workrooms and the quantity and quality of the work turned out by the prisoners. He was supposed to satisfy himself that the building was clean, the regulations all kept, strict discipline maintained, and that was all.

No reports were sent on to Wiesbaden. No inspector ever came to Eberbach. The commandant was complete master. Lally found that every day he had many hours on his hands; plenty of time to realise his loneliness, his extraordinary situation.

The whole institution was so foreign to him, and seemed within its limits so admirably ordered, that it did not occur to him to either interfere in the administration nor to throw himself with any enthusiasm into his duties; he did what was required of him, smiled, and was content to remain a figure-head.

He was sufficiently a great gentleman to keep his soldiers in awe of him, despite their knowledge of his history and the reason why he had been sent to Eberbach.

Yet he could not but be aware that they discussed him, mocked him, analysed him behind his back in no very friendly spirit, and this doubled his sense of isolation.

He stood twice alone—once in the natural solitude of the place, and once in this attitude of the human beings with whom he was forced to associate. The cathedral became a favourite haunt of his; even in decay and desecration Lutheran whitewash had not been able to destroy all the beauty of the rich carvings; some of the gorgeous windows still remained, and amid the stacks of wood and grass and last year's hay Lally found the splendid monuments of former bishops of Mainz and one to a Duke and Duchess of Nassau.

In the youthful features of the mailed warrior Lally thought he could trace a likeness to his present enemy, but it was likely enough mere fancy. The reigning Duke traced his descent by many winding and diverse ways to the ancient line.

The failure of the senior branches of the family, deaths of young heirs, decrees of European policies, had put this young man on the throne of Nassau, but lately made an independent principality. His blood was mingled with English, Russian, French; in many ways he was no proud reigning sovereign, as these earlier German princes had been, but a mere puppet of the larger powers whose kingdom might be swept away as swiftly as it had been created.

Yet Lally never looked at the presentment of the dead Duke without thinking of the living one. So, he thought, might Aurelio have looked in chaplet and mail, serene, straight-featured, cold.

It was a beautiful statue in marble nearly as fine as alabaster, probably the work of some Italian master. The detail was most delicate, yet so exquisite the proportion, the pose, and the expression that the whole effect was of manly strength and power.

The Duchess slept in veil and robe. A window above the tomb cast a faint rosy colour on to her smooth face and close-pressed hair—a golden pink, like the flush of life.

Looking at her, Lally must think of the lady at Wiesbaden who should have been of this same placid greatness, and was not because of him, and now might never come to such peace as this either in earth or heaven.

Lally felt impatient with all womenkind; they interfered unwarrantably with the easy flow of life which they were obviously designed to help. Their appeal was too obtrusive, their lure too flamboyant, their position too prominent, for an existence with which, after all, they played the smaller part.

Lally thought that there were so many things more important than women—ambition, conflict, friendship, adventure, power—aye, more powerful, too. Love lasted but a little while—it was but one among many lusts—why could it not come and go without leaving disaster in its path? He was a man who would have liked a hundred loves, but he did not want to attach much importance to any of them. They were to be the background of his life, not the main incidents, and yet he had allowed one of them to utterly pull him down.

His own fault, of course. He had chosen the wrong woman. He raged against the fate that did not permit you, without bitter consequence, to choose any woman, or to allow, Lally added cynically, any woman to choose you, for he had never found much resistance to overcome nor had to offer much temptation; so far his person had proved a passport for all his desires.

He looked at the marble Duchess with annoyance. She reminded him of the Madonna above the gate, so calm, so expressionless, and both, foolishly, reminded him of the girl Gertruda in solitary confinement.

He was vexed with himself that he even remembered this girl, for to take an interest in her was so obviously what any man in his position would do.

And he, of all men, should be, for the time at least, absorbed in one woman only. It was matter for further vexation that this memory did not absorb him, as by all traditions of chivalry it should have done, and as he must, to satisfy his own self-respect, pretend it did. He intended to behave up to any standard of honour that was demanded of him, but his inner thoughts darted continually away from the woman in Wiesbaden. He disliked to look backwards in his emotions.

According to his own instinctive convictions the incident was done with, and he alert for the next adventure, but he knew that neither the world nor the woman would have it so.

He wondered that she did not write to him. Certainly he had not written to her, but how was he to send a letter when the post went once a week by road to Wiesbaden, and any letter of his with that superscription was likely, no, certain, to be intercepted?

And he could think of nothing to write that he would not have winced to know that the Duke's cold eyes were glancing over.

But she, surely she could have written without portentous difficulty. He was glad that she had not chosen to do so. As he stood by the tomb a group of prisoners in their orange-grey uniforms came in under the charge of one soldier.

They were bringing in bundles of faggots, which they piled about a bishop's monument, It seemed strange to Lally that they did not endeavour to escape, for none were chained or bound; yet he knew that life could not be supported in the forest, and that the little Duchy, easily searched, could offer no hiding-place for any wanted man.

Still, it was strange to see these subdued creatures, most of them strong and young, meekly submitting to their bondage.

Lally would have liked to have spoken to them, but the discipline of the prison was that the commandant should never directly address a convict, and he did not want to make himself conspicuous. The sunlight that streamed in through the open door behind the men, the bundle of hay and dried clover and wood on the stained marble floor, the patches of mellow colour from the unbroken windows, even the quiet figures at their labour, made a picture of secluded peace. Lally, standing unseen in the golden dusk of the shadow behind the Nassau tomb, thought of those prisoners who never tasted this liberty, nor the sweet air of open day; those who saw nothing but the strip of sky visible through the high-set tiny window of the cell, who had to sit with idle hands, never exchanging a word with any human being, and who saw no one but the silent soldier who brought their food. Such was the punishment that girl Gertruda must endure for five years. Surely she would either die or go mad before this sentence was complete. He had been told that many of the maniacs had first been prisoners undergoing long sentences of solitary confinement.

Lally smiled as he recalled the doctor's solemn assurance that she was a witch. Poor wretch, if she had any superhuman powers would she be in such a plight? It fretted him that there was no one of whom he could ask her history; he chafed against the brutality which left all the female prisoners in the charge of men; he thought that these miserable creatures should be in charge of someone of their own sex.

He had only seen her once; it was no part of his routine to visit those in solitary confinement. There was no excuse by which he might see her again, though the key of her cell was always in his possession.

His fine hand went out and touched the marble duchess—the smooth contour of the cheek, the line of throat and bust, the piously joined and pointed hands. How would this great and gracious lady have dealt with such a one as Gertruda? Surely in ways of gentleness.

Then another thought caused his unpleasant smile—perhaps the duchess had been herself a Gertruda; perhaps, had she been a poor girl living in these times, she might have sat behind a door with "Dissolute" marked on it. There was a certain lady in Wiesbaden now—if misfortune had not overtaken her, she might have gone through life with as fair an aspect as any duchess of them all.

The prisoners left the cathedral, and Lally soon followed them into the orchard without. At the end of this was a field, now used as a graveyard. Lally could see the wooden crosses clear in the light of the setting sun; if she died in Eberbach she would have no different grave. It was foolish that his thoughts would run on her. He must see her again to satisfy himself that she was a mere ordinary peasant wanton.

Beautiful was the evening air, beautiful the placid sweetness of early summer, the vast spaces of the sky, the distant hills, the distant forest.

"To-morrow," said Lally to himself, "I will go into the wood—right into the wood." He had a longing to be away from everything, to think out, in great loneliness, certain confused problems that were pressing on his soul.

Slowly he walked round the cathedral. The buttresses sprang straight from the flowered orchard grass, and the trails of the wild rose tangled against the stern masonry.

The fruit trees were losing their last blossom with every soft breath of wind. Lally could see the tiny plums and cherries, a bitter green among the downy leaves.

He passed into the noble cloisters of the monastery which enclosed the scented square of the herb garden, and there leant against one of the columns and looked about him with the keenness of a man always sensitive to the outward appearance of things.

The lines of the cloister cut a pale sky from which the light was faintly receding, though it was still brilliant, and every detail of the stonework showed vividly distinct. In the spandrils of each arch were angels' heads, with clustered wings gleaming in smooth glazed pottery. The capitals of each column were close packed wreaths of flowers, the slender shafts of different polished stones.

The garden was divided into four by little box-edged paths; in one division green lavender, bay, rosemary, tarragon, camomile, poppy, fennel, sage, foxglove and vervain, basil and thyme, mint and parsley, and other small, plain, fragrant herbs grew bitter and fresh to the nostrils.

In the second division was newly raked ground broken by the bright green of young salads and the feathery spikes of vegetables; in the third were rose bushes clipped close to their stems above carefully dressed beds; and in the fourth a medley of lovely flowers, most purposed to have medicinal properties, a few useful for essences, such as violet, marigold, wallflower, carnation, lily of the valley, verbena, stock, and geranium. These as yet bore but leaves, with here and there a closed curled bud.

In the centre of the space three round marble steps led to the well, a low white edge, a canopy of arching ironwork crowned with a gilt statue, from which depended the ropes and the bucket, which now stood on the top step, brimming over with water.

A man was working among the roses; he was the last object to attract Lally's attention. When he did give him a careless scrutiny, he saw that it was Luy. With a subtle sense of irritation he turned away, meaning to leave the cloister, when, as he turned, he stopped short.

Snarling at him from the shadows was a colossal and terrible face, a wild animal tusked and fierce. In an instant he saw it was a huge carving in relief above a door into the building, life-like and masked in shadow.

Lally remembered the legend of the foundation of Eberbach and smiled at himself; he changed his mind, too, about avoiding Luy, and turned back into the garden and called the man.

The fellow came instantly and saluted.

"A pleasant spot, eh?" said the commandant carelessly. "And you work here?"

"I understand plants, Herr Captain. This has been my work since I came here."

"The place is neatly kept."

"I found it so, Herr Graf. The monks took a great interest in this garden, as they had a distillery."

"I did not know. And a wine press, I think?"

"Yes, Herr Graf. You should see the cellars and the old barrels."

"And the distillery, what did they make, Luy?"

"Essences, soap, and liqueurs—perhaps other things."

"How other things?"

"Who knows? Those were queer days, Herr Graf."

"The monks sold their produce?"

"I do not think they needed to, Herr Captain. The bishops of Mainz often came here, and there were great entertainments, and many princely people were guests of Eberbach."

Lally thought that he spoke with a slight accent of pride.

"You know, then, the history of Eberbach?"

"Living here, with nothing else to think of, yes, Herr Graf."

"You told me that it was haunted," smiled Lally.

"Everyone says so, Herr Graf."

"Everyone is a fool, of course."

With these words Lally sent the man back to his roses. It was nearly dark in the cloisters; Lally looked up at the boar's head, grotesque in the dimness. "A strange thing to carve in a Christian church," he thought.

A soldier came up out of the gloom; he seemed unsubstantial save for his firm footfalls. He brought the commandant a letter from Wiesbaden. Lally glanced at the superscription, hastening to the open colonnade that he might see. As he saw the well-known writing he knew that the signature would be "Pauline."

"Herr Captain," the soldier was saying, "the sergeant thought that you should know to-night that one of the prisoners, Gertruda Gerhardt, is very ill."

Lally, staring at his letter, hardly heard these words.

CHAPTER V

Lally forced himself to pay attention to the soldier, because he was afraid to betray his passionate interest in the letter. To gain time he asked how it had been delivered.

"It was left at the nearest post-house, Herr Captain, and a peasant brought it over to-night."

Lally slipped the precious epistle in his pocket.

"You said a prisoner was ill?" he asked distractedly.

"Yes, Herr Captain."

"Tell the sergeant to come to me later; I cannot attend now. What should it be to do with me?"

"It was thought, Herr Captain, that as the girl was so ill—"

"The girl?"

"—the doctor should be sent for, even to-night, Herr Captain."

Lally recalled then that the man had spoken of Gertruda Gerhardt.

"That young girl—so ill? Is there no woman to go to her?"

"No one, Herr Captain."

"Ask the Herr Pastor to go," said Lally quickly, "then beg him to come to me." He had really lost all interest in Gertruda, so completely was his being absorbed by the other woman. He had believed that her influence over him was ended, yet at the sight of that letter—

He found the curtains drawn and the lamp lit in his chamber and he walked straight to the light and tore open the thick envelope.

She wrote from Wiesbaden. Of course, she began with a reproach.

"I have been left, as women usually are, lonely, defenceless.
Could you not at least have written?

54

"I have had to gather from strangers the news of your whereabouts. They say Eberbach is an unholy place, fittingly inhabited by criminals and lunatics. What company for you, so luxurious and fastidious! The Duke has been more than generous; his magnanimity astonishes, overwhelms, and shames! I lie in the light of it, touched, passive, helpless. One sees that there are many ways of love.

"The postponement of the marriage has not yet been announced—again his delicacy, that it might not follow too quickly on your departure. I admire him in everything.

"I am too wounded to write of our affairs or feelings. I only send you this to let you know that I live and rest in the Duke's kindness.

"Forget as I forgive.

"PAULINE."

"I believe she is in love with the Duke," grinned Lally. "The jade!" he added softly. "'To let you know that I live,'" he quoted. "By heaven, I never thought that she would die of it. So she mopes and cries, and the Duke pities her, and perhaps, after all, she achieves her coronet—or might, did he not know too much."

Lally folded away the letter.

His vanity winced because she had written no word of love; because she so persistently praised his rival and his enemy, who had the upper hand now, and was the only one of the two worth courting.

"Women hate you when you fail," said Lally.

And what failure could be worse than this—to fail at love?

Well, he had failed, and this was the way she took it—already she set her lures for the other man.

Lally began to lose interest in her again; she was merely an incident once more, not a part of his present life.

He disliked her letter; vain, and calculated, and heartless he thought it seemed.

What did she mean by her reproaches? Surely she knew that he had gone into his exile, silently, secretly, as the Duke had ordered, because to resist would have meant a scandal.

The Duke's generosity! The Duke was playing with them all!

And she remained at Wiesbaden. Lally did not like that; he thought that her obvious course would have been to leave the capital—some pretext could easily have been found.

He walked about the strange, dim-lit room, this prison which love for this woman had closed round his hot ambitions. "She was not worth it," he told himself definitely.

Yet some tenderness flushed his anger when he recalled what had been between them. Surely, after all, it was not possible that she was turning to the Duke.

Well, he had lost her, and he was here, exiled, helplessly dependent on this *generosity* of the Duke! He laughed at himself; he could not subdue his buoyant spirits to any melancholy; life seemed very good to him, even life in Eberbach.

There was a zest in everything, a deep, curious, intense joy in the mere acts of moving and breathing, in the mere feel of the sun and wind on the face. It was as if there was some intoxicant in his blood that made every experience of mind and body a delight.

It was good to have loved Pauline; it was good to know that there were other women in the world, and that he was free to win them.

He would not write to her; it was so useless, and he felt so sure that the Duke would see his letter.

56

He was still in a state of subdued excitement, pondering Pauline, when the pastor entered.

Lally stared. Almost he had forgotten this creature's existence; certainly forgotten that he had sent for him. He disliked the sight of this dull, ordinary person with tired eyes behind horn-rimmed glasses and an undecided mouth.

"I have seen the young prisoner, Herr Captain."

Then Lally remembered. A flicker of interest showed in the eyes, now deep crimson brown from the rush of excited blood.

"She certainly seems ill," pursued the pastor evenly, "but it might be feigning."

Lally offered him a chair; for himself, he remained standing, one hand on his hip.

"And I was told of a very curious incident, Herr Captain."

"Yes?"

The pastor was now seated by the table; he took something from his pocket and held it out an instant.

"This was found this morning in the corridor outside the cells of the females in solitary confinement."

He laid an object both heavy and bright on the table.

Lally could not see what it was; the light was very dim. He caught up the lamp and approached the table. A broken chaplet of rich gold lay between him and the pastor. It was in the form of vine leaves, grapes, and roses, intertwined in careless profusion, all cut from the beaten gold.

Here and there the wreath was in part snapped across or worn into holes. It was dirty, stained with soft mould, and smelt of the dregs of wine long in cask.

Lally had seen such work before and heard it called Etruscan; he knew that necklaces and bracelets wrought in this manner had been found in Wiesbaden, that old Roman town.

"Someone found this and dropped it," he said, taking the thing in his hand.

"Who? Only one of the soldiers could have done so."

"Why?"

"It is obvious that it comes from the cellars; it is rank with stale wine lees."

"The prisoners never go there?"

"No—the soldiers but seldom."

"They all deny the finding of this?"

"Yes."

Lally shrugged his shoulders.

"But of course it is the only explanation, one of the men found it, concealed it, became frightened—after all, how could he dispose of it?—and flung it down where it was sure to be found."

As he spoke he put the chaplet down. The lamp was left on the table, and the yellow rays struck full on the gold that showed between the spots of dirt and tarnish.

"It was a strange thing to find in Eberbach," said the pastor.

He seemed both dull and suspicious, full of secret dislikes and enmities.

"It is not a Christian ornament," he added, "but heathen."

"I know," said Lally, "but it might have been found here. Who knows what hoards these old monks may not have had? It might be worth while to investigate these cellars," he added with a smile.

"All the treasures were taken out of Eberbach when the Duke dispersed the establishment. This, of course, must be sent to him."

"Of course," said the commandant, with his too ready sneer. "Now about this girl; it is impossible to send for the doctor to-night."

"I think it is her soul that troubles her," replied the pastor, with a sudden kindling of professional interest; "her wickedness."

"Will she speak to you?"

"No."

"What do you know of her?"

"Very little. I take no great interest in the prisoners—they are all so much the same. I am supposed only to teach the young ones—the children."

"You see them on Sundays?"

"Those in solitary confinement do not attend the services, and many of the others are Romanists. You know how liberal the Duke is."

Lally smiled; he was a Romanist himself, by tradition if not by practice.

"This girl was brought here in the usual way?" he asked.

"Yes, sentenced at the Courts in Mainz. But she comes from this neighbourhood—Kiedrich, I believe."

Lally was interested at this; had he not thought her a creature of the forest. Dissolute? He wished he knew her story.

"Will you not come and see her, Herr Captain," added the pastor, "and judge for yourself of her state?"

Lally gave him a sharp glance, but there was neither sneer nor smirk in the fellow's dull face.

He had suggested what Lally had himself much desired, though recently a more intimate interest had obscured this emotion.

"I will come at once, Herr Sandemann." He took up his keys; the pastor had left a little hand-lantern inside the door, which he used to guide himself through the long, intricate stairs, passage, and rooms.

"Do you know your way about Eberbach yet, Herr Captain?" he asked as he led the way through the dark building.

"No. There are parts of it where I have not yet been—the palace or royal suite of rooms where the princely guests stayed, the cellars, the distillery—"

"All these are shut up."

"Surely it would be worth opening the wine press and the distillery. The prisoners could work there."

"The Duke has no need to make money out of Eberbach."

"No," said Lally swiftly. "He makes enough out of his mineral waters and his spas."

The four beautiful beams of the lantern travelled over walls and floor, all whitewashed; here and again it touched a grotesque carving. More than once Lally noticed the boar's head. It made him think of a line in Pauline's letter—"They say it is an unholy place."

"What is the history of this place?" he asked abruptly. "There seems to be talk as if it had an ill reputation."

"A very scandalous one," replied Herr Sandemann. "The monks are accused of many wickednesses, orgies, and untold luxuries, even secret crimes and heathen rites. The peasantry say that St. Bernard was deceived by the boar who urged him to build here."

"How?" asked Lally, amused.

"Ah, they are just legends and fables, of course; you know how many we have on the Rhine. It is supposed that the valley was haunted by evil spirits, of which the boar was one, and that when the monastery was built they rushed in and took possession and debauched all the monks, and no blessing or consecration would get rid of them, so that while the other four Bernardine establishments in the Rhinegau were truly Christian this always secretly belonged to the devil."

"It is the wood," said Lally. "The influence of the wood is very powerful—anyone must feel that—Nature beating at the very doors of man's church. The peasants were trying to explain that when they invented their tales."

Herr Sandemann stared at him; he did not know how to continue the discussion on these lines.

"We are in the women's quarters," he said. "It is the last door."

Lally remembered it; it gave him a strange sensation to think that it would be so soon opened again.

Herr Sandemann did not seem to be much occupied with the girl; the conversation had introduced what he had made, in his dull way, the hobby of his monotonous leisure. This was the legendary history of the Rhine. He had collected, he said, many fables and tales, and had many books on the subject, if the Herr Captain would one day care to hear them.

Lally thought it a curious taste for one so prosaic, but promised to visit the pastor's study.

He unlocked himself the door above which was inscribed, "Gertruda Gerhardt, dissolute," and stepped into the cell.

At once he was touched with shame at the ease with which he had her privacy at his mercy, so small and bare was the tiny prison.

There was no light save that of the pastor's lantern and that of the moonbeams pouring full through the high, narrow slip of a window.

Their cross lights, gold and silver, revealed the girl on her straw pallet. A stool stood beside this, on which was an earthenware jug; in the far corner was a basin on a wooden shelf; nothing else in the whitewashed cell, which was pure and clean.

The prisoner lay as if she had flung herself down in an attitude of despair and then never moved. Her arms were across her face; her bare feet touched the stone floor.

Her worn and tight cotton garments—these provided by the prison—seemed to strain away from the full curves of her limbs. Across her bosom the buttons were undone, showing the white calico beneath; round her knees and ankles the poor material clung scantily. The heavy folds of her hair had escaped the common horn pins and lay across the mattress and the floor. Lally saw that it was not, as he had thought at first, brown, but a dark blonde, full of colour.

The young commandant stared, advanced, and held the lantern above her. She was beautiful in some almost unearthly fashion; her feet looked like pale gold, her arms and neck silver, in the mingled lights.

She did not move.

The pastor advanced, bent over her, and touched her; Lally winced.

"She is asleep," said Herr Sandemann, "and the fever has gone down. We had better leave her till the morning."

He spoke quietly, but Lally thought that he was moved.

"The moonlight plays tricks," he added. "She looks more like a nixie than what she is."

"Let us go," said the commandant abruptly.

As he shut and locked the door he thought he heard someone laugh.

CHAPTER VI

"Did she laugh?" asked the commandant, hesitating by the door.

"Look and see if she has moved," said Herr Sandemann.

But Lally did not want to open the door again.

"It may have been from some other cell," he replied.

"It is also quite likely that the wretch was feigning," remarked the pastor severely. "She is supposed to be a person of great resource and trickery, and has the reputation of being a witch."

"So Luy told me. It is strange how these superstitions linger."

As Lally spoke he moved away down the corridor, which looked vast in the lantern light. No moonlight fell this side of the building; the Gothic window looked on blackness. The doors of the cells, one exactly like the other, showed in a regular succession, with the neat placards above each. Lally thought of the different individualities enclosed behind each of them, and again of that other woman whose letter lay in his pocket.

"Now we are here," said Herr Sandemann, who was more friendly in his manner, "there is something that I would like to show you if you have the time, Herr Graf."

"I am not eager to return to my solitude," answered Lally negligently; his thoughts were very far from the pastor, who again took the lead through a maze of passages and stairs and stopped at a low door, which was reached by descending three steps.

Herr Sandemann, entering, held up his lantern and showed a small disused chapel, bare and whitewashed.

Lally could see nothing peculiar in the place, but the pastor pointed out the wall to the east where there had been the altar space.

63

"You know," he said, "that the prisoners have to whitewash out the building three times a year. This was done shortly before your arrival, and this chapel found to have been shut up and neglected. There, on this wall, was a crude painting of St. Bernard, much damaged, but I bid the men clean the wash off. In so doing they discovered this."

He lifted his lantern higher and showed a faint but lovely fresco painting, still half hidden by coloured, dirty wash, and partly scraped away.

"Look at the subject," added Herr Sandemann. Lally peered close.

The design, blotched and damaged as it was, showed vaguely. Lally saw dim chalky colours of blue and yellow, green and a dim rose tint; then, aided by the patiently pointing finger of the pastor, he made out portions of a strange picture—the bare limbs of women, uncouth forms of animals, wreaths of fruits and flowers, and inhuman looking creatures, horned, bearded, not pleasant to look upon.

"Now what do you make of that in the wall of a Christian chapel?" asked Herr Sandemann.

"It may have come from some heathen temple."

"It is painted on the wall."

"But the building here is very old."

"Not older than the monastery—twelfth century, built by St. Bernard of Clairvaux," replied the pastor.

"Well, what do you infer?" smiled Lally.

The defaced painting pleased him; it suggested warmth and sunshine; here and there the delicate lines of a woman's face showed smiling and kind.

"Probably this was the scene of some of the monks' private orgies that an after generation endeavoured to turn into a chapel."

"Do you believe those tales?" asked Lally, as the two left the chapel.

Herr Sandemann was quite dull and fair about that.

"I cannot say so. The Rhine land is full of wild myths, most still credited by the peasantry. You know the stories of St. Goar and St. Ritza; of the Lorelai and the Gallows Manikin; of the dance of the maidens who die betrothed but unwed; of the nixie and doomed dancers of Ranersdorf and a hundred others? Well, these things are all credited still."

"Where do you learn them?" asked Lally.

"From my pupils—from the peasants of my village. I come from Kiedrich," replied the pastor, with satisfaction. "I am collecting these tales into a book, which I hope to dedicate to His Serene Highness."

"The Duke has little interest in such things," remarked Lally. "He is straight from a serene and practical university."

"No, I suppose he has not," said Herr Sandemann unexpectedly, "or he would not allow all these noble castles, churches, and monasteries in Nassau to fall into decay."

"Ah, you do not think him perfect then?"

To this the pastor did not reply. He stopped before a small door that he said was of his apartment; he invited the commandant to enter, and Lally indifferently followed into the room.

This consisted merely of three cells opened into one, and was almost entirely lined with books. The air was close with the odour of leather and dust and lamp-oil; the furniture was plain to poverty.

Lally did not like the place, which was a fitting background for the little drab, dry figure of Herr Sandemann, and soon took his leave, not escaping, however, without the loan of an old volume which he promised to read.

Once in his own chamber, Lally lit all the candles he could find— four in an iron scone and two on the mantelpiece—besides the lamp. Luy was not waiting for him, and the building was entirely quiet. The golden chaplet showed in dimmed radiance on the poor table where he had left it.

Lally thought that it was such an ornament as might have been worn by one of the women dancing in the faded fresco. He put it carefully away in the topmost of the valises that still lay piled in a corner of the room.

He felt sleepless and excited—the cause, he thought, was Pauline's letter; the other incidents of the evening were but phantasies compared to this.

He took it from his pocket and read it again. It was clear that she was lost; he did not know whether to pursue her or let her go. Pride urged the first, inner indifference the second.

His feeling for the Duke—near hatred—remained unchanged; he hoped that time would give him an opportunity of crying "Quits!" with the Duke.

To distract himself he opened the volume lent him by Herr Sandemann.

It was ancient, and printed in Nassau, perhaps by some early successor of Gutenburg himself, the cover was parchment, the clasps brass. Lally, turning the pages, found himself in a maze of legend pertaining to another age.

He read of the building of Koln Cathedral, how the architect bought the plan from the devil with the price of his soul; of Ursula, daughter of Vionetus and Darla of Britain, who was slain in Koln by the Huns, together with her husband, Conan, and her virgin attendants, the sole survivor, St. Kovdula, fleeing from the wrath of Attila to drown herself in the Rhine and rejoin her companions, whom she beheld "like a flock of birds, beating at the golden gates of heaven," of the "Heerwisch," or marsh spirit, which was to be seen on St. John's Eve flickering his elusive demon light over the peninsula of Godorf; of

Sister Eli, the wicked nun, who, after her death, haunted the convent of Grau-Rheindorf, "appearing in an apple-tree with a green hat on her head," and sometimes as a small naked boy who was found under the altar, "curled up like a sleeping dog"; the legends of the "Meister Hammerling," who haunted the mines of Rheinbeitlach. His half-amused, half-absorbed glance went over the lines that told the tale of Genofera of Brabant and Sir Golo of Srachenfels, the sunken castle of Saach. All the crude wildness, the black melancholy, the morbid glooms, the religious terrors, of Gothic fancy; all the fierce passions, the untamed imagination, of the North were in these uncouth fairy tales, which, darkened by superstition, saddened by fanaticism, sullied by ignorance and cruelty, yet showed here and there glimpses of a yet older world, joyous, human, lovely, the age of the Pagan gods before monk and nun, ghost and demon, robber knight and goblin, came to dwell on the banks of the Rhine.

Lally closed the book with a sense of confusion. The barbarous stories left a shadow of their gloom, their awe, on him which was enhanced by the silence and the strangeness of his surroundings.

For the first time since he had come to Eberbach he definitely wished that he was back in Wiesbaden.

He longed for the music, the dancing, the gambling, the theatre—Pauline. Yes, Pauline as she was, with all her faults, rather than this life.

He raged with inner jealousy of the Duke; his hate for the man kindled his indifference for the woman. He wanted life—life as he had known it with Pauline. Going to the window, he pulled aside the coarse curtain and looked out on the moonlight, which was brilliant with an intensity that seemed artificial.

The monastery buildings were sharply defined in black and white; the sky was luminous and void of colour as of darkness; the summer night was silent and chill.

Lally thought of the different scenes the moon must have looked down on in her uprising over Eberbach; how this silver light had streamed into the cells of the anchorite and the fanatic as it now poured into the prison of the maniac, the wanton, and the thief.

His body still and his thoughts impatient, he leant against the cool stone and looked through the veils of moonshine beyond the buildings where the wood sloped to the valley.

He could distinguish the forms of the trees in the dim white radiance; nearer, he could see the gardens and orchards and the dark forms of the firs.

How easy to imagine Pauline in such a setting; how delicious to dream of going down to meet her in this mystic loneliness. With his cloak over her frail gown (he could not think of Pauline in other than silk and lace) she would cling close to him, and they would creep to the edge of the wood—the wood must be wonderful on a night like this—or perhaps they would climb together through the oak-grove and look down on the Rhinegau and the river. Would not this be a better background for Pauline and his love than the formal gardens at Wiesbaden, or a dim chamber with a servant keeping watch at the door?

This thought made him so restless that he was half inclined to go down into the moonlight and wander alone through the stillness.

Yet he felt indolent, too, and leant against the casement undecided.

A slight sound beneath his window caused him to be instantly on the alert.

Someone else was abroad then; distinctly, through the complete silence, came the sound of footsteps on the path, of something jingling, as it might have been spurs or ornaments, and then, suddenly, a breathless laugh.

Lally considered.

There were no sentries or night watchmen at Eberbach—after dark the place was locked but unguarded. He had the keys of all the gates at that moment on his table; the sergeant came to fetch them early every morning. The maniacs in the summer-house were chained and padlocked. It must, then, be one of the soldiers.

Lally leant farther from the window, and listened and gazed.

Directly underneath him something was moving—something small, dark, on all fours—an animal.

Lally could not see the shape clearly, for the creature hugged the shadow of the building, but he thought it was that of a thin pig.

Beside it was another shape, dimly white. Lally thought that he could see the breast and thigh of a woman, and a bright coronet, then both forms were blurred and lost.

"Some animals have got in from the forest," he thought, and, clapping his hands, shouted into the night.

He shuddered at the effect of his impulsive action. He had forgotten that the windows of the madmen's cells looked out the same way as his own; at his cry a hundred hoarse voices yelled in fury and alarm, chains and bars rattled, howls and groans mingled in what seemed, to Lally's horrified ears, a demoniacal chorus, while yet more desperate shrieks arose from the ferocious lunatics confined in the summer-houses. This din so distracted Lally that he forgot for a second the two moving objects that had attracted his attention; when he looked again, they were gone.

He thought that he saw something white and gleaming flash through the moon-misted orchard, and a black shadow skulking along the buttresses, but the light was too treacherous—he could be sure of nothing.

"I have been reading too many fairy tales," he told himself scornfully.

He half expected that the garrison would turn out in alarm, but evidently they were used to these nocturnal disturbances, for, as the howlings of the madmen died away, silence complete fell again on Eberbach, broken only at intervals by the wild laughter of one of the maniacs in the pavilion who had been roused to a restless fury.

"It was he whom I heard at first," thought Lally. "One cannot be sure of anything in such a place as this."

And then a sudden disagreeable idea gave his thoughts another turn. That small, dark, creeping figure that he had taken for a wild animal—might it not have been a man—Luy? It seemed foolish to suppose that the fellow, even if a spy, should go these lengths. What could he hope to discover beneath the window?

Yet Lally could not rid himself of the idea that Luy would do any-thing in the way of espionage. Perhaps he knew of the pastor's coming and the visit to the girl Gertruda; perhaps he wanted to get Pauline's letter into his possession. Lally crept to his door and opened it sharply on the dark corridor.

Something heavy bounded back against the opposite wall, and there was an instant scurrying and pattering of feet. "Luy!" cried the commandant. "Luy!!" He dashed back into the room to snatch a candle. When he returned the feeble light showed him but empty darkness.

"Oh, God!" he groaned. "I wish that it was day!"

He was not yet sure where his servant slept or he would have gone and roused him.

"Luy!" he cried again strongly.

It was with a certain relief that he heard a sane human voice answer, "Herr Captain!"

"Come here at once," he said, and went back to his room, yet when the man appeared he was ashamed of his impulse. What had he to say? That he thought he had heard something in the garden, something in the corridor?

He looked sharply at Luy; the man had hastily thrown on his uniform and seemed still half-stupid with sleep.

"Your room is near?"

"Just round the corridor, Herr Captain."

"You have heard nothing?"

"Nothing, Herr Captain."

"Not all that shrieking and howling?"

"Oh, that! One hears it every night; some little sound disturbs them and they yell like that, Herr Graf."

"I thought I saw—an animal outside my window, and again, just now, there was something in the passage."

Luy grinned. How disagreeable he was, with his small eyes and long features and that shrewd quiet look...

"Rats, Herr Graf, rats. The place is full of them."

Lally felt foolish inasmuch as he had never thought of this, yet he knew that in neither case had he seen rats.

"Or a ghost," added Luy, with a certain insolence. "I told the Herr Graf that Eberbach was haunted."

"I thought of neither rats nor ghosts, but of human trickery," replied Lally sternly, though in his heart he hardly could suspect Luy now. "Get back to your bed and remember I notice everything."

The man saluted and went.

Lally extinguished the guttering candles, reflected that Luy could not possibly have been under the window, then in the corridor, then in his room and in night attire, so swiftly.

"But he is capable of it," thought the commandant, as he sank across his bed, yawning heavily. There was now only the lamp burning, and it was very low. Lally's pulses slackened; he was at last inclined for sleep; when, raising his eyes, he saw the window nearest to his bed entirely blocked by a figure standing on the sill.

For the first time in his life the young soldier knew what it was to be in the grip of pure horror.

The thing in the window, draped, formless, dark against the pale sky, yet seemed to be observing him. After the first shock Lally's virile courage returned to him, with a warm rush of blood to the heart.

"What foolery is this?" he cried, and sprang forward to the window. The creature dropped or fell—at least vanished. Lally hung over empty space; only on the sill, pallid in the moonlight, was a cluster of white violets, chilled and dripping with dew.

CHAPTER VII

I t needed but the light of day to completely dispel from the mind of Lally Duchene all the impressions of the night.

He was absolutely convinced that all the incidents of that time (which he remembered but confusedly after his short heavy sleep towards dawn) were hallucinations engendered by the time, the place, his own excitement, the queer old book he had been reading.

The white violets were no longer on the table where he had dropped them in horror; of course, they and the figure who had appeared to leave them behind existed only in his inflamed fancy. He was sorry that he had called Luy, but was ashamed to question the man or to explain to him; indeed, in the glow of the beautiful and normal day Lally himself regarded it all with indifference.

He sent one of the soldiers into Kiedrich to fetch the doctor to the girl Gertruda, who, he was told, was neither better nor worse, but lay in a sullen apathy or swoon, and after his brief routine of duties was over he went to visit Herr Sandemann's school.

The pupils were just leaving the refectory to go to their appointed labours; an elderly prisoner was in charge of them.

All looked healthy and all wore the prison garb of parti-coloured grey and orange—clean, stout clothing, of which each had three sets, so that they were never either unclean or unmended.

"A paternal government," smiled Lally as they trooped out, each saluting him.

"They are better off than when they are at home," remarked the pastor, putting away his book.

"And happier?"

"Some of them," replied Herr Sandemann, "could hardly be more miserable. You have not observed, perhaps, Herr Graf, the lives of the peasantry?"

"They are slaves," said Lally quietly.

The pastor shrugged.

Lally watched the group of prisoners go past the low open window. He knew that all of them were being punished for some offence against the Duke's game laws—gathering sticks, grass, or leaves in the forests; killing the deer or the birds; fishing in the river—and he recalled Pauline's praise of the Duke's generosity, nobility.

The pastor wiped his glasses and suggested a visit to the old distillery or laboratory. Lally accepted gladly; he wanted to distract himself from thinking of Pauline and the Duke, and the dull company of Herr Sandemann had in it something soothing. Lally liked him, too, for his interest in the place, and pitied him for his wretched life.

The pastor was not as well clad as the prisoners. Lally had noticed his threadbare linen and the starting seams of his brown coat.

"Underpaid," said Lally to himself, and again thought of the Duke with a sneer.

The laboratories were near the herb garden, built on off the cloisters. Lally found the plan of Eberbach as difficult to follow as that of the houses in Nuremberg. There had been so many additions and alterations to the original structure, so many staircases, windows, doors, added and taken away, everything altered so from its first purpose, that Lally always had the impression of walking in a maze.

Queer slits and apertures let in the light on to twisting stairways; doors had been blocked up, walls taken down, modern masonry added wherever the convenience of the prison had required the sweeping out of any ornament, and whitewashed, so that it was difficult to discover even the original intention of the old monastery.

But the laboratories were untouched. The doors would have been sealed up had not Herr Sandemann begged that they might be left open for his investigations among these queer remnants of the past.

Two long, low rooms opened one from the other, built on to the side of the palace portion of the monastery, but approached through the cloisters and looking directly through wide englazed windows on to the valley and the forest that here seemed to swell forward like the advancing battalions of a victorious army arrested suddenly by a word of command. Now gratings, red with rust, were over these windows, and one was almost covered by a creeping rose.

There were three brick furnaces, one in the first room facing the window and two smaller ones in the same position in the second room. All were filled with retorts, stills, and distilling apparatus, and either side of them were deep shelves and cupboards filled with a medley of pots, jars, glasses, boxes, knives, and uncouth instruments, dirty and broken, while on the floor bellows, pans, baskets, jugs, bottles, and scales were piled in confusion.

In the first room, by the window, a collection of books were neatly arranged on a long table.

"My work," said Herr Sandemann, taking away the cloth that covered them. "I have mended, cleaned, and docketed them, and mean, when I have time, to transfer them to my collection."

Lally glanced at the thick parchment volumes.

Nearly all dealt with the bitter conflict waged on the banks of the Rhine during the Middle Ages by the alchemists and chimastres. Here were the works of Graterole Brachechus and Alexander of Swehtenl, Conrad Gesner, Thomas Mugetus, and Nicholas Guibert, and all the Latin works of Paracelsus, printed, during thirty years, by the presses of Westhner and Frohen.

"This does not seem to have been a scent distillery only," remarked Lally.

"No, most of these monks were alchemists. You would find, Herr Graf, that Raymond Lulli was as much admired as Bernard of Clairvaux in these establishments."

"Well, Herr Pastor, I do not think Lulli ever wrought anything as disastrous as the second crusade, for which the good saint is responsible."

"I have often thought," remarked the elder man, tenderly fingering the smooth backs of the thick calf and parchment-backed books, "that these old alchemists came very near great secrets, for all George Agricola may say. Yes, for all their jargon of extract of hares' bones, manure, coral, mother o' pearl, broken eggs, and the like; for all their wild talk of the green lion, the inflated toad, the essence of azure, cinnabar, vermilion, musical gold, and so on, I think there was something in it—in Paracelsus and his Arcana, Herr Graf."

"I think we miss much in this practical age," replied Lally.

He was not thinking very much of what the other was saying; his attention was absorbed by the climbing rose-tree that filled the window space.

The sun shone through the glossy leaves and the red healthy thorns. A few buds, folded tight, showed hard and compact amongst the twisting stems.

How full of life and mystery and joy and beauty it seemed compared to these dingy rooms, this fantastic litter, these massive tomes wherewith man had striven to learn the secrets of Nature. Not all the ravings of Paracelsus had led him any nearer to the marvel of the rose.

"Here," said Herr Sandemann, "is a rare work by Artemidoras, *The Oneirocristiticon*, or dream book, published at Venice, and here one by Jerome Cardan; and here the *Mirabilis Liber*, believed to be by Saint

Caesarius. These books must be of some value, and I shall give them to the Duke."

"If you can get an audience," smiled Lally, remembering the ante-chambers at Wiesbaden.

Herr Sandemann flushed; he had forgotten to whom he spoke. His manner became more formal.

He remembered that he ought to dislike this man whose bizarre history, heard in incredible rumours and wild tales, had always seemed to him so strange and repulsive.

He looked at Lally with furtive sharpness. The thought crept into his slow mind that the young commandant, with his queer looks and foreign air, was almost absurdly out of place in Eberbach, and that anything extraordinary might be true of a man of his appearance. Lally Duchene was certainly different in everything to the average German—a difference for which he was not loved in Nassau.

He was instantly conscious of the unfriendly scrutiny of the pastor, and for him, too, the pleasantness of the acquaintanceship was over.

"Thank you for showing me these distilleries," he said coldly. "They have certainly a unique interest, but I must not further importunate you with my curiosity."

"Ah, Herr Graf," replied the pastor quietly, "do not think that you are really curious about Eberbach."

"No?" smiled Lally.

"Your thoughts must be always with other things."

"Perhaps; but believe me, I am very curious about Eberbach. I thought to-day to go through the woods towards Kiedrich."

"You must take a guide. It would be impossible for any stranger to find his way alone."

"Yet it was alone that I wished to go. Who is supposed to be your best guide?"

"Luy, your body-servant," answered the pastor at once. "He has a most extraordinary knowledge of the Rhinegau."

"Luy?" cried the commandant. "But he has just come from Wiesbaden."

"From Wiesbaden?" repeated Herr Sandemann vaguely. "That may be—I suppose he was sent there—but he is certainly a native of the Rhinegau."

"He never told me so," said Lally, with a deepening of his suspicion of his servant. "Do you know much of the fellow, Herr Pastor?"

"No, nothing at all—he has been here such a short time—but he always seemed to me more intelligent than the other men."

Lally, with no further leave-taking, turned to go. He was glad when he was again out in the pure warm air, which was strongly perfumed with the odours of the freshly growing herbs in the cloister garth. The low, dark rooms, with their litter of rather horrible looking utensils, the disused furnaces, the row of wicked seeming books, had made an unpleasant impression on Lally.

He wanted to get away from Eberbach, for he also began to feel a prisoner, and to think out in solitude his relations with Pauline and the Duke and his plans for the future, for of course he could not stay in Eberbach—no, not even for a while.

He did not wish to take a guide, yet in his heart he feared being lost in the wood. Certainly he would not and could not take Luy.

In the orchard he found the sergeant, who was superintending the work of a number of prisoners who were disloading little ponies laden with weeds from the crops on the mountain slopes. The sergeant told him of an ass who was so used to go between Kiedrich and Eberbach that she was as good a guide as any human.

It was well into the morning when he started on his meek little steed. Though he was aware that it was against the discipline of

Eberbach for him to be long absent, he did not intend to return till evening. Bread and meat and wine he carried in a pannier at the ass's saddle, for he did not wish to be dependent on an inn at Kiedrich.

As soon as he was in the forest and had turned his back on Eberbach he began to lose sense of the present, almost of reality. The influence of the forest was powerful and all-pervading. Like the lover of Thetis drawn down through soft blue waters to the couch of the goddess; like the knights sucked into the whirlpool of the Rhine down to the coral palaces of the nixie and the Lorelai; like Sardanapalus swooning in the spicy perfumes of his aromatic funeral pyre, was Lally overwhelmed and drugged by the enchantment of the wood.

The great trees soon closed round him, so that he was completely shut in the forest; the ass twisted and turned through little worn tracks, and sometimes where there were no tracks at all, without pausing or quickening her pace.

The trees were mostly oak, of a great loftiness that clouded the sky with foliage. Yet here and there were others, from the pine to the wild cherry, growing in little open spaces that were tangled with brambles, fox-red and orange, or knee deep in grasses, wild hyacinth, and lilies.

Lally had never been so far into a forest alone before. When he had hunted with the Duke from Die Platte he had always been in company; and Nature in the royal preserves, tamed, disciplined, and in charge, as it were, of keepers, was different to this utter wildness.

Yet he reminded himself that this equally belonged to the Duke—to touch a stick or a stone, the grass or the leaves, the fruit or the flowers here, meant imprisonment in Eberbach. He smiled sourly, glad to have a cause—a good cause—to hate the Duke.

He never meant to go as far as Kiedrich, but he had lost sense of time; it seemed hours that he had been slowly riding through the forest, and yet but a few moments, when he found himself looking down into a hollow where a few houses clustered together in the shadow of a ruined castle that rose boldly on the heights the other side of the valley, one tall tower rising above a heap of fallen masonry.

Lally knew this to be Sharfenstein, the old palace of the bishops of Mainz, that had been an abode of surpassing splendour in the days when the monks of Eberbach had boasted that they could walk from their convent to Rome on their own possessions.

The little village, built in the style of a bygone age, looked dead. Lally noted the church and the chapel of St. Michael showing among the poor houses—all looked as unreal as a scene glimpsed in a dream.

The surpassing rich loveliness of the country, this garden of Bacchus, the vineyards and cornfields and orchards, the swelling hills filled with afternoon sun, the warm scents and straying perfumes, the softness of the air and the gentle heat of the sunbeams after the shadows of the forest, wrought on Lally like a spell.

He tethered the little ass to a wild plum-tree that bent above the slope, and smiled to see the beast cropping the Duke's grass; he took his ease on a shaded couch of cupped mosses and ate his bread and meat and drank his Johannisberger with infinite relish, then fell into musings without form or consistency, in which neither Pauline nor the Duke had any part.

Not till the sun had gone behind the hills, leaving the gaunt tower of Sharfenstein dark against a pellucid sky, did he rise and turn the ass back towards Eberbach.

CHAPTER VIII

Lally had not journeyed far into the forest before he realised that night—or at least darkness—would overtake him before he could reach Eberbach. He had made a townsman's miscalculation in forgetting how much sooner the day would fade in the forest than in the open country.

After he had travelled a mile or two in the obscurity of the great trees he was amazed to find that he disliked being alone in the twilight wood. He seemed surrounded by faces entirely alien and inimical, and the mood that had enabled him to believe in the figures beneath his window at Eberbach returned to him.

He was vexed to find himself so much a creature of circumstance and surrounding, and urged the ass to a quicker pace, marvelling at the sureness with which the animal, even in the dusk, found her way.

The wood was completely still; if there were wild night creatures abroad they made no sound; only the upper leaves of the great trees now and then rustled in the evening breeze.

To Lally this silence was more ominous than many strange sounds and sights might have been. He felt himself completely of the town; all the beauty of the day seemed now gathered into a menace. For the first time since his exile he whole-heartedly wished to be back in Wiesbaden. It would be the hour now for the opera or a concert or walking with Pauline in a comfortable garden, lit with a less magic light than that of sunset or the moon. Yet all the while a deep excitement and curiosity stirred the innermost recesses of his heart. It was as if some secret tempter was urging him to leave the safe guidance of the little animal and trust himself to the heart of the forest, where, in a few moments, he would be completely lost.

He tried to fix his thoughts on Pauline—he had left Eberbach with the express purpose of considering at leisure that problem, and so far had given it no consideration.

He was amazed that it was so difficult to bring his thoughts to bear on Pauline, and at his own desire to thrust her into the past. He did not care to admit to himself that his was one of those natures who live mainly in the present moment and shrink from all the ties and obligations of the past.

In his soul he really wanted to be done with the episode of Pauline. Yet that was quite impossible. He had a great responsibility towards this lady. This fretted him to the quick. He most heartily cursed the chance that had "found them out." But for that she would have been the Duchess now and he in Wiesbaden, glittering at the court.

Now she never would be the Duchess. It was useless to hope for it. Her natural honesty and honour (he still in all sincerity applied both words to Pauline) would prevent her accepting such a position, even should her arts and the Duke's infatuation induce him to offer her marriage.

No, it was unthinkable, and he would always owe her that—her missed chance of a throne—and from the tone of her letter, still lying close (though often forgotten) over his heart, he did not think that she would undervalue what she had lost nor his blame in the matter.

By the extent of her praise of the Duke he judged the extent of her reproaches for him—he could guess how she was saving them for their next meeting. Pauline had a temper as well as dignity.

When neither were aroused—when it was no question of honour or scandal, or worldly loss or gain, or shamefaced fear or selfish dreads, all of which had marred their love-making—how desirable Pauline could be!

If he could have had her now, in this forest, free of all thought for yesterday or to-morrow! His heart bounded at the bitter-sweet poignancy of the thought. That was his ideal of love, unfettered by honour or wisdom, unwatched by prudence or expediency.

Love like that was love indeed; love like this of his and Pauline was so crossed and shadowed with other things that it was but a sweetened draught that left bitter dregs behind.

The forest dusk influenced him against Pauline; he could have worked himself into anger against her—a woman who had got in his way!

As he reached an opening in the wood where the daylight was still showing he saw the light of a lantern moving towards him.

The thought of a fellow-traveller seemed foolishly strange, yet he was glad and curious to see this other who was traversing the forest at dusk. A few more paces and he saw a small pony such as the peasants used laden with two surgeon's cases and the doctor from Kiedrich.

Lally was disappointed, this man's personality jarred on the moment and the place.

The little doctor, Herr Lindpainter, was loquacious in his greetings.

"I reached Eberbach as you left it, Herr Captain."

"Yes?" said Lally drily.

"To see your sick girl, Herr Graf."

Lally was instantly aware of the suppressed leer on the flat face shown in the beams of the horn lantern.

"Is she ill?" he asked coldly. "I have not seen her, but this report was brought to me."

"Ah, I thought you had seen her, Herr Graf." Lally maintained his lie by an impassive face of formal attention.

"I should see her, Herr Graf," chuckled the doctor. "She is a very remarkable person."

"Do you know anything of her?" Curiosity forced from Lally a question he would rather not have asked.

"I know as much as any," replied Herr Lindpainter, with gratified importance. "It is not much."

"Another time I will hear the recital," said Lally.

"Ah, you think it late, and you are new to the forest. To me it is like my own garden. But they told me that you had old Katerchein, who is as good a guide as any in Nassau."

"I am not afraid of losing my way," smiled Lally, "but of detaining you, Herr Doctor, who must be wishful of returning home."

"Oh, I am used to being out at all hours of the day and night, and I have neither wife nor child to sit up for me, so if it would help you in your dealings with this girl to know her history, I can give it to you now, Herr Graf, in a few moments."

"Tell me then," said Lally, still in his grand manner.

"Well, this girl appeared first in this district last harvest-time. She said she came from Ketenlollen—was an orphan and looking for work. She had with her a troupe of others. One of them was the man Luy."

"Luy!" cried Lally, in sincere amazement.

"Yes. Luy was then in the army, but on leave. I forget the village he came from—somewhere in the Rhinegau—and he was related to some of the people he brought with him and acted as sort of captain or protector of the band. They came to Kiedrich, and easily found work at harvest-time. They worked well, but they were a noisy, rude lot of rogues, heartily disliked by the natives."

"Where had they been employed before?"

"Some at the Duke's mineral water works, some on the land and in the baths at the Spas, but they were all of the same disposition and more like a band of roving gipsies, and in many cases, where pains were taken to discover the truth of their tales, they were found to be false.

"When the harvest was over they mostly wandered off again—Luy to Wiesbaden, where he made a special application for the next vacancy at Eberbach."

"Then he is not the Duke's spy," thought Lally instantly.

"But the girl Gertruda remained."

"Where?"

"At Kiedrich—in the house of the peasant for whom she had worked. He was the handsomest man in the village, and his wife soon drove her out."

"And then?"

"With the most insolent calm she took up her abode with another man until the pastor stopped it and turned her out of the village."

"And for this she was imprisoned?" asked Lally, with indifference.

"Oh, there was a great deal more than that," said Herr Lindpainter. "I do not know how many lovers she had," he added, with a relish of malice. "No one seemed able to resist her. It was well believed that she was a witch."

"The witchery of abandoned beauty!" smiled Lally.

"She is not so beautiful now—strange. She lured two men off into the forest here; both died."

"Not by her means?"

"No. But it was all queer."

"No doubt," smiled Lally, with no hint in his demeanour as to how his imagination was stirred. "What happened in the forest that men should die of it?"

"Neither could tell—both seemed half-witted. One was found drowned; the other died suddenly of some stroke while he was dressing his vines."

"Natural causes," said Lally, "and doubtless they were out of their wits before they encountered this rustic Venus."

"That may be, but you know how full of legend this part of the country is, Herr Graf, and how the wildest things are believed, and the girl was most firmly credited with being a witch."

"Well, there was some cause," said Lally. "But it is not for witchcraft that she is imprisoned, I think?"

"No, but for the great scandal of her life that was an offence to all. So black was the case against her that she was ordered into solitary confinement, though on a first conviction."

"And now she is ill?"

"Yes, more of the mind than the body, I thought."

"Has she, then, a mind?"

"Desires, at least, Herr; first of all the desire for freedom—she was always wild and wandering, disappearing for days into the forests and hills, and never settling long in one place."

"How long has she been in Eberbach?"

"Four months or so."

"She might be allowed a greater measure of liberty now."

"It would mean an application to the Duke; of course."

"No," said Lally, "I could undertake as much on my own authority."

He spoke haughtily, knowing well enough that the doctor, like everyone else at Eberbach, was entirely in the dark as to his relations with the Duke. They always fumbled round the fear that he might still be really a favourite at court. Now the doctor's manner became instantly touched with servility.

"Of course, Herr Graf. That would be my advice, to give this creature some liberty if it is desired to preserve her life."

It seemed to Lally that there was some malice at the heart of this speech—to give such a woman any manner of freedom meant a grave responsibility for the governor of Eberbach.

"Do you take the onus of this, Herr Doctor?" he asked.

"I, Herr Graf?" The tone was yet more decidedly cringing. "It is but my advice as a medical man. Of course, if you should doubt the consequences it is different!"

Lally detected the challenge, perhaps the insult, and laughed.

"I think the restrictions of Eberbach are sufficient to control the most lawless girl," he replied. "But I must watch this man Luy," he added.

"I do not think that he followed her," said Herr Lindpainter, "because he had desired to be sent here before her arrest."

"But he never admitted to me that he knew her," answered Lally, "and he said he was a native of Wiesbaden. I never liked the fellow."

"Nor I. Get rid of him, Herr Graf—a word to the Duke."

Lally felt that the man was again feeling his ground, and, having found out all he wished from him, abruptly closed the conversation.

"It grows dark indeed, Herr Doctor," he remarked "and we must on our ways."

"Will you take my lantern? The moon will soon be up and I can find my way in the dark."

"So, I believe, can Katerchein, and if I lose my way it will be rather a novel adventure to a townsman."

"Do you think to see the erl-king or a nixie, Herr Graf? The pastor has been filling your ears with his strange tales. What a mountain of rubbish he has collected!"

"Good-night, Herr Lindpainter."

"Good-night, Herr Graf Lally. I will come over and see my patient the day after to-morrow. Again, good-night!"

They parted, and Lally watched the doctor's lantern until it had disappeared in the darkness of the trees. He now felt very suddenly alone.

While he had been speaking he had noticed the closing in of the night about him and the blotting out of the first few tremulous stars by the pale radiance of the rising moon.

He rode on into the forest. Pauline and the Duke had again left his thoughts, which were touched by the fancies roused by the story of the girl Gertruda. Always had he thought of her as part of this forest—a wild creature.

Probably she was the child of some forest woman, and had never known even a village until she wandered down to Kiedrich. Probably she had escaped the schools, the pastor—what was she to know of morality?

She should not be in prison, Lally thought, and yet he despised her as a manifest jade.

Stripped of her mystery she was stripped of her allure, and again yet—

He certainly thought of her; he decided that he would see her on the morrow and give her some liberty, setting her to some work with the other female prisoners.

Yes, he would do that. The doctor had spoken of the possibility of her going out of her mind. He did not want to see her grinning from behind the bars.

Then his thoughts veered again, and he pictured her as he had first seen her—the only time that he had seen her face.

She had seemed an image of such fresh, frank innocence. Why, he hardly believed any of these tales. The doctor was full of little spites and malice—there might be nothing in all these wild stories.

Wild tales. Well, there were plenty of them in the Rhinegau, and they did not seem so unreal in this time and place, riding through the black forest with the moonlight filtering through the great trees, and all round silence.

Was it only last night that he had dazed his brain by reading in the pastor's book of legends, and had imagined that he had seen those figures creeping beneath his window in the moonlight and that other shape standing on his sill?

He vividly recalled the cluster of white violets; their faint perfume seemed to be in the air. Certainly there would be white violets in the forest.

He rode on, and the way seemed endless. The constant rays and patches of moonlight and pools of black shadow worried his eyes and plagued him with a sense of dreaming instability. He felt as if he was going round in a circle or threading a maze; there was no sense of progress in his ride.

What a companion Gertruda would be for such a night as this! He almost envied those fools she had taken with her, if that tale was true.

Any tale might be true to-night. Why had men said that these old stories were false?

He thought of the legend of the Wartzburg. If Venus left her fastness now to wander among the sweet fruits of the earth that overflowed the Rhinegau, would not the Duke of Nassau have had her arrested as a wanton and imprisoned in Eberbach.

Lally laughed aloud. That was a strange thought—Venus a prisoner in his charge, he ever a worshipper of Venus, and she bound and at his mercy! The idea intoxicated. Perhaps there was something of Venus in this girl Gertruda.

His laugh echoed in the forest and seemed to be taken up and repeated by a hundred other voices. Lally paused, checking the ass. Not a whisper disturbed the night.

But he felt a desire to get out of the forest; aye, quickly, quickly to ride out of the wood. He experienced that sense of pursuit so common to those who travel for a great while alone, and found that he was breathless and with a damp brow when the trees thinned and he saw beneath him the towers of Eberbach in the moonlit valley.

The effect of coming thus on this immense lonely building, so palatial and grandiose, set in the midst of this wild, unspoiled Nature, was most extraordinary. Lally felt now—as he had done the first time he saw the monastery—a sense of unreality.

How much more fitted for the worship of heathen gods was this building, placed in this rich garden of Nature's fairest fruits, than for the rites of a spiritual religion!

Lally remembered the defaced painting in the chapel, the coronet found in the cellars. Perhaps Eberbach had known mysteries that he could only dimly guess at.

He rode past the great gate, now locked, and looked up at the three great figures of Mary, St. John, and St. Bernard that towered into the moonlight filled air.

So fantastic was the light and black shade, so unsteadied his mind by strange thought, that he imagined that the Madonna's robe changed to a flutter of Attic drapery; that her hood had gone, showing a face that was not the face of Mary; and that the two saints were transformed into laughing fauns that towered gigantic, menacing, above him.

As he stared stupidly the ass gave a start and a neigh of violent fright. Lally looked swiftly down. Something was moving by the gate, then out into the light and towards the forest.

It was a small boar.

CHAPTER IX

The next day Lally received a letter from the Duke. Even the sight of the familiar handwriting put Gertruda and his ride home from Kiedrich out of his thoughts.

Even before he received the letter, Pauline, with the daylight, had become again the pressing problem, the others mere phantasies.

He mentioned the wild boar to Luy when the orderly brought him his breakfast.

"This time I was not mistaken," he said; "the wild animals do come up round the prison grounds."

The soldier seemed indifferent.

"It is likely enough, Herr Captain; the forest must be full of them."

"I rode through it last night and saw nothing."

"You kept to the beaten track," replied Luy.

"I saw no track at all."

"But the ass did, Herr Captain, else you had lost your way."

Lally laughed.

"I suppose so. Of course, you are a clever fellow, Luy."

He meant to let the orderly see that he knew something of him, but the soldier's queer face remained impassive.

Lally thought, not for the first time, what an unpleasant countenance it was—the features small, yet the cheeks and neck thick and the teeth long, the hair shaven so close that it was impossible to see what colour it was, and the eyes blurred and reddish.

"Why did you want to come to Eberbach?" asked Lally sharply.

"The Herr Captain is misinformed," replied the soldier.

"You never asked for the first vacancy here?" demanded Lally.

"Never, Herr Captain."

"And this girl, Gertruda, did you know her formerly?"

"I met her at Kiedrich during my last leave."

"You did not tell me that."

"Was it of the least importance, Herr Captain?"

Lally felt annoyed that he had paid any attention to the doctor's gossip, but he answered drily, "It might have been."

Luy was not in the least discomposed. "I am sorry, Herr Captain; I had almost forgotten. I only knew of the girl as did everyone in Kiedrich."

Lally could not question further.

"And that boar you saw last night, Herr Captain."

"Did I say it was a boar?"

"I thought so, Herr Captain."

"Well?"

"I believe they often come, several of them, about Eberbach."

"Surely strange."

"Perhaps they have some affinity with the place, Herr Captain. It was a boar discovered the site for Eberbach."

"It was an unholy alliance on the part of St. Bernard."

"Perhaps that is why the place is haunted, mein Herr."

"Is it haunted?"

"That is the repute."

"What do you think yourself?" smiled Lally.

"I always said it was haunted," replied Luy rather sullenly.

Then the Duke's letter came, brought by the peasant who fetched the mail from the nearest post-station.

Lally read it when his daily rounds were over. He went into the cathedral and seated himself on the ledge of the tomb of the early Duke of Nassau.

It was a glorious day, the sun strengthening hourly. Through the coloured windows the light streamed in a flood of blue and gold, yellow and scarlet; through those open to the air the pure sunlight flooded, fresh with the perfumes of the living green. Piles of fresh fodder and newly lifted roots concealed the bishops' tombs. The air was full of strong, growing, fragrant things, of spring deepening into summer, of the promise of abundance.

Lally broke the seal that bore the blazonry of the arms of Nassau.

He could picture the Duke's fine hands stamping this seal. What a different world it was—Wiesbaden. Why did it seem small compared to Eberbach? He played with his curiosity. Why had the Duke written? It was a surprise, and gave voice to much speculation. Was it a peace offering or a challenge? Had the Duke decided that Pauline was not worth the dispute? Or did he really care enough for Lally to overlook all offences? Perhaps this was a recall to Wiesbaden. The latter disappointed all these surmises. The Duke wrote with the utmost formality, though more as Lally's superior officer than his sovereign.

He asked for a report on Eberbach; stated his interest in the establishment, and his desire to effect improvements there. He had heard, he said, that Eberbach had been much neglected in the reign of his predecessors, and he wished to put it on a level with other reforms that he had undertaken in Nassau.

Lally smiled awry.

He never remembered the Duke, though he had something of the pedantry of college about him, being in the least interested in his subjects.

"I wonder if he knows that people get five years here for poaching in his rivers and three for gathering sticks in his forest?"

The Duke went on to ask if there was any industry that could be conveniently and profitably started at Eberbach, to give the prisoners some employment besides supplying their own needs. Lally thought instantly of the disused distillery and the empty cellars. Both perfume and wine-making took his fancy and seemed suitable to Eberbach.

There was no more in the letter, which ended, as it had begun, with great dryness. No hint of what there was between these two men; no offering of any solution of that great difficulty that both must face—Pauline.

Lally was half-vexed, half-relieved—vexed that the Duke did not more plainly show his hand, relieved that the whole issue was suspended.

On such a day as this he could not long for action. So balmy was the air blowing against his cheek, so pleasant the view of blooming orchard and azure sky through the great Gothic door, that he felt quite content to sit here, leaning against the marble Duke. This letter removed a certain onus from him; it would be easy to take the same tone—to be calm and formal and wait.

He was already composing in his mind a stiff reply to the Duke when the pastor entered the church. He looked rather like a bat in daylight, and moved a little uncertainly, as if baffled by so much sunshine.

"Good morning, Herr Pastor," said Lally, adding on an instinct of the bravado that came so naturally to him, "I have heard from my good friend, the Duke."

The pastor bowed at mention of the august name, but it was more with an old-fashioned courtesy than with the servility that the doctor used.

"He is interested in Eberbach," said Lally, rising and leaning against the tomb.

"He proposes a visit?" asked Herr Sandemann, with eagerness.

"No," smiled Lally, "but he suggests reforms."

"There are many needed," replied the pastor simply. "This church, restored and treated as a place of worship instead of a granary and storehouse, would be a noble monument to the House of Nassau."

"His Highness has little connection with these," said Lally, lightly touching the cheek of the sculptured knight.

"Yet he holds his throne through them and surely would not care for them to be thus?"

"My friend the Duke is not interested in the past. You will not find that he will be stirred by your old legends or your decaying cathedral."

"Well," said Herr Sandemann placidly, "there are plenty of reforms in the present that he can put his hand to. This place is well done within limits, but they are very narrow ones."

Lally was slightly irritated by this acumen in one whom he despised.

"Can you suggest any reforms?" he suggested drily.

The pastor was full of the subject; evidently he had thought about it for years. He came up to the ducal tomb, and, nervously fidgeting his ugly hand up and down the marble coils of the Duchess's hair (a sight which further irritated Lally), he propounded his suggestions.

There should be a larger staff—two resident doctors, young, clever men. The lunatics should be separated entirely from the convicts under the charge of a special professor. A new schoolroom was needed, and a schoolmaster as well as a clergyman. Baths were required; there was a sunk part of the old walled garden that would do very well for an open-air bath in the old-world style. The educational library was out of date—Lally knew this was all true; it was also very dull. He would send a list of grievances to Wiesbaden, just to vex the Duke; meanwhile he wished Herr Sandemann's monotonous voice would cease.

"I will write about the laboratories," he said, "but I do not think that you will be allowed to search for gold, Herr Pastor."

"I will find gold in honest ways," replied the other quickly. "Very valuable perfumery could be made here, I know something of the art."

"How many hobbies have you?" smiled Lally.

"I have had a great deal of time and a great deal of loneliness since I came to Eberbach, and study has been my one friend."

"Well, I will put you in charge of the laboratories."

"I shall be glad; there will be much to purchase, and we shall have to be content with little at first. I shall need two or three assistants."

"The girl, Gertruda, has been ordered some occupation, by the doctor," said Lally lightly. "Will you have her?"

The pastor was not, as Lally had maliciously hoped he would be, shocked; he was no gossip like Herr Lindpainter, and this girl to him was no worse than any other in an establishment where everyone was either a criminal or a maniac.

"Why not," he replied, "so she is teachable and not too stupid?"

"The work is easy then?"

"Quite easy."

Lally sighed and yawned.

"I must go and see her. Will you accompany me?"

He really wanted to be rid of the old pedant, but he felt a curious dislike to interviewing the girl alone, and there was no one else whom he could ask.

The pastor agreed as a matter of course, and the two left the cathedral.

Lally felt his spirits rise as the softness of the outer air touched his face. The day was glorious beyond words; the whole earth seemed breaking into a wealth of fruit and flowers; from the great vineyard, the Steinberg, came the sounds of busy labour.

They passed through the orchard, and he noticed the firm green apples swelling amid the small greyish leaves, and the tiny cherries like jade beads hanging from the smooth round stems.

"It must have been a fine life to be a monk here, Herr Graf—this without and books and comfort within."

"Yet no doubt one yearned after the cities, Herr Sandemann—"

Lally's words were checked by a thin, dismal scream, jarring indeed, in such a place. He knew that it came from the summer-houses where the worst cases of lunacy were confined, yet he shuddered.

"It is that wretched woman," said the pastor, with an air of interest, as they entered the cloisters. "They have to keep her chained. Hers is perhaps the most curious story of anyone in Eberbach."

He paused, and in the same tone pointed out a little plant growing in the cloister garden.

"That is a plant useful in perfumery," he said, "and outside Eberbach is a grove of bitter oranges, not fit for eating, but one could get from them the perfumes they call 'Neroli' and 'Petit Grain.'"

Lally noticed that they were standing under the carving of the boar's head that he had noticed his first day at Eberbach.

In the daylight the thing was crude and grotesque, yet still showed that ugly look of menace and ferocity.

Lally's fine brown fingers idly traced along the shaggy stone neck which they could just reach.

"Here's a thing for your Christian monks to carve!" he said. "I wonder what is the truth of that story of the boar? I saw one last night quite close to the great gate."

Herr Sandemann gave an exclamation of astonishment and was about to speak when again a dismal wail from the lunatic woman cut the air.

"For God's sake come on," cried Lally, in a sudden flare of impatience. "Cannot that wretch die or be cured?"

They entered the building.

"She has often attempted to take her own life," said the pastor. "That is why she is chained. She is troublesome now, poor soul, but for days together she will be quiet. I think that she will never be cured."

"What is her story?"

"She meddled in black magic."

"You believe that?"

"Put it that she thought she did, Herr Graf; it comes to the same thing."

"What did she do?" asked Lally, speaking with a faint and idle curiosity.

"She tried to raise the spirit of her future husband on St. Thomas's Eve."

"And this crazed her?"

"The consequences did. She is from Hiegenach, where the superstition is very strong. These are the rites—the maiden lays a table at midnight in her father's kitchen, with a clean cloth and two plates and two knives, no forks, and a loaf of newly baked bread with two double-edged knives enclosed in it. As the church strikes twelve the maiden throws open the outer door and flings in the direction of the river the shift she has worn for a week, rolled into a tight ball; she then repeats a doggerel invitation to the lover, whose spirit is supposed to appear and seat itself at the board."

"And this poor fool worked this so-called incantation?"

"Yes, and, according to her tale, the phantom entered and took his seat opposite to her, plunging his knife into the loaf and disappearing into thin air. When she examined the bread there was only one knife in it, and that none of her own; the other two had vanished. Her shift she found at her feet, torn to tatters."

"And what was the result of this unholy rite?" asked Lally as they turned into the long corridor leading to the women's quarters.

"She had recognised in the ghost a neighbour's son. Seven days after he came wooing her; in seven times seven more she was a wedded bride. For seven years she lived happily with her husband, bearing him seven children. At the end of this period she began to feel an unaccountable aversion both for her husband and her children, and after a brief struggle yielded to the tempter and on St. Thomas's Eve again attempted the foul rite.

"All was done as before, but this time through the open door came no lover—no man even—but the awful figure of death himself, holding an hour-glass in which but a few grains of sand were left.

"This is the strange part of the story. That night the husband dreamed that a voice bade him search in a certain old chest belonging to his wife. He did so, and found his own knife, lost seven years previously, and the tattered shift. The truth flashed on him, and he rushed off in search of his wife. He found her cowering before the apparition on the threshold, and began violently upbraiding her for the agony she had caused him when she had forced his spirit to appear before her. In his hand he still held the rusty knife, and with it he threatened her, while he recounted the tortures she had caused him. Then, observing her preparations for a new rite, he, in a frenzy, flung the knife into his own heart. He lived long enough to tell the neighbours his version of the tragedy and died cursing his wife, and she became as she is now."

They stopped before the door of Gertruda's cell.

CHAPTER X

Lally had forgotten that the sergeant carried the keys of all the cells, and for a moment he stood at a loss. Then he remembered that he possessed a master-key, a symbol of power that he was so new to his duties as to have overlooked.

With this he opened, not without a feeling of shame, Gertruda's door, and when it was open he hesitated.

Herr Sandemann, too used to prison routine to feel any delicacy about intruding on a criminal's privacy, glanced at him in surprise, and himself stepped into the cell.

Lally followed, by no means at his ease. The Duke could hardly have found a man more unsuited to this post than Lally Duchene.

The girl was standing in the attitude in which he had first seen her—leaning against the whitewashed wall beneath the narrow slit of window through which flowed the pure, fresh air.

The clean, rough prison dress of orange and grey was, as before, put on carelessly, and slightly disarrayed.

She altogether lacked the neatness of the other female prisoners. Her hair, which grew in naturally stiff waves, was held loosely by a few horn pins, and she was, against the regulations of the prison, barefooted.

When she heard the door open she turned on the intruders that long, mournful glance that Lally had seen once before and never forgotten.

"Do you speak to her." He addressed the pastor, filled with distaste for his task.

Herr Sandemann responded at once.

"We have come to see you," he said, "on the doctor's report."

Then for the first time Lally heard her speak.

"It is good of you," she murmured.

The quality of her voice was peculiar; so was the accent. Lally would have taken her for a foreigner. She was facing them now, the curving lines of her figure showing dark against the pale wall, on which Lally could discover faint tracings of a painting that had been whitewashed over—dim figures, and probably of those saints that this girl could least bear to consider.

"You do not look ill," said Lally, forgetting his embarrassment in his curiosity.

She was indeed the embodiment of florid health, perfectly put together, poised and modelled with rich colour in her flesh, her eyes, her hair.

Lally thought of the chaplet so mysteriously found outside her door; he fancied how magnificent it would look pressed down on those waves of hair in which gold and silver, iron and ebony, seemed mingled. The girl did not answer, but looked at him with steadfast eyes.

She was of a type quite unknown to him—inhuman, with the god-like look of some noble wild animal. The face was peculiar; not beautiful according to the Wiesbaden standard of beauty, but compelling the gaze and swaying the senses. The features were small, yet blunt and broad; the brow low, the eyes far apart; the nostrils wide; the lips very full, yet firm; the chin slightly cleft. Her colouring was luscious and indefinite, and seemed to change with the light and shade that played over her as if it was compounded of all the rosy whites, faint purples, and amber gold of flowers and fruit.

Lally had never before seen anything like her; she bewildered him, so little did her appearance fit in with her story.

"How is it that you are here?" he asked, in genuine amaze.

"I wonder," said Gertruda simply.

"Do you not know that you could have done so differently with yourself?" asked Lally.

"I never thought about it." The speech was primitive as her appearance; as simple and as alluring.

The pastor pointed to a distaff in the corner.

"That was given you that you might employ yourself," he remarked serenely. "Why do you not use it?"

"I do not know how to spin," she answered calmly.

"A German maiden, and not know how to spin!" cried the pastor.

Gertruda laughed.

The laughter made her cell seem absurd—some huge joke. She gave Lally the extraordinary impression that she could, if she wished, shake the walls about her and walk away. He took his eyes from her with an effort to be stern and practical.

"The doctor said that you should have fresh air and exercise, Gertruda Gerhardt, so I think to release you from your solitary imprisonment and employ you with the other women."

"It is a great concession," said the pastor drily.

"What can you do?" added Lally.

"Do?" she repeated.

"I mean, what work?"

"No work at all."

"Did you not work at Kiedrich?" demanded Lally.

"No."

"You could labour in the fields."

"I know nothing about it," she replied simply.

"Yet men employed you at Kiedrich?"

"Yes, men employed me."

Lally felt himself flush.

"Then there is some kind of work that you can do?"

"*Those men all loved me*," replied the girl gravely. "They liked to see me in their vineyards and their fields."

"You see that she is a shameless jade," said the pastor warmly.

"*Love brings a blessing on the harvest*," said the girl gravely. "The crops are poor at Eberbach because there is no love."

Then she did an extraordinary thing. She looked straight at the commandant with her warm-coloured, innocent eyes, and added, "*or was not until you and I came here, Lally Duchene*."

The pastor, usually so gentle, was shocked into anger.

"Your insolence is beyond bearing, woman. Do you know who this gentleman is?" he said.

"Why, Lally Duchene, who was sent from Wiesbaden because of love."

"Who told you that tale?" demanded Lally. "It was Luy," he added.

"Perhaps it was Luy," she said calmly.

Lally worked himself into anger against her.

"I perceive you have no mind to be reformed, but require severe treatment," he said. "The Duke thinks to restart wine-making and perfumery at Eberbach."

"But wine has never ceased to be made at Eberbach," said the girl.

"But the vineyards and cellars have been let off to farmers. The Duke thinks to take it in his own hands and employ the prisoners in this labour."

"Oh," smiled Gertruda, "the Duke is young and beautiful, they say."

Lally was deeply angry now.

"You need much discipline and chastening," he said hotly. "Herr Sandemann here shall heal you with penance and fasting—I will set you to work under him at the perfumes, and I will see that he is very rigid with you."

"Are you angry that I spoke flatteringly of the Duke?" asked Gertruda calmly. "Will you be so angry if I say that you please me well, Lally Duchene?"

"Your arts are crude," said Lally sternly, but his heart was beating fast.

She looked at him with those strangely steadfast eyes.

"Why did you bring this old man with you?" she asked. "Were you afraid to come and see me alone?"

Lally was furious that she had divined the exact truth. He gazed at her with bitter coldness. "Why do you go barefoot?" he asked. "I insist you wear the prison hose and shoes."

The girl looked down at her feet.

"Are they more beautiful than these?" she asked.

Both the men glanced away. Her feet were of perfect beauty; Lally remembered them as they had shown silver in the moonlight. How was it that a peasant girl had such feet? It seemed incredible.

"Ah, Lally Duchene," said the girl mournfully, "you go against your heart when you persecute me."

"I, persecute you!" exclaimed the young man violently. "Do you forget where you are? In prison for a shameful offence."

So obvious and distressing was his sudden emotion that the pastor interfered.

"Let us leave her, Herr Graf; it is useless to argue with these people."

That he thought the commandant had already gone beyond his dignity showed in his manner. Lally flushed, and, without daring to look at Gertruda, again left the cell.

It gave him some satisfaction to firmly turn the key on her cell.

"I understand why they call her a witch," he said.

He seemed unnerved, almost like a man who has been frightened. Herr Sandemann's placid nature was stirred and uneasy.

"There is certainly something strange about her," he remarked. "I never noticed it so much before. A child of nature, utterly untaught. Perhaps the law is too severe for such as she."

"Instruct her in religion," said Lally.

"I shall have a hard task; she seems entirely careless and wanton," replied the pastor. "Perhaps it were best to leave her as she is, in close confinement."

"No," said Lally quickly, "I cannot bear to think of that. The doctor said that she might become mad."

"She seems to me very far from insanity, but to be perfectly composed."

"She must leave that cell," asserted Lally, wondering how he should pass the day without seeing her again.

"Well, you take the responsibility, Herr Graf," remarked Herr Sandemann drily, and Lally knew that he was condemning what he thought was a libertine's interest in a desirable woman. He felt the anger of a man misjudged at this definition, yet he could not himself have named his feelings differently.

To check the vexation of his unbidden thoughts he began to talk quickly on another subject, expounding the letter he would write to the Duke and what he should say about the perfumery and wine-making.

Herr Sandemann was voluble and pedantic on this subject.

It was, he said, absurd to suppose that the Duke could take on the wine-making at Eberbach.

The Steinberg, the large vineyard at the back of the cloisters, was one of the finest in the Rhinegau, and produced in great abundance the finest Riesling grape. It was let to several farmers, who worked as the paid servants of wine brokers, and they also hired the larger portions of the cellars for storing the wine in casks.

The big farm at the end of the valley was kept for the sole purpose of supplying manure for this vineyard, the dressing and tending of which gave employment to nearly all the surrounding peasantry, who, though the pay was poor—far less than could be got in the silver mines—yet were eager for the work on account of the feasts provided at the harvest festivals.

"And how," finished the pastor, "can the Duke, with these prisoners, very few of whom are trained in agriculture, take over their organisation? It would be to rob the whole district of employment and to make himself very unpopular."

"He could buy up the whole concern," said Lally, who hated these practical details and was becoming intensely irritated by this man's presence.

"It is his," explained Herr Sandemann patiently. "These people are his tenants, paying a yearly rent."

Lally, of course, had known this; he lifted his shoulders in vexation at the correction. "He can withdraw the concession then; he will do as he wishes with his own property, of course."

"And throw honest people out of work to give it to untrained convicts?" insisted the pastor, with a tiresome air of reproach.

"Well," said Lally, who would have liked to have been violently insolent, "you may be sure that His Highness will do as he pleases."

"Which means that you will, Herr Graf," replied the clergyman obstinately, "and that you have set your heart on this whim."

"Do you think that I have so much power with the Duke?"

"If you have," said Herr Sandemann, "I hope you will use it to dissuade him from this idea. There are so many reforms more needed at Eberbach."

"And your perfumery?"

"That can only be a small matter to begin. I have not too much time, and not many of the right kind of flowers grow here; but I will make a beginning whenever I receive the necessary materials."

"Make a list of them," replied Lally negligently, and the two men parted in the cloisters, the pastor to return to his duties, Lally to wander round the cloister garth, which now seemed pressed full of sweetness and fragrancy.

The girl Gertruda!

Something was grotesquely wrong with things as men had made them. Here was such a day as this, golden-purple, odorous, winelike, the epitome of early summer. There was the valley, the wood, the river, all full of secret beauties, potent as magic to charm the senses. There were the long hours ahead to the beautiful twilight, which thrilled the pulses to think of, and there was that girl, wonderful as an opening rose, under lock and key, in a monk's cell, with two feet of sky to gaze at. And he held that key, and must be her jailer, and walk here alone and think of his duties and his honour—and Pauline. Pauline, who had been foregone for these same conventions—Pauline, who held him in a barren land and made the ends and purposes of love a farce. Here was a waste of all life's best things, and youth was so short!

His mental infidelity to what should have been a great devotion vexed him as being trivial and common, but he could not reason it away. He knew that he was quite ready to love this peasant wanton, and forget Pauline. He compared them—the fine, delicate features of the court lady with the girl's strange, simple face; the pale colouring, slyly helped by art, of Pauline, with Gertruda's rich glowing hues; the artificial figure, the tight satin waist, the bust rising from lace and whalebone, he compared with the limbs which conveyed firm softness through the cotton dress, and shaped the poor stuff into noble curves, waistless, low bosomed, unconfined, ready to emerge perfect from the cheap shift as a flower from the withered sheath, whereas with Pauline, her dress was part of her. Even at night she was powdered and adorned. Lally, sickening at himself, tried to recall some duty to perform.

The clock struck mid-day and he turned to the kitchens; it was his business to sometimes see the lunatics fed.

In the great low room, clean and full of sunshine, rows of female prisoners were bending over the brick fires and ovens that lined one side of the room; on the spotless wooden tables what seemed end-less lines of bowls full of steaming soup and plates of meat and bread stood ready.

Lally went to one of the windows, away from the smell of the cooking. He was cruelly glad the girl Gertruda was locked away from this; he would not have liked to see her with these other dull, patient women waiting on maniacs.

The door at the end of the huge kitchen opened, and the lunatics streamed in, both guided and driven by a couple of soldiers.

With fierce and uncouth shouts they fell upon their food, each bearing away a portion and instantly devouring it with unrestrained voracity. The kitchen was a confusion of senseless sound.

Lally turned away, eager to get into the fresh air.

CHAPTER XI

Lally composed a suitably formal reply to the Duke, striving to allow malice to show beneath the smoothness of the words.

He sent a list, composed in irony, but reading like official gravity, of the reforms and improvements needed at Eberbach, beginning with the restoration of the church and ending with the project of open-air baths for the prisoners.

He wrote of the perfumery and the wine-making and the difficulties in the way of each, and in conclusion begged the Duke to send some other officer on a visit of inspection to Eberbach, and not to take his word or opinion for anything.

He said this, not only to show that he disclaimed all responsibility in the post to which he had been so hastily and incongruously appointed, but because he longed to see and speak to someone from Wiesbaden—from the old world. As he had at least an acquaintanceship with every gentleman of the court, the Prince could send no one who was a stranger, to whom and from whom he would not be able to glean news of what was said of him in the society from which he had been so summarily thrust, and what was the gesture and expression of those who now regarded in amaze the empty pedestal on which he once stood.

To Pauline he did not write at all—he could not bring himself to do so. Her image was blurred and broken, and seemed shut completely out of his present life.

He knew that he should never be allowed to forget her; that some day she must return, probably with violence, into his life; but meanwhile he would do nothing to keep in touch with her, and he hardly thought of her at all.

Of Gertruda he thought too much; his own contempt at his swift yielding to the first fair face encountered after separation from the object of his last infatuation controlled him far more than any notions of prudence or honour or loyalty.

His intelligence was always apt to sit in judgment on his senses and instinct, and in this case at once scorned and restrained as well as condemning.

He heard reports of her. She was either sick or sullen, would not spin, weave, or sew, nor wear the rough footgear provided; the doctor maliciously reminded him of his promise to give her some liberty, and he looked forward, half in dread, half in excited anticipation, to the day when she would work in the perfumery.

For then he would, in the usual routine of his duties, have to see her daily, and could teach himself to loathe or despise or ignore her peculiar allure.

The days slipped by like the even turning of a wheel, with regular, soothing monotony. The peace, the beauty, the strangeness, lulled Lally like draughts of some drug. In place of his usual eager energy he became touched by sloth.

His light duties once over, he would loiter in the orchard, in the old cathedral, or the cloister garden, with some ancient book of legends borrowed from Herr Sandemann, or roam for hours in the wood that was, with every visit, more like a place of enchantment than before. Sometimes he would climb through the grove of oaks and look on the Rhine and rich country beyond, viewing the distant city towers with a curious sense of bitter sweetness, half longing to return, half clinging to his drowsy exile.

The days were splendid in unbroken gold. The peasants predicted a hot summer and autumn, and an ideal harvest. Last year, they told Lally, it had been poor, for the early frost had set in before the grapes were all plucked.

Lally found himself looking ahead with pleasure to this harvest, of which he heard so much and which was celebrated with such lavish festivals and rites almost pagan, more fitting the worshippers of Bacchus than Christ.

He visited the Steinberg, the great vineyard attached to the monastery, which seemed to occupy half the valley, and watched the quiet peasants and the docile ponies coming and going with the cartloads of dressing for the vines, which were beginning to show a foot or so above the ground, adorned with tendrils and leaves of a pink amber hue.

His only further interest beyond these lingerings and wanderings was the preparation of the laboratories.

He had them cleaned out and lightened by the whitewash so beloved of Herr Sandemann, the rose-tree cut ruthlessly away from the window it darkened, the furnaces mended, cleaned, and tested, the sinks and vessels put in good order, and many new things ordered from Wiesbaden.

The pastor, in his ingenuous honesty, was uneasy at all this trouble and expense, and continually repeated that the whole affair was just an experiment which must be long before it could justify itself. German perfumes were despised, and could never compete with those of the East or France.

"The Duke can make them fashionable at Wiesbaden," said Lally negligently.

Herr Sandemann was worried about the flowers, too; the violets were over, the roses not yet on, the other flowers capable of yielding perfume were few at Eberbach. To buy musk, ambergris, frankincense, or castor would be expensive.

Lally listened without interest to these complaints. What did it matter to him whether the distilleries yielded a single saleable drop of perfume or no, or if the Duke's money was wasted? He merely wished to give this last darling of his fancy a background suitable to her strangeness; to amuse himself by dabbling in a curious art which rather attracted him. He had not even the Duke's authority for his expenditure, but he ordered lavishly everything that Herr Sandemann mentioned as likely to be required.

July was wearing out with a daily intensity of heat, the weather, like Lally's life, set in a golden calm which was yet creating harvest, bitter or sweet, for the near future, when Lally was interrupted in the distillery by a message that there was a young officer who wished to see him—a young officer who had ridden from Wiesbaden.

The news came as a shock to Lally, a reminder of that other world that now seemed so far away. Of course this was the visitor he had himself requested. The Duke had taken him at his word then, though after some delay—perhaps seized the opportunity to send a spy.

Old suspicions flashed up in Lally's mind, and he stood irresolute, wishing he had not brought this vexatious interruption on himself, for his mood had changed now and he wanted no news of Wiesbaden. With impetuous bad temper he bade the soldier see to the stranger's horse and comfort and then turn him into the cloister garden to wait.

"I shall not be free for half an hour or so," he added.

As the man went to execute these orders Lally stood silent, considering if this stranger's coming meant the end of an epoch; if this false calm was to end suddenly. There might be news—letters from Pauline, from the Duke.

Lally's brow lowered; he wished that he could have had the distillery ready and Gertruda liberated before there was a spy on his actions. Days ago he had fretted for her freedom, but Herr Sandemann was resolute that there was yet no work for an assistant.

Now he was alone with Luy, who had helped continuously in the task of clearing up the laboratories. Lally disliked him more and more, but found him remarkably quick and clever at any kind of work, very different to the other soldiers, who were dull and heavy when taken from their daily duties.

The two were without their coats, for the heat was great in the low room; the fine lawn shirt and the rough cotton one were both soiled and dishevelled. Lally's thick dark hair was gathered untidily into a black hair-ribbon. Luy's ugly reddish crop showed damp. The walls, shelves, furnaces, and tables were clean and bare, but the floor was covered with litter.

Lally had been arranging a collection of old glass bottles that he had discovered, and which gave him great pleasure to handle. They were of foreign, perhaps Venetian, make, and in many unusual shapes and colours. He could see Gertruda pouring essences into them or handling them with lazy movements.

On the floor in front of him were small hand tincture presses, tap funnels and stills, maceration pans, and pots and jars for the oils, ottos, and pomades.

All the metal, porcelain, and glass was new and clean and shone pleasantly. On the table by Lally, near the old glass bottles, were small quantities of oils in common bottles—bergamot, bay, and balsam of styrax camphor, cassia, orris, cinnamon, sandal, and other Asiatic perfumes which were so well corked that they gave no perfume to the air. In muslin bags there were nutmeg, tonquin beans, dried thyme, marjoram, and origanum. These, gathered from the convent garden and still fresh, gave forth the slightly medicinal yet fragrant odour of herbs.

Lally liked the surroundings; he liked to lean out of the low, long window and watch Luy rinsing out the vessels, first with water and then with spirit, and then wiping them with fine, clean cloths.

He did not wish to meet this officer who must most certainly disturb and even alter his life. He had a desire to be rude to him; to send him back to Wiesbaden that very evening.

He lingered, unintentionally discourteous, his thoughts rebellious, his lazy gaze fixed on Luy. How ugly the man was; the thick neck and full cheeks, the long nose and teeth, the tiny eyes, the coarse reddish complexion, gave him the appearance of a grotesque; he was not, Lally thought, unlike one of the hideous mediaeval carvings of Eberbach.

Suddenly the man looked up, as if conscious of this idle scrutiny.

"The officer is waiting, Herr Graf," he said respectfully, and rising, fetched Lally's braided and laced coat.

But the commandant wilfully put it aside.

"It is too hot," he said briefly, and strolled out into the garden.

It was a glorious hour of late afternoon. The colour and substance of everything seemed rarefied into pure gold. Every sense was penetrated by the sense of sun and summer peace and beauty.

Lally put the disordered hair back from his low forehead. The intense light made his locks show reddish; his complexion had browned since his stay at Eberbach, and looked dark above the white shirt; the faint scent of tonquin and cassia clung to him. He walked slowly, his eyes narrowed in unconscious defiance.

As he entered the cloisters he saw at once his man, leaning against the well-head and looking at the pigeons that circled round on the paving stones, trailing their pure white tails, and their wings delicately stained with a purplish pink, like faded blood marks.

He had his back to Lally, who thus had leisure to observe the stranger as he sauntered through the shadowed cloisters.

The newcomer was young, elegant, and wore the Nassavian uniform under a light travelling coat. Beneath his hat his hair, of a light dull bronze tint, was confined by a silver buckle. Lally knew that fashion of hairdressing, and the unusual colour of those locks.

He no longer idled, but hastened into the garden. At the sound of his step on the flags the stranger turned. Lally's incredulous conviction was confirmed—it was the Duke of Nassau.

"Good evening, Lally Duchene," he said gravely. Lally flushed, aware of his appearance, of the time he had kept his sovereign waiting.

"I never thought that it might be Your Highness," he said, with a tinge of bitterness through his confusion.

"How should you? I call myself Major Schomberg, who has come to see Eberbach, and these needed reforms."

"Your Highness puts me in a cruel position," said Lally.

"I thought," replied the Duke quietly, "that it was the other way about, Lally Duchene?"

"I mean, here, in Eberbach," insisted Lally, "if you are to stay here—in disguise."

"Theatrical, you think? But I could not come here openly. It would have been a great scandal. I cannot afford that. I am supposed to be at Die Platte."

Lally felt despair invade his soul, as if he had been delivered to his enemy.

"Let me go, Highness," he said. "The sight of me must be an offence to you. In a few hours I can be out of Nassau."

"Herr Jesus, no! Do you think that I have done with you, Marquis?"

"If you have not, I beg your Highness to let me know what you want of me," said Lally impetuously.

"Not now," answered the Duke, with sudden uneasiness. "I am tired—tired of Wiesbaden. I had a great desire to be away from it all."

Lally stood silent, sullen.

"This place is very beautiful," added the Duke, almost wistfully.

"Your Highness means to stay here?"

"For a while. I have left my suite at Die Platte. Edgar Sylvanus knows what to say and how to forward letters."

Lally had no doubt of that; the devoted, obsequious, secretary knew more about the government of Nassau than the Duke himself—more about most things. He had always been Lally's enemy, and it was his observation and warning that had caused the downfall of the favourite. The thought of him drove Lally further into anger.

"How am I to treat Your Highness? I have not even any rooms—any servants—"

"There must be rooms enough in Eberbach," smiled Aurelio. "One of your soldiers can wait on me. You will treat me as a fellow-officer."

Lally could have imagined no scheme more hateful, the more so as he was entirely ignorant of what was passing in the Duke's mind—some elaborate plan of revenge, he feared.

"Your Highness will hate Eberbach," he said sourly.

"They say I do not know Nassau well enough—let me begin with the Rhinegau," replied the Duke. "I want to know, too, about this wine-making. I think to work the Steinberg myself, next year at least. Sylvanus says the farmers make a great profit."

"You would make more," said Lally, "with pressed labour."

"I should pay the peasants. We must look into it. And this perfumery?"

"Oh," answered Lally, more and more angry, "that is the most foolish experiment, undertaken, Highness, by the pastor here and myself because there is not enough to do at Eberbach."

"It will interest me," said the Duke calmly. "Have you ever put perfumes in scales, like music?"

Considering the manner in which they had parted, he spoke, Lally thought, with astonishing ease. How had he obtained so much mastery over himself in so short a time?

Lally respected and hated him for it. His enemy seemed to have got beyond his reach—and no word of Pauline. How long were these antagonists to circle round each other in the dark?

The Duke was still leaning against the well-head, looking down in a musing fashion almost as if he had forgotten the presence of Lally, who stared at him with bitter keenness.

Aurelio Johann Georg Wilhelm, Prince, Duke, and Plazgraf, with titles that the heralds would take half an hour to recite, born on both sides of some of the oldest blood in Europe, and established, by curious turns of fortune, in this minute and absolute sovereignty, was then in his twenty-sixth year and the fifth of his reign, having left Heidelberg College for a throne on the death of his cousin.

He was an only child and had early been left an orphan, being brought up in Germany, Holland, and France in a proud and courtly seclusion.

He had always been serious-minded, fastidious, silent, haughty, keenly intelligent, sensitive, overtrained in the duties of royalty, inclined to austerity, but nurtured in class prejudice and aristocratic principles—a young prince not easy to govern or persuade.

He owed more to the great Dutch house from which came his heritage and to his French mother than to any German ancestor. He had nothing in common with the heavy, gross electors and margraves who were his neighbours.

In appearance he was tall, with a slenderness that might conceal strength, wide in the shoulders, palely dark, with little colour either in his dull, bronze-tinted hair, in his grey eyes or his clear complexion. The features were straight and of almost classic perfection; his profile on his coinage was the best likeness taken of him. In the presence of Lally his personality was completely overshadowed.

CHAPTER XII

"There is one man here who will recognise Your Highness," said Lally sharply.

"Yes?"

"A certain Luy, my body-servant, who comes from Wiesbaden. I am sure he knows you by sight." Lally spoke with some malice.

But the Prince remained indifferent.

"It is likely that several of the soldiers here know me," he answered, "but they are bound to respect my incognito, and if I call myself Major Schomberg, to treat me as such."

"And the scandal that Your Highness is afraid of?" For the first time the Duke showed signs of feeling of anger.

"It is not *I* who am *afraid* of any scandal," he replied.

It seemed as if the moment had come when one of them must mention the name of Pauline, but the Duke caught himself up and asked abruptly if Lally would show him his lodgings. Lally, too, soon had himself well in hand.

"I must beg your Highness to take my rooms. There are none others prepared."

"Marquis, I absolutely refuse to take your rooms. There must be others in Eberbach."

The Duke spoke with such sharp haughtiness that Lally flushed.

"There are the old state apartments," he answered, "but they have long been shut up."

"Anything will do. Let us go and see them. You have the keys?"

"I do not think there are any keys. I fear you will be utterly uncomfortable," replied Lally stiffly. "However, I am in your hands, Highness."

The situation seemed to shift from tragedy to comedy. Now he was inclined to smile at the Duke's whim, which would react more on himself than anyone else.

The truth was that Lally's love of life would not suffer him to be long depressed by any circumstances, however untoward. He looked up at the purpling sky, cut by the fine lines of the cloisters, and scented the air fragrant with living green, and felt it was no longer in the Duke's power to greatly discompose him—but, then, he had forgotten Gertruda.

He led the Duke round the outside of the convent to the magnificent old door that led to the state apartments, once occupied by the bishops of Mainz and other princely guests of Eberbach.

There, long disused and neglected, overlooked the great vineyard, the Steinberg, the farm at the end of it, the wood and the hills, and was near the old chapel that the monks had turned into a press house.

"The harvest was the great festival of the year with these holy heathen," said Lally, "and the guests liked to be near the vineyard."

"I should like to see the harvest at Eberbach," replied the Duke.

"Your Highness means to stay as long?" asked Lally drily.

"I hope," said the Duke, "that my business will be settled before then."

"I hope so, or one of us dead," replied Lally.

The Duke looked at him strangely, and the two passed into the building, the heavy door giving at a push.

"This should be mended," remarked the Prince.

"There was nothing within to steal and no one ever comes here," was Lally's quick excuse. Though, as a matter of truth, he had never troubled about this part of the building, nor set foot inside it before.

They ascended a noble stone staircase, chill with damp and foul with dust. The light, filtering through the deep-set lancet window, showed colourless and unearthly.

Lally shivered in his thin shirt. The Duke in silence offered him his travelling cloak. Lally, in silence, put it aside.

The walls were covered with rude carvings. Lally noticed again and again the boar's head.

At the top of the stairs was a fine suite of apartments, opening one into another, and looking, by means of fine arched windows, into the huge vineyard and the press house, which was adorned with large figures of St. Bernard and the Virgin.

The first three rooms were entirely without furniture. In the fourth was a massive bed standing on a dais in an alcove, a black cabinet, and several black chairs covered in leather faded to a smooth orange colour, and a set of green worsted tapestry on the walls.

"I will stay here," said the Duke. He went to the window and looked curiously on the scene below.

The peasants were just leaving the vineyard, which they had been weeding; the rows of vines showed precise and regular along the bare, dark earth; the white handkerchiefs of the women gleamed along the wide tracks left for the carts; the four lines of the roofed wall looked hard and straight, strange in this wild spot.

Beyond, a party of convicts were moving slowly homeward through the orchards that reached to the vineyard wall.

The Duke looked at them, and Lally looked at him, wondering what emotion he felt—of shame or compunction or remorse—at the sight of these wretched people, nearly all of whom were expiating some personal offence against himself.

But the young man's regular features showed no sign of feeling.

"The prisoners' quarters are not near here?" he asked.

So he was merely considering his own comfort. Lally sneered, glad of an opportunity to scorn his enemy.

"No," he replied, "they are all housed in the other modernised part of the building; so are the maniacs."

"The maniacs?" repeated the Prince. "I had forgotten them."

"I daresay they will rouse Your Highness to-night," said Lally. "The least disturbance causes them to cry and howl, and those in the pavilions you are bound to hear."

"Horrible," said the Duke. "They should be moved to a separate establishment."

"I believe that has been suggested to Your Highness."

"I know, Marquis."

"And you have not pleased to attend to these matters."

"Marquis," said the Duke, with dignity, "I have not so long come to my inheritance, and I have been somewhat distracted."

Lally bowed; the sarcasm of the gesture was obvious.

"My little kingdom, Marquis, is yet a great responsibility."

"Many men would find it so, Highness," said Lally drily.

"I have never been a fribble," replied the Prince, as if defending himself.

Lally lifted his shoulders as high as he dare. "Why, no, the opposite, Highness," he said, and was gratified by the young Duke's flush.

"A pedant you mean, Marquis? Well, that also can be cured."

Lally bowed again.

"If Your Highness would study the penal laws of Nassau you would find many spots and flaws—"

The Duke moved from the window with sudden alertness.

"I have come here to study other things, Marquis," he said. "If you will have a bed sent into this room, and to-morrow have it cleaned and put in order—"

"Your Highness makes your quarters here?" asked Lally.

Certainly the spruce, almost over-groomed figure of the Duke looked almost grotesquely out of place in the deserted, dusty, forlorn state chamber.

"I am not an effeminate, Marquis," he replied. "This will suit my purpose well enough, I think."

"And Your Highness's meals? This is a long way from the kitchens, and we are short of service."

The Duke hesitated for a second, then said with a slight effort:

"I will eat with you. It will cause comment were I to do otherwise."

"Then I will show Your Highness my apartments. Supper will shortly be ready."

The two, so ill-assorted, so antagonistic, left the darkening rooms together, walking side by side after the manner of friends, talking quietly, each full of hot and bitter thoughts.

As they crossed the twilight orchards they met the sergeant, returning from conducting his batch of prisoners to the convent.

Lally, with quick malice, delivered the Duke to this man's charge, bidding him see to Major Schomberg's comfort and that supper was set for two.

Having thus disposed of his enemy, he returned to the distillery, where Luy was still working by the light of a lamp.

Lally flung on his coat and laughed.

"Fellow, your master has arrived," he said quickly.

Luy rose from his polishing and wiped his hairy red hands on the leather he held. His queer face was flushed and looked stranger than usual in the uncertain light of the lamp.

"My master?" he repeated.

"The Duke," said Lally, leaning against the table of perfumes.

"The Duke!"

"Aye, play the simple fool," smiled Lally. "I know you are his spy."

Luy made no answer; he did not seem even interested.

"I suppose," continued Lally, "that you told him that I was getting out of hand, and that it were best for him to come and see for himself."

"I do not know what you are talking of, Herr Graf."

"Bah! You know perfectly well. You are not one of these peasant fools. You know why you are sent here, and why the Duke charged you to spy on me."

Luy lifted the last of the vessels that had cumbered the floor to a shelf. During his captain's absence he had made the distillery precise and neat.

"You are quite mistaken, Herr Graf," he said quietly. "I have seen the Duke, but he certainly has never seen me."

Lally hesitated, doubtful what to believe.

"And to tell the truth, Herr Captain," continued the man, with his respectful but indifferent air, "I am not at all pleased that the Duke should come to Eberbach."

"What difference does it make to *you*?" demanded Lally.

Luy, putting on his coat and buckling his buff Nassau belt, made a strange remark.

"This pedantic young man from the city," he said, "will spoil everything."

This speech, and the manner of it, was so unlike anything the man had said before, or what any common soldier would say, that Lally felt a faint sense of discomfort.

"How—spoil everything?" he asked, leaning forward.

Luy, in replying, showed his disagreeable teeth.

"Herr Graf, Eberbach is a strange place—it does not suit everyone. You, perhaps; the Duke, no."

Lally laughed lightly, though he felt an odd excitement.

"You are not what you pretend to be, Luy," he said.

"I was many things before I was a soldier," replied the man.

"And you like Eberbach?"

"Yes."

"And wish to stay here?"

"Yes."

"Yet you say it is haunted?"

Luy smiled.

"You have not been troubled of late, then, Captain?"

"I have seen nothing since the boar the night I returned late from Kiedrich."

"The boar," said Luy blankly. "What had the boar to do with phantoms?"

"I thought he was one himself, my friend, so near the convent; and there is this association between Eberbach and the boar. There are too many boars' heads where I was to-day."

"Where was that?" asked Luy sharply.

"In the old state apartment; the Duke lodges there."

"Well, well," said Luy. "I wish he had not come to Eberbach."

This was spoken in such a manner that Lally felt as if he had an ally in the man. He could hardly believe that Luy was such a fine liar as to be able to deceive him thus, and he dismissed the idea of his being the Duke's spy.

Secretly he was rather pleased that this queer creature should be antagonistic to his own enemy.

"You will wait on us at table to-night," he said. "And be attentive to the Duke, who passes as Major Schomberg. Tell them to send up good wines, with a bottle of Cabinet for the dessert."

"Yes, Herr Graf."

He put out the lamp, followed Lally into the cloister garden, and locked the door of the distillery.

"The Duke will be interested in this perfumery business, Herr Graf, and in Gertruda Gerhardt," he said.

Lally swung round in the dusk.

"Herr Jesus! What do you mean?"

"Do not think me impertinent," replied Luy calmly. "I am no more an ordinary soldier than you are an ordinary officer. I might be of use to you."

"How?" sneered Lally.

They were standing so close in the aromatic garden that each could feel the other's breath on his cheek.

"Distract the Duke with Gertruda and he will let your Pauline free."

At mention of this name Lally flamed with a sense of sudden madness. That Luy should dare! And the fury of the thought that his enemy might cheat him of the other woman! He seized hold of Luy and shook him to and fro.

The fellow twisted himself free and laughed.

"You are not so up in the stirrups that you can choose your friends, Herr Graf!" he cried. "And I could help you to—Pauline."

"Herr Jesus!" answered Lally, beside himself. "It is the other I want."

At this there was such a burst of laughter that his blood was cooled by a sudden panic.

"Is that you, Luy?" he cried, for the moon was not yet up and the garden completely dark.

The laughter continued; it seemed to echo from every wall in the convent.

"The fellow is half-crazy," said Lally aloud and angrily.

He went quickly to his own rooms.

Lally's evening meal was not a pleasant one. He was himself in dangerously high spirits, and drank heavily in defiance of his guest. The bottle of Cabinet, served with the strawberries and cherries that formed the dessert, he drank by himself.

The Duke was grave, sad, restrained, and would not drink. Luy, who waited on them, had something odd in his manner, and showed a thinly veiled antipathy to the Duke that amused and pleased Lally.

The Prince took his departure early, the sergeant conducting him to the distant apartment he had selected, which had been hastily arranged for his convenience.

Lally thought he had a good nerve to take up such a lodging in such a place as Eberbach, and Luy grinned maliciously to see him go.

Lally, who was intoxicated for the first time since he had been at Eberbach, loved the fellow for that grin.

"I hope your ghosts will plague the young fool, Luy," he said, almost before the Duke was out of earshot.

"You never believed in them," replied Luy drily, as he cleared away the dishes, "and I never spoke of ghosts, Herr Graf."

"I saw them," said Lally, "saw them!"

Luy paused in his quick movements and looked round sharply. Lally, taking no notice of him, continued to talk loosely of the figures he had seen beneath his window and the boar that he had met at the state gateway in the moonlight.

"That cursed beast haunts the whole of this place," he said. "Everywhere I see a likeness of him which reminds me—of someone—"

"Herr Captain," interrupted Luy quietly, "you are drunk. Do you want it known? Go to bed and be ready to meet the Duke to-morrow."

Lally rose, holding on to his chair. He was a dishevelled, rather wild figure, with excited eyes and flushed face beneath his dark fallen hair.

"You are a good fellow, Luy," he muttered. "You'll help me to outwit this jackanape, eh? I stole Pauline from him, but he shan't steal this girl from me."

"Go to bed, Herr Graf," said Luy, taking him by the arm, "go to bed."

CHAPTER XIII

Lally woke next morning full of sullen remorse for his behaviour of the night before, and of dismay at the thought of the Duke at Eberbach.

The exultation of yesterday evening had gone; he felt dull and foolish and at cross purposes with life. He was angry to think that the Duke might have left him in scorn—"A rake, a sot," Nassau might have said, with that pedantic air of his—and Lally felt himself a fool for giving these points into his enemy's hands. He had fallen on his bed fully dressed, and he searched in his pocket for the pass key. If Luy had not been trustworthy he might have secured that when he helped Lally from the supper-table. He was, perhaps, not so much trustworthy as uninterested. At any rate, the key was safe.

Lally made himself as spruce as he had been in the old Wiesbaden days, and waited for the Duke at the breakfast-table.

But the sergeant came with the message that Major Schomberg had been long abroad and had broken his fast with bread and milk at the farm; he requested, later, Captain Duchene's company on a visit to the Steinberg. Lally assented with a bad grace. Why was Nassau fooling in this manner?

"The fellow ought to have been a monk," grumbled Lally, when alone with his servant. Luy grinned. He seemed to dislike the Duke as much as Lally did.

It was another golden day, perfumed, hot, a day that made all thought of work or duty hateful.

Lally would have liked to have wandered off to the woods, the hills, or the banks of the Rhine. Rebellion against every trammel of convention was hot in his blood. He went through his routine sullenly, and sullenly waited on the Duke at the appointed place.

This was the wall of the great vineyard nearest the convent, pierced with several doors to allow of carts passing in and out and near the press house, the entrance to the cellars and the open-air vaults where the choicest of Cabinet wine was stored.

The Duke was there already when Lally arrived. He was unpowdered and looked pale; his manner was as it had been yesterday—cold, sad, and civil.

"Come into the press house," he said. "It is curious; the monks have turned a chapel into what is really an altar to Bacchus."

"Your Highness slept well?" asked Lally drily.

"As well as I am used to sleep of late, Marquis."

"There were no noises or disturbances then, Highness?"

"None; your poor maniacs were quiet."

"And the evil spirits, too?"

"There are evil spirits in Eberbach?" asked Nassau, pausing at the entrance to the press house.

"It is very firmly believed; the whole country is full of legend."

"Ah, yes; the only place where one does not hear them is Wiesbaden."

They entered the press house. It had not been altered from its original design. The walls still showed traces of frescoes in blue and red and green. The eastern windows were yet of painted glass, and a large gilt wood statue of the Virgin had been left on a niche in one corner.

In place of the altar were ten large wooden wine presses, and round the walls were arranged the pails, baskets, scissors, pruning knives, and all the implements used in the vintage.

Two old peasants were working at one of the presses, which they were filling with sacks full of last autumn's lees—a thick, yellowish, clayey fluid.

They stopped respectfully at the entrance of the two officers, but the Duke, approaching, bade them get on with their work, and began to ask several questions as to the wine-making, which they answered with the eagerness of men allowed to speak on the one subject in which they are expert and interested.

Lally leant against the wall, antagonistic and silent; he felt that his enemy was playing with him, and hardly disguised his resentment. He had to listen against his will to the speech of the peasants; their voices, rough and unmodulated, filled the close, wine-perfumed air of the chapel.

They earned, one said, a shilling and a half a day, working from five in the morning till seven at night. They could have got more in the silver mines, but everyone would rather work in the vineyard—there were a great many goblins in the mines.

The Duke asked them about their present occupation. They said that this was last year's wine which had been fermenting in casks all the winter and racked for the first time in the spring, and again now, six weeks after; in each stuck cask, they added, was usually about ten gallons of lees and thick wine. This they were now pressing in the sacks; the resultant wine would be used for filling up.

The wine would be racked every spring and autumn until four years old, when it would be bottled.

"I am going to see your vineyard," smiled the Duke. "I do not know as much as I should of the principal industry of Nassau."

"It is the finest vineyard in the Duchy," said one of the old men, watching the yellow drops oozing from the press. "As large again as the Johannisberg, and producing better wine."

"But sometimes you have a bad year?"

"Yes, and then that is misery for all of us. There is nothing else but the vines and the mines."

"But the Duke employs so many in bottling the mineral waters and at the baths."

"One cannot live on what he pays," answered the peasant simply, "and must not touch a twig to light a fire, pick up a handful of leaves for fodder, or let a beast graze on a scrap of grass. Everything belongs to the Duke, you see."

Lally looked at Nassau, but that young man betrayed no sign of confusion.

"I hope you will have a good harvest this year," he said quietly.

"There is every sign of it if the weather holds and we have an early frost. Last year it was November before the grapes were fully ripe, and after that the bitter weather came too soon."

"I shall hope to see your festivals," replied the Duke, and, beckoning to Lally, left the chapel.

"What does your Highness mean by this?" broke out Lally in uncontrollable exasperation.

"It means that I am really interested," said Nassau. "After all, a man generally is in his own property."

"Wiesbaden used to content Your Highness."

"One changes," answered the young man briefly. "And my taste for pleasure has been spoilt."

Opposite them was the small building where the best wines were pressed and the outdoor vault where they were kept; this was protected from the sun by shrubs and trees. The Duke asked what it was, and on being told smiled and said:

"The wine that you drank last night at dessert, and would have been better without, I think, Marquis."

"There are times," replied Lally, "when it is better to be drunk than sober."

They passed through one of the open doors in the roofed wall of the vineyard and saw it spreading before them—a long oval, which covered the hill of the Steinberg. Two pavilions broke the even rows of the vines, and beyond the most distant wall the wild beauty of the wood tossed against the blazing blue of the cloudless sky.

The Steinberg was entirely planted with the short-wooded, small vine, called the Riesling, which grows slowly and ripens late, so they now showed little foliage, the majority being pruned away to two branches, one upright and left to grow for next year, one outstretched and supported on stakes. This long cane, now covered with shoots of leaves and beginning to form buds, was being stopped by women, who were pinching off the tops above the sixth leaf. Some of the vines were dressed in the peculiar fashion known as the Rhenish basket, each of which carried three to five branches bearing fruit spurs.

The heavily manured ground was clear of even the smallest weed, and to Lally at least the scene was disappointing. It entirely lacked that opulence, that riot of colour and jollity associated with wine, and only conveyed the sense of unremitting toil for a bare livelihood.

Yet when he had come alone before, he had enjoyed his visit.

He pointed out to the Duke the different parts of the vineyard, that which produced the best wine being known as "The golden beaker," while that bearing the second quality being called "The garden of roses."

"I do not see why the prisoners should not work this," said the Duke.

"The farmers and the peasants would be thrown out of work," replied Lally quickly, "and we have no one among the convicts who knows the work of these *Weinberg Hofleute*, who have given their lives to this study of its culture."

"I could employ them as well as the farmers do," insisted the Duke obstinately, "and there are other vineyards where these peasants could find work, and the mines."

Lally looked at him with dislike, and the two left the Steinberg.

The Duke expressed a wish to see the cellars, and Lally, who had never been there, was making some demur when they were interrupted by the approach of Luy.

The man's face and manner were indifferent, as usual, but his news was startling, at least to Lally. One of the prisoners had escaped.

Who?

The girl Gertruda.

Lally's bitter and involuntary curse caused the Duke to flush and frown.

"Who is this girl?" he demanded sternly.

Lally bit his lip in vexation too deep for words.

Luy replied briefly and respectfully:

"One of the prisoners in solitary confinement, Herr Major."

"Her offence?"

"Dissolute conduct."

"Her sentence?"

"Five years."

The Duke seemed to wince a little. Lally, in angry malice, hoped that he was thinking of Pauline.

"Her age?"

"I do not know, Herr Major. A young girl—perhaps eighteen."

"And she has escaped?" The Duke took a tone of authority which reduced Lally to a state of galling silence.

"This morning," said Luy composedly, "when her food was taken to her, the cell was found empty—the girl gone—"

Lally broke in furiously:

"Why was I not told of this when the report was made to me this morning?"

"It was hoped to find her, Herr Captain, somewhere in the building. The sergeant was very unwilling to give the alarm."

"Who has the keys?" asked the Duke.

"The sergeant, Herr Major."

"But you"—he turned to Lally—"have the pass key?" His eyes finished the sentence: "And you were drunk last night."

"I have the key, and it has never left my possession," answered Lally swiftly.

But all the while he was thinking of the stories the doctor had told him; and his hatred and suspicion of Luy revived in full force. But stronger even than these feelings was his sensation of wild regret at the loss of Gertruda.

She had been safe, locked in, guarded, his prisoner, waiting his pleasure; it had been in his power to see her any moment that he wished; now she had escaped him before he had even touched her hand.

He was silent, for fear of humiliating himself by a show of futile rage before the Duke, but his eyes shot furies at Luy.

The Prince, being disinterested, treated the matter coolly, and in a practical fashion.

"She cannot be far away," he said. "It is well known that escape from Eberbach is quite hopeless."

"Why?" asked Lally.

"Where can these people go in a country where there are no large towns? Only to their own homes, where they would at once be sought for, or the woods or valleys, where they would die of hunger."

"Let us send a party to search the woods," said Lally.

"By all means. It is strange there should be so much commotion over an affair so simple," said the Duke coldly. "Tell your sergeant to send a search-party to the woods and surrounding country," he added, turning to Luy.

When the soldier had gone, he spoke again to Lally. "Marquis, you were drunk last night, and that fellow took the key to let his wench escape."

Lally was silent in sheer amazed wrath—first, that the Duke should so accurately have discerned the situation; secondly, that Luy should really be in league with Gertruda, a thought in which he was confirmed, since it had so instantly occurred to a stranger.

"I did not like the fellow last night," continued the Prince. "He knows me, and will do all the mischief he can."

Here was the end of the last of Lally's suspicions that Luy was the Duke's spy.

"Let Your Highness get rid of him. It is easy to send him back to Wiesbaden."

"No," replied the Duke, "he knows my identity—perhaps more than that. I could not openly anger him."

"Clap him up!" cried Lally.

"Marquis, I am no tyrant of the Cambyses type," said Nassau indifferently. "The fellow can scarcely trouble us."

"But the girl! Where has he hidden the girl?"

"Hidden her?"

"Of course he knows where she is."

The Duke laughed.

"I think she will be found. Is it so important?"

He looked sharply at Lally, who answered sullenly.

"Such a thing has never happened before at Eberbach. I do not wish the discredit to fall on me."

Nassau interrupted:

"How often have you seen this girl?"

"Twice."

"She is beautiful?"

"I hardly know."

The Duke marked his angry reluctance.

"Ah, Marquis, is it possible that you are interested in this—this jade—after—"

He nearly stammered the name that had so often nearly burnt the lips of each, but checked himself and took a few turns about in deep distress and agitation.

His emotion communicated itself to Lally, who felt suddenly stirred to his heart with intolerable feeling.

"Duke, speak to me," he said passionately. "Let us get this matter clear between us."

The Duke clutched his arm.

"Come into the press house. I saw the old men leave it."

Together they entered the old chapel. The reek of wine was strong on the air, the floor and walls wet with spillings and scattered lees from the press; the face of the gilt Madonna smiled down at them with features so typically feminine that they seemed to Lally to be sometimes those of Gertruda and sometimes those of Pauline.

"I do not know how to begin," said the Duke, pacing about.

He had totally lost his composure; his nostrils were distended, his lips strained to distortion.

"Oh, for God's sake!" cried Lally. "You have the whip hand—say or do what you will."

He looked down at his sword, wishing they could settle it that way. All this bother over a foolish woman—how intolerable! He wished he was in the forest with Gertruda.

The Duke was still silent.

"You wished to speak, you came to speak," said Lally, "of Pauline?"

At last the name was out and the crisis upon them; the Duke turned to face his enemy.

"Yes," he answered in a faint voice, "I wish—after all—to marry her—that our marriage shall take place as we meant—"

Lally's astonishment sobered him; his emotions lightened into a desire to laugh.

"And she—is willing?" he managed to say.

"Yes."

Lally's thoughts were grotesque, compounded of scorn and admiration of women, and marvel at the audacity of this one.

"And what do you want to know?" he asked cautiously.

"If there is any reason"—the Duke was forcing the words out—"why—if there is any obstacle to this marriage."

"Have you not her word for it?" asked Lally quickly. "Is not that enough?"

"I want yours."

Lally stared at the wet and reeking wine press; he did not care to look at the man who was being so fooled. Once he had been fond of the Duke.

"My word?" he repeated.

"Shall I put it plainly?" asked the young Duke, in anguish. "Your word that the Margravine of Rüdesheim was never your lover."

CHAPTER XIV

Lally could not control himself to the conventional look, gesture, or answer; the thing had fallen from the grotesque to the ridiculous. He was annoyed to think of all the forces that had been working to make this question possible—the man's weakness and passion, the woman's guile and astuteness; all the influences of expediency, policy, and desires; all the folly of a man very young and chivalrous and all the wisdom of a woman experienced and subtle.

Lally leant against one of the wine presses, smearing the sticky ooze on his uniform.

He laughed, pressing his handkerchief to his rebellious mouth.

"Why do you laugh?" asked the Duke, in a terrible voice.

Lally rallied to the old standard. The woman must never be betrayed; in this case it was also to his own interest to deceive.

"I laugh that Your Highness should ask such a question; that you should ever have had such an idea."

"Appearances—" stammered the Duke.

"You judged them?" asked Lally, on a fine note of scorn.

"What else? What did you think you had been sent to Eberbach for?"

"Appearances," echoed Lally, with malice. "I never thought that Your Highness believed—that you had come to such crude—such gross conclusions."

"My God!" cried the Duke. "What was I to think?"

He spoke in a tone of self-defence, and Lally knew the day won. His predominant thought was, "Now I am free of Pauline." A triumphant throb of relief went with it.

"The Margravine has spoken to me," added the Duke, "with her heart on her lips—confessed a passing infatuation, a rebellion against a Court marriage, a wilful desire to hurt and defy, the caprices of a beautiful woman chained—but all in pure innocence."

"In pure innocence," repeated Lally.

"Taken advantage of by you, Marquis, in a most unknightly fashion."

"I lost my head," murmured Lally, "at favours so undreamed—"

The Duke interrupted hastily, as if unwilling to dwell on this aspect of the matter.

"The Baroness Klanvitz, the Margravine's constant guardian, has sworn to me the harmlessness of this—crazy love affair."

"The Baroness?" said Lally, in an expressionless tone.

He remembered her; she was a figure only less vivid in his memory than Pauline herself. She had always liked him, the gay fair woman, and despised the Duke.

Without her connivance his intrigue had been impossible. He could see her now, a smiling, jolly figure, letting him out at postern gate or pressing a note into his hand in the midst of some Court function.

Meanwhile the Duke was saying:

"The integrity of such a gentlewoman is not to be questioned. I could hardly doubt her. Her father was one of my father's friends, and with her word and yours, and that of the Margravine—"

Lally finished his sentence for him:

"Surely you may be satisfied."

The Duke took a restless turn about the floor that brought him closer to Lally.

"I *want* to be satisfied. I—I—all my happiness is bound up in this marriage, Marquis."

Lally pitied and no longer in the least feared him. The youth was in the grip of an infatuation; at the worst moment of his pain he had never broken the marriage off, only postponed it; it was clear that he could not easily be rid of the enchantment of Pauline.

"When will the marriage be?" asked Lally, as if all hint of the tragedy was over.

But the Duke shrank at once. The wound was still raw, and his was not the nature to boldly decide on any new course.

"There is nothing settled," he said quickly. "We will talk no more of the subject."

"I would only ask this—how do I stand with Your Highness?"

"We can tolerate each other," replied the Prince, with a faint smile.

"I am still in disgrace?"

"You will remain at Eberbach."

Lally was not ill-pleased.

"And Your Highness will return to Wiesbaden at once?"

"I also shall remain at Eberbach," said the Duke. Lally's relief was clouded.

"He still doubts," he thought instantly. "He has come here to muse and brood over his suspicions. Pauline may lose him yet."

"In a few days I shall return to Die Platte," continued the Duke. "But I really wish to look into the government of Eberbach, and the place pleases me."

Lally bowed.

The young Prince's clear grey and innocent eyes gave him a long look, before which he was slightly abashed.

He no longer hated this young man because he no longer feared him; indeed, he really liked him better than he liked Pauline. He had only taken her part from convention and expediency. And Lally was one to whom the lie always came more easily than the truth.

"Well," said the Duke, with a sigh, "go your ways, Marquis. I have promised to visit your pastor in his new laboratories. He seems a very earnest man."

He did not speak as one just satisfied on a vital point, but Lally was indifferent. He took his dismissal gladly, and went with a bounding step out into the hot sunlight.

He was free of Pauline—no need to even write to her. She could want nothing more of him. With infinite pains she had set herself to win back the Duke, and with marvellous success had induced him to believe the incredible. It was clear that she meant to be Duchess of Nassau, and equally clear that she would sooner or later attain her object. These two might safely be left to each other; he was free of them—free to think of Gertruda.

He pulled out his watch. It was not yet mid-day; long hours of daylight were before him; he would go into the woods and look for the wild girl.

His blood tingled at the thought. The Duke might stay and ponder his problems; Herr Sandemann might maunder round with his books and perfumes; but he, Lally Duchene, would get away into the woods.

Everything—the blue air, the rich trees, orchards, and gardens—seemed powdered with gold; every breath of air so flavoured with the scents of budding fruits that it was like wine. Lally avoided the building and the ground where the prisoners were working, and, skirting the long wall of the Steinberg vineyard, came out on to wooded hillside.

This time he did not trouble to even think of a guide, but recklessly followed the first track that led through the great trees, and soon was completely shut away from the outer world by huge trunks and dipping, spreading branches.

Where the sun could penetrate the close midsummer branches it sent patterns of dazzling gold on to the ground and caught on the leaves of plants in lines of yellow light, dazzling against the deep shadows of the undergrowth.

The sward was fragrant with wild strawberries. Lally crushed the trails of scarlet fruit at every step. The foxgloves were out now, and the wild rose was in full bloom, but grew sparsely in this shade. The huge oaks were intermingled with elder-trees, cherry-trees, and little sloe-bushes, the white flowers of the first twisted with the boughs of shining red fruit borne by the second, and the yet unripe sloes showed a purplish green amid the crooked thorns.

Lally took off his hat; he was minded to fling it aside. He walked on for a while without purpose or direction. It was curious, even to himself, how this wild loneliness pleased him, who came from a world so different; whose tastes hitherto had been for anything rather than for Nature in her solitude.

He handled the leaves that touched him as he passed; stooped to the purple spotted flowers that nodded as high as his waist; caught at clusters of the fruit for the joy of plucking it; listened eagerly to any sound of bird or beast that seemed to indicate the pulse-beat of the life of the forest.

Though he was walking without direction or purpose he felt as if every step was bringing him nearer to Gertruda.

She was, to his imagination, so essentially a part of the forest that he saw her in every quivering shade to which the shape of leaf or bough gave the semblance of a human form.

Then, as he came out on a little open glade, he saw her, in flesh and blood, before him. It was a little valley in the forest, so narrow that it was shaded overhead by the interlacing boughs of the trees growing either side.

In the depth of this valley was a pool, thickly grown with maiden hair and other luscious ferns, cool, green, and damp, while beyond, on the other slope, was the wildest tangle of midsummer flowers, their hues all dimmed by the translucent shade.

Here by the pool lay the girl, her body pressing down the delicate ferns, in the deepest shade, not a ray of sun touching her, yet her white flesh seeming to give out a radiance as of light.

She no longer wore the prison clothes, but a strange, straight shift of purple, sleeveless, low on the bosom, and open at the sides to the knee. This was girdled by a wreath of milky-white berries, the name of which was unknown to Lally. They had curious curling leaves, and long tendrils that clasped her figure close and lovingly. Other clusters of these dim white fruits were knotted in her heavy hair.

She was looking at a green-and-gold lizard that glowed and shone in a shaft of sunlight, but as soon as Lally paused on the edge of the incline she slowly turned her head and glanced up at him.

As he saw her face an extraordinary emotion of pure delight touched him. He had an incredible desire to turn and fly, crashing blindly through the forest; it was as if he had looked on some immortal nixie or dryad in her secret haunt.

For the face turned up to him out of the green shade was more awful than beautiful; the wide eyes, the distended nostrils, the parted lips, wore an expression of cruelty, like the look some fabled monster might have given on seeing a victim approach. Lally controlled himself with a strong effort, and rubbed his eyes. When he looked again it was only the peasant girl, Gertruda, glancing up at him from a bed of fern, tricked up with the wiles of her class.

"I am like to make a fool of myself," thought Lally. "I shall become as crazy as no doubt this poor creature is."

And he thought of her plots with Luy and hardened his heart against her.

"*Olla!*" he cried, putting aside the branches roughly.

In his uniform and sword, with his high boots and his hat under his arm, he looked a strange contrast to the fantastic, half-nude figure of the girl.

"It is a strange chance that you have found me, Lally Duchene," she said calmly. The lizard darted away, a streak of gold-blue light.

"I was not searching for you," answered Lally.

"Why did you come into the forest?"

"To be alone with my thoughts. But now that I have met you, wench, I must take you back to Eberbach."

"What were your thoughts?" she asked, ignoring this.

He laughed, trying to speak rudely and with authority, as he would have done to any other prisoner.

"You and your friend Luy were fools," he said sternly. "This will mean another year on your sentence and disgrace to him."

Even as he spoke he was conscious how incongruous his words were with this scene—with this woman.

To steady himself he tried to speak yet more harshly.

"What does all this mummery mean? Do you want to be led back to Eberbach like that?"

She raised herself on one elbow and, looking at him steadily, asked:

"What harm have I ever done to you?"

Unconsciously—for he indeed knew not of his own movement—he came a step or so nearer to her. A strong perfume came from her vicinity, either from her body, the fruit she wore, the pool, or the ferns. This drew him against his will.

"Come, what harm?" she insisted. "Not as much as Pauline."

"Ah, that villain Luy has been talking of me to you," cried Lally, in hot jealousy and vexation.

"What chance has anyone had to speak to me?" she asked.

"Luy set you free." She laughed.

"How do you know?"

"He stole the pass key last night. He was the only one who had a chance to do so."

"Luy never touched your pass key or came near me."

He was relieved to hear her say this, even though he knew himself a fool for being so.

Even thus must the Duke have felt in listening to his lies about Pauline—relieved and thankful, while his heart was full of doubt and suspicion.

"Why should I listen to you," he answered, "when your very livelihood is falsehood?"

"You do not know much of me," she said. She put her hand to the ground and rose quickly.

Lally had never remembered that she was so tall—unnaturally tall she looked now, yet, when he approached her, her head but came to his shoulder.

"Leave Luy in Eberbach," she said. "He will be your enemy else."

Lally interrupted; now that he was so close to her he was fast losing his self-control.

"Luy loves you?" he asked abruptly.

Gertruda answered gravely, as if she pitied him:

"*Luy loves no woman and I love no man*, Lally Duchene."

"But I have heard of you—"

"*You will hear all the follies of the world imputed to me.*"

Lally moved away from her and stared down into the pool, where her long reflection showed dim but distinct.

"Remember that you are a prisoner, and for what offence."

"That is the blindness of men," she answered. "Look at me—am I a thief to keep in prison?"

But he dare not.

"Who are you?" he asked.

"*A woman*," she said.

She put her hand on his cuff; he glanced down at the long, firm white fingers, which seemed as strong as beautiful.

"*I have no history*," she added, "*that is not the history of all the world as well*. Why are you disturbed? How men waste their youth! Come with me. I know a cave near by where I have stored some strange old wine."

"I shall believe you," said Lally unsteadily, "to be the witch the vulgar report you to be."

"If I am a witch what does it matter, if I can give you some happiness?"

Lally had no answer. He was free of Pauline; he did not know what held him back from this woman.

The hand slipped down to his; the cool fingers touched his hot palm.

Why should he resist her? He could think of no man who would do so—save the pedantic Duke, with his heart full of Pauline.

Pauline? Why, Pauline was but a handmaiden to a Helen compared to this girl. She pulled her hand away from him, and he followed where she beckoned—through the glade into the recesses of the forest.

He noticed strange blooms that he had never seen before—a gorgeousness in leaf and tree, a blazing glitter in the sunshine, an enchantment over the commonest object.

"Am I in love with this jade?" he thought.

She led him on swiftly; her colouring seemed to blend with the colouring of the forest, so that she seemed part of every leaf and flower.

Lally thought that she led him farther and farther from the monastery, and that every moment the heart of the wood closed more completely round them, but a sudden dip and opening in the trees showed him Eberbach lying just beneath them, brilliantly clear in the cloudless sunshine.

"You risk much so near your prison," he said, and thought how long ago that morning seemed when he had talked with the Duke in the press house.

Gertruda drew him back among the trees.

"I love Eberbach," she said.

She led him through a short grove of ancient oaks (he had often noticed them from his window) to where an entanglement of wild roses climbed over some clear grey rocks. These flowers she parted, and showed him the entrance to a grotto, flooded with daylight from an aperture above.

He followed her through the rose thicket and across the thick grass. They stood together, enclosed in the golden embrace of the sun that blazed directly overhead.

CHAPTER XV

Lally was dazzled, half-blinded, made giddy, by this shower of golden light coming so suddenly after the green gloom of the forest. He caught at Gertruda as a man will catch at something to save himself from falling. She was as firm beneath his touch as if he had leant against a perfectly poised statue.

"The light is too strong?" she asked. "Come again into the shade."

He followed her guidance blindly, and after a stumbling step or so found himself in a curious little rock chamber, the walls of which were grown with mosses and trails of small white and purple flowers, and which was lit by a natural window which opened full on the slope of the hill and showed, through a veiling of delicate creeper, the wood, the great vineyard, and the monastery of Eberbach amid the gardens, like a picture in miniature.

"This is the *Reganherte Hohle* of which I have heard the pastor talk!" exclaimed Lally.

And he stood looking out of the rude window at the scene below in a strange way, faint and dizzy, as if he was indeed in the enchanted cave of which so many wild legends were told.

There was a faintness over him, spirit and body, like the ebb-tide of passion. He tried to remember the Duke, Pauline, the old life, but he knew that he only wanted to stay with Gertruda in the cavern.

He turned from the view of sunshine to look at her as she moved in the violet shadows of the cave. From some recess or fissure in the living rock she had drawn a dark bottle of antique shape; it seemed to be of black glass, but the surface was rough, crusted with dim gold, and shot with vivid colours.

Lally stared stupidly at the shape and whiteness of the woman's arm and the rosy firmness of her fingers as she held this bottle up against the dark purplish wall of the cave. The light here was clear but dim, as if it filtered through water; about everything was a faint, transparent look. The outlines of Gertruda's figure were half-elusive, but the substance of her—the curved limbs, the luminous flesh, the rich hair—glowed with radiancy.

"This is wine brewed at Eberbach when the monks pressed the vintage; no such liqueur is made now."

"How did you find it?" asked Lally.

She smiled, as if the question was not worth answering.

"I believe," said Lally unsteadily, "that you are a nixie."

Her smile became, he thought, mournful. She took up from the mossy floor, it seemed, a long glass of opal and gold and began to pour out the still wine that had, contrary to the German wines that Lally knew, a slight rosy tinge.

He half closed his eyes. The impression she made on his senses was so acute, so extraordinary, that something in him fought against it; he had never before thought it worth while to struggle against the allure of a woman, but he did now.

As he watched her pour the wine, old tales and legends awoke in his mind and tormented him cruelly. He thought of Circe, of the Sirens, of the Lorelai, of the Rhine maidens, of Venus herself, supposed to be still holding court in the Venusberg; of the terrible fate in earth and heaven of those who had meddled with these unholy things.

For the first time in his life the spirit dominated the body, the mind, the senses; his blood began to run cold. He saw the woman's beauty, but only as a man might see the wine in another's cup without wishing to taste of it himself.

Gertruda his prisoner, Gertruda in her prison dress, locked into her whitewashed cell, Gertruda working under Herr Sandemann in the distilleries—under these aspects he could have fearlessly loved her; not like this. All that was in him of ordinary humanity, of the court, of the city, shrank and turned from the scene, the woman.

She came towards him with the glass in her hand. Now the wine was in it it looked a thick amber colour, powdered with gold. Lally thought of the doctor's story of the two men who had followed this woman to the forest and afterwards died miserably. Perhaps it was here that she had brought them.

He thought of Christ on the Cross and other holy things that had never before moved him. Gertruda came close to him, holding out her glass with the simple gesture of a child.

Lally leant against the window—leant out of it. The fine tendrils of the creeper clung across his face, his hands scorched on the burning rock and were pricked by the red thorns of the brambles that guarded the rude aperture.

Coming up the hillside he saw two of his soldiers, weary and bent beneath the sun in their heavy uniforms. He knew that these must be the two searching for Gertruda. Probably they had been to Eberbach to report their ill-success and were now returning to their task.

Lally leant forward on his hands, regardless of the painful sting of the rock and bramble, and leapt out of the window, out on to the burning hillside.

He heard the woman's voice behind him calling: "Lally! Lally Duchene!"

Heedless of this, which was like a sigh on the hot breeze, he put his wounded hands to his mouth and shouted. The sound travelled clearly in the still air; the two soldiers looked up.

"Here," said Lally, "is your prisoner."

He found himself running down the hill, then stopped and stood still as the two soldiers, at the salute, passed him.

He could not resist looking back, but he did so with a throb of terror.

The girl had followed him, and stood in front of the bramble thicket. Her figure looked small and sombre; the wood behind her seemed to leap up with a sudden dark menace.

Lally turned away again, put a violent curb on his shuddering feelings, and walked slowly down the hill.

The whole valley was full of light, the sky like one vast sun; so intense was the refulgence that the whole air glowed with gold.

The monastery, like the buildings of a fairy tale, shone as if built of some unearthly material. Lally hastened on, and did not look back again.

Without considering where he was going, he passed through the orchards, now in full leafage and fragrant with ripening fruit, to the cloister garth, where the unshaded herbs were fainting with perfume beneath the blazing skies, to the low door of the laboratories.

As he paused on the threshold, his eyes dazzled by the sudden gazing into the dark room, he perceived Herr Sandemann and the Duke leaning on the table.

With a start Lally pulled himself together. Normal life was closing round him; he could now dismiss the afternoon's adventure as a piece of foolishness.

The real issue of everything lay with this young man.

"Come in, Marquis," said the Prince, looking up. "Where have you been? You left me to dine alone."

"I went into the wood and lost my way," answered Lally.

"Oh," said the pastor, "I was telling Major Schomberg about the wood. He certainly ought to go there. He ought to go to the wood, eh, Herr Captain?"

"It is like any other wood," said Lally sullenly. "Major Schomberg knows Die Platte. The woods there are more beautiful."

"But cultivated," answered Herr Sandemann eagerly. "This is wild as it was in the days of the bishops of Mainz and the old electors and princes, nixies and elves."

"You think they live there still?" asked the Duke gravely.

"Ah, you Court gentlemen laugh, I know, but it is so long since any of you were in touch with Nature that you don't know anything about it."

The Duke smiled.

"I suppose cities have spoiled some things for us," he said.

"This at least. Now I am making, as I told you, Herr Major, a collection of the legends of the Rhinegau, which I hope to dedicate to the Prince."

"He will be flattered," answered the Duke. "What do you think of him?"

At this question, which he considered vain and cruel, Lally frowned impatiently.

The pastor answered frankly, without apparently any thought for the fact that he was talking to two courtiers who might very well be friends of the man under discussion.

"Of course he is just a fashionable gentleman given up to town amusements, and almost a foreigner, too."

"He comes from the family that has always ruled in Nassau," said the Duke.

"But only through a distant connection. What does he know of his Duchy beyond Wiesbaden and Die Platte?"

"They say that he has no vices, and never misses church service," said Lally drily, and was gratified to see his enemy flush.

"Ah, well," replied Herr Sandemann, "I do not know much about him except that he is very different from his ancestors—men like the

Duke buried here, who lived in the forests and hills; real rulers and warriors of the old German breed; mighty soldiers and fearless hunters—hunters of the boar. Why, at Die Platte I hear the deer come to eat out of your hand."

Again the Duke coloured.

"We are all of us of our age," he remarked. "One of your grisly warriors would ill fit the present times." Then, with an abrupt change of subject, he turned to Lally.

"Observe this scent-making, Marquis; it is very interesting."

He moved to one of the furnaces that Luy had cleaned and pointed out one of the new stills which had been just filled with cloves.

This still was much the same in shape as those broken ones left by the monks, and consisted of a copper pan with a dome-shaped top, which terminated in a coiled pipe which passed through a bucket of cold water and came out in the form of a tap, which was placed on a large glass pot standing on the floor.

The furnace was closed in by iron doors so that it heated the room very little, but the water in the still was boiling, and Herr Sandemann pointed out how the steam passing through the twisted pipe became condensed in the cold water of the bucket before it could reach the tap.

He showed Lally the fragrant liquid—smelling indeed too intensely of cloves—that ran into the glass jar, and the funnel with a stop cock that was used for separating the two portions into which the distillations divided after standing a short time.

In this way, he said, most of the essential volatile ottos were obtained, and he remarked with satisfaction that the monks had so taken advantage of the natural springs of Eberbach that the laboratory was constantly supplied with pure water, there being a row of taps at the back of the furnace whereby the condensers could be kept constantly supplied with cold water.

Lally listened without interest. His head and his eyes ached; the room was too hot, and too oppressive the mingled odours of the perfumes.

He did not know why he had come here; he had been walking blindly, merely anxious to get away from the wood—from all sight of the wood.

The Duke seemed really absorbed and by no means disposed to dispense with Lally's attendance. There was no trace in his behaviour of the passion he had showed that morning.

Lally felt that the deepest reserve had again closed over the subject of Pauline. Was the Duke really satisfied?

If so, why did he not at once return to Wiesbaden, impatient to meet his bride? Lally did not like this calm delay; it looked to him as if the Duke was brooding, wondering, dallying; as if Pauline's chances were not so good as she might perhaps think them.

The Duke's cool voice broke in on his reflections.

"We are going to make a new perfume, Herr Sandemann, and I—to be called—Pauline."

"Pauline?" repeated Lally.

The pastor smiled at the Duke, quite unconscious of what this word meant to these two men. He had heard vaguely of the scandal that had ruined Lally, but he did not know the lady's name.

"Pauline," repeated the Duke. "It must be a rare and elusive perfume."

He returned to the table where he had been standing when Lally entered.

On it was a large porcelain pan filled with pure white fat and covered with the petals of white roses.

"Fresh petals have been added five times," said Herr Sandemann, "and still the fat is scarcely perfumed. I doubt if our roses are strong enough; to make a good otto one requires the flowers of the East, or of France, Spain, or Nizza, in Italy."

There were baskets of roses, white and red, on the table, some whole blooms, some shredded leaves. The Duke put his hands into one of them. "I should like to make a perfume of our Nassau roses," he said.

Lally could no longer endure this dalliance.

"How long does Major Schomberg intend to stay in Eberbach making scent?" he asked.

"I hope you have permission to make a long visit, Herr Major," said the pastor, who thought Lally's words discourteous and sincerely liked the other officer.

"I may stay as long as I wish," said the Duke.

Lally turned away impatiently; the heat and the odours were becoming quite unendurable. He went to the door, eager for fresh air. The Duke followed him.

"Let us, Marquis, go into the gardens for a while."

The two young men stepped into the garden. The rigour of the sun was now diminishing; the blaze of gold was dimmed; colours, intense, soft, and deep, began to show in the building, in the garden, in the sky; the natural perfumes of evening mingled with the artificial odours that came from the door and open window of the distillery.

"Highness," said Lally impatiently, "what is this jest you play?"

"No jest," answered the Duke grimly. He turned and looked at Lally, who was bareheaded (he had lost his hat in the forest) and dishevelled, but flushed and animated into a warmth and richness that touched his distinctive good looks into beauty.

The Duke, as usual, calm, cool, haughty, reserved in word, look, and gesture, was eclipsed by this vivid personality, as he had been at the Court of Wiesbaden. Lally found his entire aspect irritating. Vexation urged him beyond prudence.

"I thought that Your Highness was satisfied. Why, then, should you linger in Eberbach?" he asked.

They were walking now along the purple-shadowed cloister. The Duke frowned and looked up at the carving of the boar's head Lally had so often and so unpleasantly noticed.

"Why is this beast met with so often here?" he asked.

Lally was vexed at this evasion of the matter in hand. Briefly he told the Duke the legend of St. Bernard and the boar.

"I saw one last night, looking from my window—a small boar by the press house," said the Prince.

Lally shuddered, though he could not have told why, and felt a wild desire to change the subject.

"The forest is full of wild beasts," he answered quickly. "They often come up to the doors of the monastery."

They passed into the orchards; the sky was lilac-coloured behind the grey-green of the fruit foliage; the close grass was full of the hard green fruit that had been blown down; behind was the wood, dark on the hillside, like the hunched shape of a crouching beast. Lally lifted his glance to it and turned away.

"It is cool here," said the Duke. "It was hotter than I realised in the distillery." He paused a moment, and then added in another tone: "Why, they have found the prisoner."

Lally looked over his shoulder. Through the trees came the two hot, tired soldiers, leading Gertruda. At sight of the officers they paused.

"Herr Jesus!" cried Lally, in a rage. "I thought you had brought her back long ago!"

"She chased through the wood like a spirit, Herr Captain."

The girl raised her head. Her face looked curiously broad and flat; there was something almost unhuman in the contours; her hair hung round her thick neck like the long ears of an animal; the robe that had

155

seemed of such a marvellous weave and colour in the forest now looked dull and coarse—the usual weave of any peasant. The berries had gone from her hair, and round her waist were but a few withered leaves.

"What fools fancy makes of us," thought Lally. "She is but a common creature after all." Yet he was full of furious rage because she was looking, not at him, but at the Duke, a gaze which the young Prince was returning with absorbed intentness.

CHAPTER XVI

Luy, with his usual air of slightly sneering indifference, brought Lally the most stinging of news. The Duke, in a moment, had done what Lally had been longing and intriguing to do for weeks. He had set the girl Gertruda at liberty—as much liberty as that enjoyed by any of the most well-behaved prisoners. She was already, in these early morning hours, knee-deep in the hay.

Lally cursed the news, the Duke, and Luy.

"Why did you not do it yourself weeks ago?" asked the servant. "I never could understand why you hesitated, Herr Captain."

"I am not the Duke, to do as I wish without question," raged Lally. "My position here has always been false. I was afraid of my reputation," he added, with a sneer. "What scandal would there not have been had I interfered with this girl?"

"Whereas Major Schomberg may do what he likes," finished Luy. "Everyone sees already that he is a good youth."

Lally glowered at the servant; somehow he had come to make a sort of unacknowledged confidant of the fellow, to find him necessary even, while he hated him—or tried to hate him. There was, after all, much that was akin between them.

"When did this happen?" he asked, blinking as Luy pulled aside the serge curtains and admitted the full blaze of the sun.

"The Duke gave his orders yesterday evening, on his way to his lodgings."

"He puts my authority coolly aside?"

"He has taken care to give himself a higher rank," grinned Luy, "and to let everyone know that he represents Nassau."

"He has behaved with the sly unfairness of your virtuous men!" fumed Lally. He flung himself out of bed and thrust his arms into his velvet dressing-gown. His rich hair was tumbled on his shoulders, his eyes bright and clear from a long, deep sleep.

"He was out with the dawn," added Luy, setting the breakfast things, "watching the haymakers."

Lally raged again.

"Is it possible that he is pursuing that jade? He with his cloistered dignity!"

"He would not be the first," grinned Luy, frothing the chocolate.

"It is not possible," Lally consoled himself, "he is infatuated with another. And, after all, it does not matter. I could always take my revenge."

By telling the truth about Pauline, he meant. At times, when his rage and hate overcame him, he was quite capable of sacrificing the woman to wound the man.

Luy's thin grin lengthened, as if he understood what Lally meant.

"Why do you submit to this young man's caprices, Herr Captain?" he asked.

"Because he has it in his power to break me, you fool."

"Only in Nassau. What is this little Duchy to you?"

"I should become a penniless adventurer," replied Lally, with his crude frankness. "I have a little property here and my pay; elsewhere—nothing."

"A man like you, Herr Captain, does not count the cost so nicely."

It was true; Lally knew that he had it in his blood to ride away one morning and leave the Duke and Pauline to settle their problems by themselves. He would never lack for a livelihood, or even for pleasures—the Duchenes and the O'Neils had introductions at most of the courts of Europe.

"Why do you linger?" asked Luy. "There is London, Paris, Madrid, Rome, Herr Captain."

"Would you come with me?" demanded Lally suddenly. "You are the sort of rogue who would be useful to a gentleman."

Luy shook his head. His puffy face, with the coarse-grained skin and narrow lips, tiny eyes, and cropped, bristling hair, looked stranger even than usual, Lally thought. It reminded him of someone or something—then, before he could fix the recollection, it was gone.

"I like Eberbach, Herr Captain," he said. "I want to stay here."

"So do I," answered Lally. "I, too, like Eberbach."

Luy shot him a red glance.

"Why?"

Lally was going to have answered truthfully, "I do not know—" when he caught himself up with a realisation that the man was becoming too familiar, and silenced him with a haughtiness which seemed to make but little impression on Luy, who licked his lips with his sharp tongue in a way Lally did not like.

When he had, with an ill grace, got through his parade and inspection without seeing the Duke, he went to the hayfields which filled the valley at the bottom of the Steinberg slope.

It was another day of perfect summer, the sky one vast refulgence, the earth one vast perfume and blossom.

The air was seething with gold, the shadows the colour of honey; everywhere was a scent of ripening corn, hay, milk, and the sweet breath of animals.

Several prisoners, men and women, were working in the hayfield; the mown grass, almost ready for carting, lay in long swathes across the shaven ground.

The soldier in charge of the party told Lally that it was such a fine year that they might hope for a second crop.

Lally turned to where Gertruda stood, resting on her rake.

She seemed transfigured by the light that played over her hair, face, bare throat and arms and feet, all bloomed and dusted with gold. The odour of the cut wild flowers clung to her rough clothes. She stood in a twist of red clover, the heavy long blossoms of which were the colour of new wine. Her background was the distant wood that rose against the mountains that shimmered into the dazzle of the sky.

She looked at Lally with serene eyes, fearlessly.

"So you have your liberty," he said. "No doubt you will try to escape to the woods again."

"I am well guarded."

"You were well guarded before."

"Not so well. I suppose you blame poor Luy for my escape?"

"If it was not he, who then?"

"Why, no one. The soldier who brought my supper was called away in a hurry and he forgot to lock my door. I waited till nightfall—then escaped, that is all."

"How did you get clear of Eberbach?"

"I know secret ways."

"Ah, how is that?"

"I used to know the monastery when I was a child."

She began to rake over the clover swathe at her feet, and Lally, painfully conscious of the curious glances directed to him, went his way, nor did he look back at the hayfield.

With an agitation not easily explainable, even to himself, he went to the Duke's lodging in the old state apartment.

The Prince himself admitted him, and greeted him with that maddening serenity that Lally would have given a good deal to disturb.

The apartment that had been diligently swept and cleaned was now sweet and fresh; the great windows were open wide on the sunny vineyards; the dusty hangings had been removed from bed and walls; the old pieces of furniture polished and rearranged.

The Duke's travelling case, of a plainness that shamed the ostentation of Lally's appointments, stood on the ornate bureau; a plain camp bed with soldier's blankets stood at the foot of the state bedstead; otherwise the room showed no sign of occupancy.

In the centre of the floor was an old spinet which the Duke, a clever musician, was taking to pieces in an endeavour to repair it; a lovely little object, covered with faded painting, it gleamed with rich gilt and colour in the sunshine.

Lally could not look with patience either at the Duke or his occupation.

"Oh, God!" he cried, "first the vineyard, then the perfumes, now the music—why has Your Highness come here?"

Aurelio smiled.

"To play the harlequin, you think?"

"You must decide—on some actions," said Lally, with a violent effort at self-control.

"Leave me in peace," answered the Duke sharply. "I sorely need peace. I am not the same manner of man as you—things matter more to me—and I come to my conclusions slowly and with pain."

"There is a lady in Wiesbaden—waiting."

"She owes me that," replied the Prince sternly, "to wait."

"Till when?"

"Till the smallest flicker of doubt is dispelled, Marquis."

He looked steadily at Lally for a second, then turned away to the window.

"I thought you were satisfied," said Lally softly.

The Prince was silent.

Lally passed his fingers over the smooth keys of the spinet. A little mirror behind reflected his strong hands.

"This seems a strange way for men to settle their difficulties," he said.

"A strange way?"

"I never could give any woman the importance Your Highness gives this lady."

"It is by remarks like those that you make me doubt everything," answered the Duke quickly.

"Ah," cried Lally recklessly. "We shall always be at cross purposes, you and I, Highness, if only from the fact that you are the master."

"Not a hard one, Marquis."

"Oh, you have been generous."

"I have tried to be just," said the Prince, with a deepening of his clear colour.

"That is more difficult than generosity," flashed Lally. "But I make no complaint—it is true that I treated you ill."

"There is someone you treated worse," replied the Duke, with emotion.

Lally checked a reckless answer. He felt no compunction at all towards Pauline; he thought that she could be safely trusted with her own destiny. He knew that he was in a mood to say dangerous things, so changed a perilous subject.

"Your Highness has liberated the girl Gertruda Gerhardt, I see."

"I was told that such was your intention," said the Duke courteously, "so I gave orders for it to be seen to at once. I do not think this has infringed upon your authority. I would not do that."

By the words and the Duke's manner Lally felt reassured.

"It was my intention to employ her in the distillery," he said.

"I know, but Herr Sandemann had no work for her this morning, so I sent her into the fields."

Lally, soothed, lingered on the subject.

"A queer creature, is she not?"

"Beautiful, I think. There cannot be evil in her, only wildness. A pity one cannot find some honest man to marry her."

"Marry her! You know her story?"

"No."

"It is the most wanton piece in the Duchy," said Lally maliciously.

"Doubtless there is some mistake. The creature seems to have neither home nor friends. She is so young, healthy, and simple that I cannot believe much wrong of her."

"Has Your Highness been speaking to her?" asked Lally, with a fresh pang of jealousy.

"Yes, I spoke to her in the hayfield," the Duke answered with indifference, and returned to the spinet.

"It is unplayable," said Lally, who could get no sound from the pretty keys.

"Yes, very nearly so. The wrest pins will not stand the strain of the strings, but it is so beautiful that it may be kept and admired for that alone."

Then they looked at each other. Lally was thinking of Gertruda, but the Duke had had Pauline in his mind when he had spoken of the lovely instrument.

"You must come with me to Die Platte," he added quickly. "There is something enervating in the atmosphere of this place. I find, after all, that I cannot think clearly here."

"Why should I come with you?" interrupted Lally dully, staring at the profile of his enemy thrown against the wide, light space of the window. He marked the great beauty of it with a certain contempt.

"I cannot lose sight of you," returned the Duke, with an effort, "until everything is clear between us."

"How can it be clearer?" asked Lally, with a sensation of despair. He had hoped that the Duke would have been satisfied with his lie. If he was not, what was before him? A long, tortuous struggle to arrive at the truth? More lies, until they were all absorbed and entangled in them?

Lally sickened at either of these prospects. From his own point of view the thing was done with. He had been most relieved to think that Pauline would be Duchess, with no grievance therefore to reproach him with, and he clear of the whole incident, which had already assumed more importance than it was worth in his life.

And now the Duke was reverting to this air of doubt and suspicion, tormenting himself with pros and cons, neither so infatuated that he could marry the woman risking her possible tarnish, nor so level-headed and free from her fascination that he could detect her obvious falsehood.

This whole attitude thoroughly vexed Lally. If the Duke had not been in the position of his master he would have had passionate things to say.

And he did not want to leave Eberbach; he wished the Duke to leave him there alone.

"My office here is not quite a sinecure," he answered. "I can hardly leave it at a moment's notice, Highness."

Then he was sorry that he had spoken, because he feared the Duke might appoint another commandant.

"The sergeant can take charge for a few days," said the Duke. "The place almost runs itself. I mean to return myself; some alterations are really needed. I have sent to Wiesbaden for workmen to make the open-air baths, and I think the maniacs should be moved as soon as a new establishment can be built, for their noise and cries are horrible."

Lally listened with scant patience to this speech.

"What a pedant you will be when you are fifty," he thought.

"Meanwhile," added the Duke, with increasing heaviness, "we will go to Die Platte, where we shall be quite alone."

"But I have nothing more to say," answered Lally desperately.

"But I have a great deal."

"Oh, one can always find words. But what is the use of them? You have had—"

The Duke snatched the word from him.

"—the truth?"

"Yes," said Lally, and his eagerness to have the lie accepted gave warmth to his manner, "her word and mine. Is it not enough?"

The Duke sighed.

"Ah, Marquis," he murmured, "if you could but have dealt honestly by me—"

Lally was moved, but moved to further impatience. He would have liked to have dismissed the whole argument as futile, to have declared no woman worth so much talk—not even Pauline, who had, after all, been lightly won, whatever price she put upon herself now. It was even in him to disclose the truth, and suggest that the Duke could win her without sacrificing his pride by marriage, but he knew how wild and evil this would sound to the man who stood before him.

"I had to deal honestly with someone else, Highness," was what he answered.

"Pauline?" The Duke's flush was womanish as he pronounced the fatal name.

"Naturally"—he thought that he saw a chance to further convince the Duke of the tale he wished him to believe—"having induced the Margravine to a wilful indiscretion, I was pledged to see her through with it, though I knew that I was being used as a catspaw."

"To what end?" asked the Duke, with great animation.

"To the end of securing your affections," dared Lally. "She always thought you cold."

He ventured this because he was quite sure that a man of the Prince's type must be a poor lover compared with himself, and he knew that the serene youth had had no experience with women. His first love of any kind had been his serious devotion for the woman he had wished to marry.

The success of his chance shot was shown by the Duke's agitation.

"But she knew—she always knew that I—" he faltered.

"Perhaps she knew, but she wished to make you show it—to pique you—and she went too far, being a vivacious woman who did not reckon on the strength of the passions she was arousing."

Lally, having dared thus far, went confidently on to further boldness.

"I do not think that a woman like the Margravine ever for a moment thought that Your Highness' suspicions would take the crude form that they have done."

"That is what the Baroness said," admitted the Duke, and Lally blessed the shrewdness that had been so like his own.

He thought he had won the day, and that the Duke would turn back at once to Wiesbaden and Pauline.

But though the Prince looked relieved and pleased, he still hesitated, and ended by saying:

"Still, you will come with me to Die Platte?"

CHAPTER XVII

Lally loathed the thought of going to Die Platte; it belonged to his old life, and the very remembrance of it jarred on his present mood.

There he would be virtually the Duke's prisoner, enclosed in a narrow compass, spied upon, probed at, goaded by the Duke's cold virtue till he would be tormented into flinging out the truth and bringing stark tragedy on all of them.

He thought the Duke was a fool, and a dangerous fool, because he had power in his hands, and he chafed bitterly under the domination of his enemy.

The Prince affected not to notice his hesitation and reluctance, his ill-suppressed rage, and ordered their departure for the following morning, coolly making the arrangements to leave Eberbach in charge of the sergeant and Herr Sandemann.

His excuse for taking Lally away was plausible enough; the Duke, he said, would be at Die Platte, and they must go there to consult him about the proposed improvements in the prison.

There was no one in a position to say they considered these proceedings strange, even if they thought so. Herr Sandemann made no comment beyond expressing his delight that the Duke was at last taking an interest in Eberbach.

For the rest of the day Lally saw nothing of his enemy, who was supposed to be out in the woods. This thought filled Lally with a vague jealousy, but he was glad to be rid of the other man's presence.

He took his supper alone, avoiding the Cabinet wines, but drinking heavily enough of the Johannisberger and Rüdesheimer that filled the private cellars of Eberbach.

Luy waited on him with taciturn efficiency. He made no reference to his master's approaching departure, and Lally also was silent on the matter.

He had decided, from complicated motives, of which perhaps the leading was malice, to take Luy with him to Die Platte. It was most natural that he should take his body-servant with him, and a privilege that the Duke could hardly refuse.

Lally had from the first made up his mind to this. He knew he could not bear, for one thing, to leave Luy with Gertruda, and for another, he wanted this strange creature, whom he regarded as a secret ally against the Duke, with him.

The night was incredibly hot. Even with the curtains drawn wide from the window Lally's stone chamber seemed to give out heat from walls and floor, and the air tingled yet with the sun that had been allowed to stream in all day. Lally rated the servant for this carelessness.

"When I am out you should draw the blinds," he said sharply. "I must have shutters fixed. This heat is unendurable."

"It would be cool outside, Herr Captain," answered the man calmly. "And this weather will be splendid for the harvest. Only in very hot summers and warm autumns do we get the very best wines."

"You are always thinking of the harvest," said Lally, but the prospect excited him too, in a vague, strange way.

"It is so important," answered Luy. "Drink this, Herr Captain, since you are so hot."

He set on the table a long bottle of bright greenish-yellow Moselle, and poured the wine slowly into Lally's great round, green glass goblet, that was studded with twists and knobs of gold-coloured glass.

"This is a good drink for summer," added Luy, "cold and very dry. It should not be so green, but they train their vines too high, and are careless in the making."

"You should have been a wine-grower," smiled Lally, with something of a sneer.

Luy looked up. His face across the candles, that were dispelling the summer dusk, looked very ugly—so red, wrinkled in the cheeks, so sharp and long in the nose and mouth, the coarse hair so bristling, the little eyes so inflamed and sparkling.

"My family have always been interested in horticulture, Herr Captain," he answered. "I know all the vineyards in Germany—Schloss, Johannisberg, Rüdesheim, Berg, where they grow the Orleans grape in terraces, the Geisenheimer Rottenberg, the Marcobrunner, and all those pleasant places in the Palatinate from Lorch to Ath. Do you know the red wine of Arsmannhausen and Ingelheim? And the Hochheimer from the Maine? And the wines of Hesse, second in quality, but agreeable?"

"Nay, I am no such expert," replied Lally, emptying his glass. The cool Moselle was certainly pleasant to his dry throat.

"Do you know the different grapes, Herr Graf?" asked Luy. "The Oestreicher, Kleinberger, and Kleb-Roth, and the Riesling, which is better than any."

As he spoke he filled the goblet again.

"This is very wholesome and now at its best," he added. "Nearly ten years old, and it will keep no longer."

His words and his face were so incongruous with his uniform that Lally began to laugh.

Luy looked at him and laughed too. Only the candles divided the two faces, which were thrust close together across the table, Luy leaning forward and resting on his hands.

"You will enjoy the harvest, Herr Graf," he said, "and the festival—"

Suddenly he threw his head back and began to sing, in a curious, thin, yet shouting voice:

> Ich nehm mein Gläschen in die Hand,
> > Vive la Compagnia!
> Und fahr damit in's Unterland,
> > Vive la Compagnia!
> Vive la, vive la, vive la va,
> Vive la, vive la hopsassa,
> > Vive la Compagnia!

Lally threw back his head and laughed again and again. It seemed to him that he was on the verge of discovering something important, that he would soon be able to tell who Luy was—who he reminded him of.

With his head held up like a dog baying at the moon, the servant continued singing:

> Ich heb' mein Gläschen wieder empor,
> > Vive la Compagnia!
> Und halt's an's recht und linke Ohr,
> > Vive la Compagnia!
> Vive la, vive la, vive la va,
> Vive la, vive la hopsassa,
> > Vive la Compagnia!

Lally rose.

"Stop," he said. "I thought I heard someone at the door; I thought I saw someone at the window." Luy continued singing:

Ich setz mein Gläschen an den Mund,
> Vive la Compagnia!
Und trink es aus bis auf den Grund,
> Vive la Compagnia!

As he shrilled off into the doggerel chorus, Lally felt himself shouting:
"Why, you are—you are—"

Luy was instantly silent, and Lally put his hand to his head stupidly.

"I forgot what I was going to say," he said stupidly.

Luy began to clear the table.

"Do you like the old drinking song, Herr Graf?" he asked, and, without waiting for a reply, went on in a lower voice:

Dem Gläschen ist sein Recht gescheh'n,
> Vive la Compagnia!
Was auten ist, muss oben stehn
> Vive la Compagnia!

"Stop," said Lally.

Luy picked up his tray of plates and dishes and left the room. Lally could hear him singing down the corridor:

Das Gläschen muss nun wanderen,
> Vive la Compagnia!
Von einem Freund zum anderen,
> Vive la Compagnia!
Vive la, vive la, vive la va!
Vive la, vive la hopsassa,
> Vive la Compagnia!

Lally turned to the window. There was no moon, and the stars were beginning to show in the deep purple sky; beyond the orchards and the valley was the dark shape of the wood.

Lally's mood was one of phantasmagoria; nowhere could he put his hand on reality.

The Duke, Pauline, Gertruda, Luy, all seemed equally fantastic figures involved in an endless dream; as real as they seemed the grinning boar's head on the cloister walls, the three great statues over the gateway, the dancing Bacchantes painted on the walls of the disused chapel, the rows of monks whose portraits hung forlornly in the monastery, the marble Duke and his wife in the chapel. Lally could not distinguish false from true to-night, human being from phantom. That tall gilt-and-blue statue of the Virgin now seemed Gertruda; the face that he had thought he saw looking in at the window was the face of all three, and yet not human at all; the sound he had heard outside his door had been at once the tap of a court shoe, the tread of a bare foot, and the scrape of a hoof. He wished Luy had not sung that song. Who was Luy?

He had spoken of Eberbach as haunted, and now it seemed to Lally that this was true, and that Luy was in league with the phantoms.

He leant far from the window, hoping to feel cool air on his face, but there was no breath of wind to relieve the intense heat.

He thought of the forest. It would be cool in the forest. He wondered if the Duke was there.

The night was full of the wailing and howling of the maniacs in the orchard pavilions. It seemed to Lally to be full of other sounds and voices, footsteps, and the movements of figures in the dark.

Lally thought of the golden chaplet that had been found in the corridor outside Gertruda's prison—it had been put away in his valise and forgotten till this moment.

He went and fetched it. Through the dirt and the tarnish the un-alloyed gold gleamed here and there in the candlelight.

Lally rubbed it with his short ruffle, turning it about with a certain satisfaction in the delicacy and beauty and mystery of the thing.

The shape and twisting of the leaves and berries was like that of the coronal worn by Gertruda in the forest. He thrust it into the depths of his uniform pocket. This was the last night he would see her for some time—perhaps for ever.

His return to Eberbach seemed most uncertain. He had not the faintest idea of how things would shape at Die Platte, but however matters came to stand finally between the Duke and himself, his return to this strange post seemed unlikely. If he was reinstated the Duke could do no less than offer his return to Wiesbaden; if the Duke discovered his lies and at last shook himself free from Pauline, why, then it was not reasonable that Lally should remain in his service or in Nassau at all.

So this, upon facing the position, seemed likely to be his last night in Eberbach.

And as they were to leave early in the morning it seemed hardly possible for him to see Gertruda again.

He walked up and down the hot room, listening to the wailing of the chained lunatic in the garden pavilion, which was like the baying of a distracted animal.

Lally tried to visualise the wretch, crouched in his prison, making this sound, but he could not do so. To his fevered imagination it seemed to come from a thousand evil spirits, circling round the monastery and groaning in chorus.

He fancied the ancient building to be suddenly full of these forms. Of what? Nixies, devils, pagan gods? Strange beings at least, twisting from altar to garret, running in between the great tuns of wine, dancing in the empty chapels, climbing over the tombs in the deserted cathedral.

He put his hand in his pocket; his fingers tightened over the cold, hard shape of the master key of Eberbach.

For just a moment he stood irresolute, then took up and lit the dark lantern that had been used to conduct the Duke to and from his apartment.

With this he went out into the dark corridor. There and then a high-placed lamp was left burning all night; these gave the only light, as the open windows showed nothing but the darkness of the moonless night.

Lally knew his way now about the twisted passages of Eberbach. Despite his sensation of light-headedness, and of the nearness of this world of phantasmagoria that seemed to so press about him and cloud his senses, he went directly to the upper floor, where the women prisoners were in solitary confinement, and straight to the door of Gertruda's cell.

He set the lantern on the ground and took out the key.

Twice he looked over his shoulder in the certainty of seeing someone behind him; thrice he paused to listen, sure he had heard someone call his name. At last he turned the key and pushed open the heavy door.

He had an instant impression that the cell was lit by a clear white light that instantly flickered and went out as he entered, yet he knew that this must have been a delusion, for none of the prisoners were allowed lamps or candles.

Darkness now bewildered him. He turned, picked up the lantern, and held it over his head. The four widening rays of pale light crept up the four walls of the narrow cell; one of them fell on the figure of the girl, standing, as Lally had seen her before, beneath the small high window, through which no light fell now, but a great rush of sweet air that seemed to Lally infinitely cooler than that which came into his chamber.

In the moonlight she had looked like an image of silver; now her bare shoulders, bust, arms, and feet seemed, in this pale light, to be carved of faint-coloured gold. Her heavy hair looked the bronze hue of a water lily leaf under water; her straight, austere, and strange features were untouched by any expression; her full eyes had a blind look, like the orbs of a statue.

The scent of hay clung to the coarse garments that did not serve to conceal the round contours of her limbs.

"Lally Duchene," she said quietly.

He laughed unsteadily, put the lantern down, and closed the door. It slipped from his fingers and slammed heavily, as if caught by a sudden gust of wind.

"Why do you shut us in?" asked the girl. "Let us go out into the forest."

"You bear me no malice?" asked Lally.

She looked at him as if she did not understand.

"I betrayed you," he added. "But for me you might be in the forest still."

It was as if she had not heard.

"Shall we not go out?" she asked.

"No, for then you would escape me—I might never see you again."

She said: "I should always come back to Eberbach, one way or another."

"I am leaving Eberbach to-morrow with the Duke." She looked at him with sleepy eyes.

"And what do you want to say to me to-night?"

He put his face against the wall and groaned. He did not, could not, answer; he was torn by the most terrible longings and yearnings, remorses and fears.

The five beams of the lantern reminded him of the Five Wounds; he saw in a little vision of curly gold clouds the monk who had once occupied this cell; and he seemed to be praying for the soul of Lally Duchene.

"The woods are so beautiful at night, and there will be no one there," said Gertruda, "save perhaps the Willis maidens seeking lovers."

"I would not have them dance me to damnation," answered Lally. "I want flesh and blood in a woman."

"Let us go out into the wood," she repeated.

Lally set his back against the door.

"Wench, I want none of your spells. I am stronger than you think. Stood I at the gates of the Wartzburg, Venus herself could not entice me in."

Gertruda took a step towards him; he thought her strange face had an expression now, and that it was one of cruelty.

"Who do you think I am?" she asked.

Lally stared at her. Her eyes seemed like the holes in a mask—windows through which he peered on curious lands and seas. She seemed to tower above him as she had towered in the forest; she put her hand on his shoulder, and it was as if something hot had touched his flesh through his clothes.

Lally suddenly caught hold of her, whether on an impulse to strangle or embrace her he could not have told.

Instantly his senses swooned away from him. He thought that he was falling backwards through water or the endless leaves of the forest trees; that the roof of the cell had broken, admitting great stars that pressed down on his eyes and lips, and that somewhere in a beam of cold light the face of a wild boar was peering at him.

"Jesu!" he cried, and the vision broke into utter darkness.

He awoke with the dawn to find himself lying face downwards across the threshold of his room. He fumbled in his pocket for the key. It was still there, but the gold chaplet had gone.

CHAPTER XVIII

Die Platte, the Duke's hunting seat near Wiesbaden, was well known to Lally. Often had he spent what he then considered happy hours there, the favoured guest of the Duke. Now, after Eberbach, the place seemed dull and stale.

The familiar woods were uninteresting after the wild splendours of the Rhine's forests; the deep jungle formed by beech-trees planted a few inches asunder, with their lower branches interlaced, cut with narrow artificial paths to enable the deer to wander; the boughs and foliage entwined at regular intervals so as to form an aperture through which the huntsmen could shoot the tamed animals, filled Lally with disgust—much the same sensation of distaste that he had felt when he had seen the torn roses in Herr Sandemann's macerating pan. Since his visit to Eberbach he had conceived a firm, deep love of wild things. He could not consider with pleasure the destruction either of the roses or the deer, and he was astonished at his own relief that this was not the hunting season.

The house itself he had always liked. In the old days it had seemed an ideal refuge and rest place during the heat, and was associated in Lally's mind with many pleasant hours of idleness.

The severe white stone building, without gardens, terraces, or any conventional approach, stood on a ridge of the Taunus, looking over the forest down on Wiesbaden, Mainz, Frankfort, and the immense fertile plain beyond.

The sole ornament to this cubic house, which was of no great size, consisted in two huge bronze statues of stags either side of the entrance.

The interior comprised a large hall, a great staircase, and lofty apartments severely furnished, the only decoration being antlers ranged along the wall, and all the furniture, mirror frames as well as smaller objects, being made of buck-horn.

This was not the present Duke's taste—Lally had even heard him say that he disliked it—but he had made no attempt to alter the arrangements of his predecessors. A pastel portrait of Pauline in his bedchamber had been the one personal note in Die Platte.

An old huntsman and his wife were in charge of the house. They provided the simple service required by the Duke. He seldom brought any other servants to Die Platte, therefore his coming there alone now with Lally caused little comment among the few peasants and keepers who had to know of his arrival, especially as it was not unusual for him to use the house out of the hunting season.

The first evening of his arrival Lally stood in a black mood, leaning against one of the prancing bronze stags and looking down at Wiesbaden, which lay about twelve hundred feet below him on the plain, bounded on one side by the Mainz, on the other by the Rhine.

Pauline was somewhere in that mile of formal white stone houses set at right angles to each other between the two rivers. The thought gave Lally an odd sensation which certainly was not one of pleasure.

He was glad to have left Eberbach. His experiences of the last night there he now put down to crazy hallucinations—he was sure that he had not visited Gertruda's cell—but it was good to leave a place where such delusions were possible. He had snatched at this hated journey to Die Platte as a relief.

But now that he was here, his loathing of the place and the position returned with great bitterness upon him.

He shuddered at the contemplation of the long, empty days ahead when he would have to wait in idleness the Duke's mood and pleasure.

Of his enemy he thought with increasing contempt. The Duke's first occupation on his arrival at Eberbach had been to try over on his beautiful spinet some chords he had arranged to represent perfumes, these composed under the inspiration and guidance of Herr Sandemann.

He had also shown Lally a floral clock he had painted, consisting of a bunch of flowers for each hour, some laborious botanist having discovered that a different bloom opened for every hour of the day. That the workmanship was exquisite made Lally despise him the more. Only his reluctant sense of duty towards Pauline and his secret yearning for Gertruda prevented him from riding away from Die Platte and Nassau.

As he looked down now on the capital he thought how typical it was of Pauline—formal, stiff, bright, and shining.

And he began to wonder quite wearily how it was that he had ever loved her. The Duke came out of the house and joined him. Lally's sideways glance showed him that his enemy looked pale and overwrought for all his air of bitter composure.

"Does not Wiesbaden look small?" he said.

"Yes, I was but thinking so," returned Lally sourly.

"Everything is smaller than we think it, I believe, Marquis."

Lally lifted his lip in a sneer.

"Then why all this seriousness over the smallest thing of all, Highness?"

"The smallest thing?"

"A woman," said Lally, with an unpleasant flash of his cloudy dark eyes.

The Duke caught his breath.

"I believe you are, after all, a rogue," he said quietly.

"Why does Your Highness trouble with me?" challenged Lally.

The Duke looked at him with deep-seeing eyes.

"I loved you once," he answered quietly.

Lally laughed in sheer incredulous surprise. Of all possible aspects of the case, he had never considered this—that the Duke should have loved him. He had looked upon their friendship entirely as the domination of a strong mind over a weaker one, and he had had a certain affection for his generous, easy patron.

But when the Duke had discovered him, turned on him and exercised authority, Lally had at once and directly hated him, and believed that his hatred was returned.

That the Duke should further complicate an already impossible situation by reference to their former affection seemed to Lally sheer bathos.

"I am as surprised as flattered," he said, on the quick end of his laughter.

"I said *loved*, Marquis." The Duke emphasised the past tense. "I thought you were going to be something splendid. This—misconception of mine made everything more difficult for me."

Lally did not laugh again.

"Of course I was," continued the Duke in the same tone, staring with straight glance down at Wiesbaden, "a fool. I thought that you and the Margravine were—oh, very far from common clay!"

"I at least never pretended to be," answered Lally; but he remembered in a flash a great many incidents in his Wiesbaden life that the Duke had never known of, nor guessed at.

"Did I not say that I was a fool? I do not strive to justify myself."

"You are still a bigger fool than you'll ever dream of," thought Lally impatiently, "seeing that woman can trick you so!"

"We talk too much, Highness," he said aloud. "We talk away our manhood and our youth—for what purpose?"

"To arrive at the truth," cried the Duke, with sudden passion. "Do you not see that my whole life hangs on that?"

181

"But I swore to you. You believed."

"Yes, yes, I did believe; I should be a knave else. But—"

His hesitation was painful. Lally, however, had no pity.

"But—Highness?"

"But I have to get used to my belief," finished the Duke.

"Which means that you still doubt," said Lally, inwardly raging at these niceties.

"No," answered the Prince heavily, "no."

He turned away quickly and walked back to the house, while Lally remained leaning against the bronze stag, looking down at Wiesbaden between the two shining rivers.

So passed several days of summer idleness. The tension between the two men, outwardly so coolly civil, was, to Lally at least, almost unendurable.

And daily his longing increased for Eberbach. His final grievance against his enemy was the Duke's absolute refusal to allow Luy to come to Die Platte, and Lally was irritated to think of the fellow at Eberbach so near Gertruda; possibly in league with her; even, perhaps, contriving at her escape. She was as free as the other prisoners now, out daily in the fields or working in the laboratory if Herr Sandemann was ready.

Reports came from Eberbach, but they were addressed to Major Schomberg, and the Duke never showed them to Lally.

While he was most anxiously revolving in his mind how to end, by some direct action, this mental dallying of the Duke, help came from a most unexpected quarter.

In front of the road was a wide green roadway, fifty feet or so in breadth, one of several that, besides the deer tracks, traversed the forest for the convenience of the huntsmen.

Lally was wandering down this, late one afternoon, when he was overtaken by a rider coming up the hillside—a woman, Pauline.

His complete amazement reduced him to foolishness. The lady checked her horse and smiled, not without bitterness.

"Have you no greeting for me, Lally Duchene?" she asked. "I guessed that you might be here at Die Platte."

"Only guessed?" he managed. "You did not come, then, to see me?"

She shook her head coldly. She was not in the least embarrassed.

"No, I came to see the Duke."

He began to discover the meaning of her extraordinary conduct and to recover his own composure.

"You are alone, Margravine? It is an impossible thing that you have done. The Duke is the last man to endure it."

"It was an impossible position I was left in. I suppose neither of you thought of that?"

The sharpness of her voice was like the stinging flick of a whip to Lally's disordered nerves. He stood silent by her horse's head, frowning down at the thick, carefully tended turf at his feet.

It certainly had been overlooked by both of them that Pauline might take an active part in this affair. He had always pictured her as waiting, impatient but controlled, in Wiesbaden, for their good pleasure.

This bold move of hers was certainly as startling as displeasing.

"You received my letter?" she asked, in the same tone of voice.

"Yes. There was nothing I could say."

"Ah, the man's usual excuse! I suppose you have nothing to say now?"

"I am sick of words," said Lally sullenly, still without looking up.

"So am I—and of waiting. Take me to Die Platte."

"I cannot. The Duke will think it contrived between us."

He felt, at this, her attitude of alertness become even more acute.

"Is he, then, suspicious?" she asked.

Lally took a half-turn away. He resented her implication that they were fellow-conspirators. The last time that he had seen her he had held her close in his arms; now he almost disliked her—if any emotion could span the gulf that had opened between them.

"Yes, he is suspicious, Margravine."

"What have you told him?" she said, in instant doubt and terror.

Lally looked up now.

"The usual lie, of course," he said.

She had the grace to wince, at which he was surprised; her mouth trembled.

"Oh, it is easy for men," she answered.

"I'm ruined," he reminded her, "and in a damned position too."

"You are chivalrous!" she said hotly.

"Forgive me," returned Lally, with a sneer too fine for her perception. "Your favours, I know, outweigh everything—a man's whole life."

She was gratified, but alarmed.

"That is all over. You understood as much from my letter?"

"Yes, I understood."

He looked up at her, wondering why he had ever desired her. Against the soft background of the beech foliage her slim figure, in the dark-blue riding habit, her fair features, shaded by the brown curls and the plumed hat, showed to advantage, yet she seemed to Lally no more than pretty and graceful, and it seemed to him that the calculation and caution with which she had been, during the last few months, fighting for her own interests, was beginning to show in her face, robbing it of bloom and giving it a look of hardness and sharpness.

"Why did the Duke come to Eberbach?" she asked quickly.

"To get the truth from me."

She lifted her gloved hand impatiently.

"I convinced him; I and the Baroness convinced him! Why must he come to you?"

"You had convinced him—almost; but he has a mind must dwell and brood—"

"But I swear I convinced him," she repeated angrily.

"I admire your capacity," said Lally. "I myself should never have tried to put such a crude deception on one of his intelligence."

"What do you mean?" she asked, flushing.

"I pay a tribute to your charm, to your fascination. I want to assure you that you need not fear to lose the throne of Wiesbaden; you are clever enough to achieve more than that."

She looked down at him, frowning over this speech. Lally hated her air of virtuous reserve. Did she think he had forgotten what she had been a few months ago?

"If you can persuade the Duke to accept so monstrous a lie," he added.

She cried out on him for these outrageous words.

"Well," he said, "if you remember how we were caught—"

Again Pauline checked him with a hot exclamation of anger.

"Am I the only liar?" she asked. "You are in this, too."

"No," said Lally. "I never thought a lie would be any use—the thing was so flagrant. When I learnt from him what you had said I was so amazed that I could hardly keep my countenance—and then I was forced to lie, to support you."

"It was but plain duty on your part."

"Was it? What of the Duke?"

Pauline did not falter in her proud composure.

"He loves me."

"He loves what he thinks you are."

"I shall make him happy."

"You are not thinking of that, Pauline, but only of the throne of Nassau."

She drew a deep breath.

"How cruel you are!" she said. "If my marriage is broken off I am ruined. Already there is a scandal in Wiesbaden. It has taken some courage to face it. You were well out of it at Eberbach."

"But no one knows."

"They guess. He *must* marry me, and soon. Only as Duchess of Nassau will my position be tolerable."

"Marry me," said Lally, from a reckless desire to test her. "Let us leave Nassau together?"

"Your jest is stupid," she answered angrily.

"I am only an adventurer, eh?" smiled Lally. "Well, you seemed once to—"

"Be silent," she commanded; "it is over. I must marry the Duke, and you must help me."

"You will not further your ends by this journey," he answered.

"I know what I am about and the man I deal with. I have my own hunting-box here on the Taunus; I am staying there with the Baroness. The Duke is supposed to be in Hesse—and the scandal cannot be worse than it is."

She spoke rapidly, and with an air of courage, but Lally noticed that her hands shook on the bridle, and guessed she was desperate and conscious of a task most beyond her powers. But he had no pity for her; he was merely impatient of the whole affair.

"Where is the Duke now?" she added.

"I do not know."

"I will go up to the house and wait. I am glad I saw you first."

"Yet we had nothing to say," answered Lally.

Again Pauline winced, conscious at last that he no longer loved her. It was more convenient for her plans that he should be cured of his brief passion, but her woman's vanity found the knowledge hateful.

Slowly they went up the wide green alley towards the blank white house, he walking by the horse's head, she with glance on her saddle bow; both thinking, despite themselves, of certain past moments when their flushed faces had been pressed together, their hearts beating close, one against the other, a warm pleasure enveloping them, a sweet oblivion enfolding them—

At these recollections the woman shivered and the man smiled.

CHAPTER XIX

The Duke was in his private chamber, a large room above the entrance door of Die Platte, plain, light, and austere. At one side a door led to his bedchamber; on the other was a cabinet containing a complete library of hunting books, this collected and arranged by the late Duke and untouched by the present owner, who had really very little interest in it.

The one thing he had added to the formal furnishing of the room was a beautiful harpsichord, painted with a scene of darkling gardens where silken couples danced in the twilight.

The Duke sat before this, his fingers idly wandering from chord to chord searching for the notes with which to express the gamut of odours he had written out on a sheet of stiff paper.

He was full of this whim to choose a bouquet that should be named "Pauline" and this he wished to accord with the elements of music as well as those of the science of perfumery.

He had long studied the various strengths and values of aromatic odours; some which have a complete and distinct smell in themselves and correspond to a full tone; others with such a slight degree of difference that they take a gamut, or group, to convey the sound of a complete note.

He tried two bouquets—one of F major, then passed to that of E minor—and he liked the latter, and played it over again:

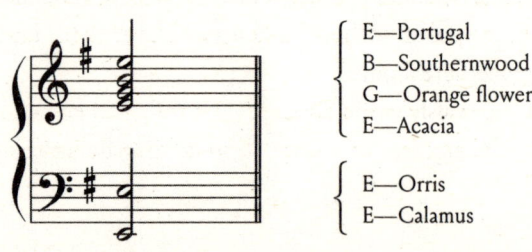

{ E—Portugal
{ B—Southernwood
{ G—Orange flower
{ E—Acacia

{ E—Orris
{ E—Calamus

Did that express Pauline?

He listened to the thin melody as it was shaken into the hot air, and then played the first bouquet to F—musk to jonquil—including tonquin bean and camphor, tuberose and rose.

This was richer, exotic, the camphor, tonquin, and musk lending an air of foreign lands—of the East.

Was not that Pauline, with her grace, her ease, her finish, her composed air of mystery, her allurement?

He was about to play the chord again when Lally entered.

"Forgive me, Highness, but I could not send old Dietrich or his wife on this errand. The Margravine is here."

The Duke rose and stood with his back to the instrument. As he had now been some time without a valet he lacked the exact spruce-ness that distinguished him when he came to Eberbach. He wore his uniform without a sword, and his dull hair was unpowdered.

To Lally his whole personality seemed lately to have become less assertive, less haughty and self-assured; his composure to be more the result of apathy than any effort.

Now he looked almost insignificant as, fingering his embroidered pocket flap, he said:

"Pauline?"

"Pauline," repeated Lally firmly. "She is waiting in the entrance. She is staying with the Baroness at her hunting-box on the Taunus. I met her in the avenue."

It gave him a certain satisfaction to speak the truth; the big decep-tion there must be, but he liked at least to be honest about little things.

"You have spoken to her?" asked the Duke; then, immediately, "She has come here alone?"

He was obviously vexed about that, as Lally had known he would be. Apart from any fear of a scandal, something delicate in him was outraged by what seemed an indelicate action on her part. Why could she not wait? That was so obviously the woman's part. These thoughts showed clearly in his expressive face, but he only said briefly:

"I will go down to her."

Before he left the room he folded up the paper on which was written the gamut of perfume; a discord had spoilt the harmony that should have been called "Pauline."

Lally followed him. He could not remain in the bedchamber, and there was but one staircase.

Pauline waited by the entrance, the sunshine pouring in behind her over the stone floor, the brown chairs, and the plaster heads to which the huge antlers were attached. These stared from the walls like skulls—symbols of the lust of destruction that blots out life and beauty for wanton caprice. Lally hated to see them, as he had hated to see the roses consigned to the macerating pot. A dead beast and a dead rose—are they not both unnatural? The robbed antlers are as hateful as the robbed perfume. Thus Lally's thoughts as he came down the wide staircase, a pace or two behind the young Duke.

Pauline looked up at both of them. The fashion in which the man she must woo and win was eclipsed by the man she must forgo did not please her; she wanted passionately the Duke to dominate, to be the finer man; but if he did, or was, she would not, she reflected bitterly, be in these straits now, for he would have held her from the first. She gave him no greeting as he kissed her hands, but she stayed Lally, who, with a brief salutation, was passing out into the wood.

"Marquis, I wish you to stay and hear what I have to say."

He paused, sullen, inwardly accusing her of selfishness and vanity. She saw his dark look, but was not minded to spare him in any way.

"What I have to say both of you may—must hear."

So she was going to make the most of it, thought Lally, as he paused, frowning.

"I wish you had not come," said the Duke gravely.

"What is the possible gossip of one or two peasants against the scandal I face daily in Wiesbaden?" she demanded. "Has Your Highness thought of that?"

"No one knows anything, Margravine," he replied, flushing.

"They know that my marriage is postponed," she said.

She glanced from one man to the other with a desperate look; it was obvious that she was straining to the limit of her temper.

"You both of you leave me, first one and then the other, without a word. I will not endure it. I am more than a woman, being a princess and a ruler in my own right. I will have, before both of you, an explanation."

It was a bold challenge. Lally admired her nerve, but he did not think it the kind of nerve a woman should have. If she had been innocent it would have been admirable; as it was, she was only embroidering a lie, and that she wanted him as witness showed her shameless, in Lally's opinion at least.

"Come outside," said the Duke. "The voices echo so in this hall."

"Still thinking of that?" she asked scornfully. "Voices have echoed already, my lord, through the whole of Germany."

But she led the way on to the smooth space of gravel that was all that separated the house from the beech-forest.

Directly below them spread the sheer magnificence of the view— the two rivers and the town; but none of them looked farther than each other's faces.

"Margravine," said the Duke softly, "what do you want to say to me? And do you require the presence of the Marquis?"

"I do," she answered instantly. "You brought him here to discuss me with him. I have a right that he should hear what I have to say."

"There were no discussions," said the Prince.

She looked him full in the face, noting with pleasure his easy flush.

"But you went to Eberbach to ask him what you asked me. Do not seek to deny it; my intuition cannot be at fault."

Both the men were silent, and she breathlessly followed up her advantage.

"You had my word, given under you know what circumstances of distress and humility; you had that of the Baroness. You shattered me with the grossness of your suspicions, and I stooped to dispel them; then you went to ask this man—to ask Lally Duchene if he was my lover!"

Her voice broke hysterically, and she stood rigid, twisting her riding whip, which she grasped in both hands across her habit skirt.

The Duke was as agitated and moved as a man suddenly wounded or insulted; he seemed quite unable to command himself. Lally was sorry for him, but with the usual accompaniment of scorn.

He wanted to say something to help him, but would not speak to support Pauline's lie.

"I was willing to break off our marriage," she continued. "It was you who insisted on a new postponement."

"Pauline, Pauline!" said the Prince, in a tone of anguish.

"What is your hesitation?" she demanded. "Why do you draw back and linger? Do you dare to doubt me?"

It was excellently done; Lally thought that she would have deceived him had he been in the Duke's place. He would remember this for use in his future dealings with women. Why, if she could lie like this, Gertruda might indeed be the wanton that rumour named her. He turned aside to hide his bitter smile.

Meanwhile the Duke was excusing himself as if he had been the one wholly in the wrong from the first, yet with a certain dignity, and not perhaps with that complete surrender that Pauline had expected.

"Margravine, I have been very heart-sick of late, and came away to cure myself. I sought the company of a man who was once my dear friend—who might be so again—whose soul I wished to know, whose behaviour I wished to understand. There should be no cause of offence in this to you."

"But why should you be heart-sick," she demanded, "if you were satisfied that I spoke the truth?"

"There was much," he said, "that you did not deny."

"Nothing that should so have moved you, my lord."

"Ah, Margravine, you admitted folly, wilfulness, caprice, wildness, a fancy strong enough to drive away discretion."

She interrupted, at a loss, and covering it with rising temper.

"And what is all this, in a woman placed as I was?"

"You should have been placed above all temptation," he replied.

Pauline turned and involved Lally in her defence.

"Your friends," she said hotly, "should have been men you could have trusted. Had I not found Lally Duchene's importunity daily at my door—"

At this, which so cruelly and unjustly implicated him, showed him up as the secret libertine, the would-be seducer of his friend's betrothed, Lally gave her such an ugly look that she feared she had gone too far, and a sick dread that he might fail or even betray her invaded her whole being, sapping her courage, so that she had to lean against the bronze stag for support and put her handkerchief to a mouth that quivered beyond control.

"That is what I wanted to know," said the Duke sternly, "how far he was—infamous. I thought that you had never been frank with me," he added to Lally, who knew that he was condemning him as a wretch whose miserable designs had only been defeated by the innate virtue of Pauline. Lally saw, too, how this belief on the part of the Duke would help the woman, reinstate her, and whiten her as much as it would blacken him. This was obviously why she had flung the full weight of guilt on him, and it would be useless and foolish for him to attempt any justification.

Chivalry, of course, bade him be silent; but from the first Lally's chivalry had been reluctant as far as Pauline was concerned.

She glanced from one to the other of the disturbed faces, her eyes furtive, afraid, yet desperately bold.

"You see, he has no word to say," she murmured.

Lally was already her enemy—at least, he no longer loved her—and if he was base enough to consider betraying her—well, she could lie better than he, and the Duke was already won to her side. But still, not as enthusiastic as she desired. She had counted on her presence evoking more emotion than this; she had thought that in this remote, unconventional meeting-place passion would have come to her aid. Instead the Duke hardly seemed like a man in love.

It angered her so to see him standing grave and irresolute, looking, not at her, but at the dark sullenness of Lally Duchene, that she resolved on her final move—one that she had hoped not to be forced to make.

She raised her full weight on to her feet again, but stood with her bare hand resting on the hot metal body of the stag.

"I do not know why I trouble you at all," she said, "only I have some jealousy for my honour; yet it does not matter, since I have come to say good-bye."

The Duke did look at her now.

"Good-bye?" he repeated.

Anger that he was not more moved lent fire to her speech.

"Oh, there are convents in Germany. I am minded to join the Catholic faith and take the veil."

"That is fantasy," he answered, still calmly, but the trouble in his eyes was deepened.

Pauline turned towards her horse, tethered under the beech-trees.

"At least I will serve my own fantasy," she said. "I have served yours too long."

He was following her at once, as Lally saw with pity, catching her hand and pleading with her eagerly.

"Pauline, you do not know what you are doing; take time."

"There has been too much time taken," she replied hotly.

"Only a few months, Pauline; only a little while—and it might have been all our lives spoilt."

With a fine simulation of passion she shook off his hand and placed hers on his shoulder.

"Do you believe me?" she asked, and let him look deep into her candid eyes.

"I do, Pauline, I do."

Her touch took him beyond reason or thought; she saw this, and instantly drew away.

"Very well," she said, "we can part in peace, Duke."

"Do you still talk of parting?"

"Yes."

"Where are you going?"

"Most certainly to my convent."

"But—Pauline—I believe you. I ask pardon for everything."

"I am glad, but I am going."

"Why, since I believe you?"

"Do you think," she asked, with fine scorn, "that I came here to beg you to marry me?"

The move was clever, but she made the mistake of not reckoning on the fineness of the material she dealt with.

The Duke drew back at once.

"No, you are right, I could never ask you to marry me. I see that—I see it is all spoilt. Your discernment is truer than mine. I thought it could have been mended, but you see truer than I. I came here to think how it might be mended, but you have shown me that this is impossible."

These words, spoken rapidly, confusedly, with the appearance of sincere anguish, pierced Pauline with bitter vexation.

She had gone too far; in endeavouring to persuade him of her spotless innocence she had impressed his sensitiveness with the fact that his suspicions were so outrageous that no amends on his part could be other than an outrage, and that to withdraw himself entirely from her sight was his sole possible form of penitence.

As she had come to Die Platte with the object of winning the Duke to an immediate marriage she felt herself most foolishly defeated.

What could she do but lean against the bronze stag and weep, hoping that her tears would evoke a flood of emotion in which all these fine scruples would be swept away?

Through her weeping, which was genuine enough, she saw Lally Duchene smiling behind the Duke's back.

This was unbearable! She shot one of her sharp woman's shafts.

"See what I am become," she sobbed, "a mock for a rogue's laughter."

The distracted Duke turned and looked at Lally, who had not contributed to the scene by a word or gesture.

He, too, saw the smile with which the man regarded the woman, and he stared for a little at both—the tears and the smile—in a silence that held them; then he walked into the house, leaving them gazing at each other, like two actors whose audience has suddenly left them.

CHAPTER XX

Lally hated the whole scene—the artificial beech-forest, with the interlaced boughs to keep wild things away; the broad, straight avenue cut for the hunters, with those treacherous loop-holes for them to shoot at their prey; the formal cubic house with the straight windows and white curtains; the formal town shining below between the parks and squares; and, most of all, the pretty figure of the woman leaning against the bronze stag.

He longed for Eberbach as once, in the first days of his exile, he had longed for Wiesbaden.

Pauline waited until the Duke had disappeared into the house, and a little pause of silence had followed, then she did what Lally was expecting her to do—turned on him with intense, if hushed, fury.

"Come nearer," she said, and he approached until there was but a foot or so of hot gravel between them.

"I hate you," added Pauline. "This is the second time that you have ruined me."

"Oh, la, la!" answered Lally. His dark look should have warned her that she dealt with no malleable material here, but she was too distraught to take heed.

"You have made a fool of me. He saw you smile!"

Certainly it had been the wrong moment for him to smile, and he had not meant the Duke to observe him; but he could not credit that infatuated young man with sufficient wit and clear-headedness to correctly interpret that smile at its true meaning. And he told Pauline so, roundly.

But she was in no mood for such consolation.

"He is not a fool," she answered. "He saw your look. He turned and left us both as one who is tired of a play."

"You should never have come," said Lally sullenly.

She continued to talk, to accuse him, to lament; though her words were well chosen and her accent well bred, yet she conveyed an atmosphere of railing—the intolerable nag of the shrew. She had given this scolding touch to the whole affair ever since she had taken a personal part in the matter.

The Duke and Lally might hate each other, but there had been sadness and dignity in this hatred, a certain sweetness in their antagonisms. The woman had introduced spite and malice and fury; dragged the whole thing down to the level of a petty backstairs intrigue.

Every word she said showed her smarting vanity, her childish temper, her overweening selfishness.

Both the Duke and Lally had from the first considered her; she did not consider either of them. She was eager to sacrifice Lally and deceive the Duke in her frantic egotism.

"It would be better for you to go away," said Lally. "If he knows we are talking here he will think us fellow-conspirators indeed."

"I cannot go like this," she answered hotly. "I risked a great deal to come here, though I made light of it. I cannot return to Wiesbaden save with my marriage immediately in view."

Lally took a half-turn away; he was sick with the business of this protracted payment for a brief passion.

"Since you think he guesses, why not confess? Maybe you would win him that way—humiliation, an appeal."

She was vehement in her refusal of this expedient, apart from the risk of failure. Nothing would induce her to descend from the pedestal of virtue on which she had enthroned herself.

It was a counterbalance to her wounded self-esteem to pose as martyred innocence before the world. Only Lally and the Baroness really knew; before the rest of the world she could still maintain the position of the spotless great lady. She would scarcely descend from this pose even to become the Duchess of Nassau; to be wedded for pity would be intolerable.

She told Lally so, with hot anger at his heartless stupidity.

"But if you marry the Duke under this deception neither you nor he will be happy," he answered.

Pauline was not playing for happiness, but for safety. Moreover, she was of a temperament on which secret shames would weigh lightly enough to ensure her a pleasant life.

"Do you suppose," she said, "that he will regret his marriage? He loves me and will never be happy without me."

"I wash my hands of it all," replied Lally.

"You do not ask how you can help me."

"Well, how can I?"

"Bring the Duke here to me again," she answered.

"Help you set the stage for another piece of acting?"

She stamped her foot.

"How I loathe you, Lally Duchene!" she cried, with soft fury.

They had to keep their voices low, for they stood just in front of the house, and all the windows were open.

Both knew that the Duke would never spy or eavesdrop, but they knew also that any raised word might, on the still air, reach him wherever he was, and show him the truth beyond any hope of concealment.

"Then I will go to him," she said. "He loves me. It is impossible that I cannot do what I wish with him—he loves me," she repeated through dry lips, in the tone of one seeking reassurance from the sound of their own words.

She took a step towards the villa, then turned and said:

"Has he met another woman at Eberbach or here?" Lally was amazed.

"What makes you ask that, Pauline? Here there is only old Dietrich's wife and at Eberbach only criminals and lunatics—all peasants."

"Still, was there one he noticed—one that you noticed?"

It was rare for the blood to deepen in Lally's dark face, but he felt a flush burn him now as he inwardly cursed her vixen's intuition.

"Who should there be?" he asked. "Why do you put such a question?"

Her lip lifted; her grey eyes were heavy with anger. To her keen watchfulness he had betrayed himself.

"Both of you were in love with me when I last saw you," she said, speaking crudely to this man before whom it was useless to attempt any disguise. "Now you are indifferent, and he—he is not as I left him. There is some woman at Eberbach."

Jealous vexation began to rouse Lally. He had never since the first moment troubled about the Duke and Gertruda, but was it possible that Pauline was right—had that witch snared him also?

"He saw her but once—or twice—" he began, and Pauline instantly darted on the admission.

"Who is she?"

"One of the prisoners."

"Her offence?"

"A wanton, Margravine, a wanton!"

"Ah! And what is she like?" demanded Pauline.

"Oh, la, la!" he answered impatiently. "Like a witch—like Venus—"

"Beautiful?"

"To a man."

"Like me?"

He laughed.

"She has a wide waist, bare feet, and goes in rags. I think she could strangle you without losing breath, yet she is fine as a water lily."

Her frowning brows cast wrath on him.

"You—*want*—this creature," she said flatly. "Well, where is your difficulty?"

"All women are not of equal—kindness," he answered.

She had the grace to flush and shift her ground.

"And the Duke? Of course, she is playing for him."

"A boy like that, fastidious, romantic, his head full of you! I think he has hardly noticed her."

"If she be half what you say he has certainly noticed her."

"Well," said Lally, with an angry grin, "he certainly will not make her his Duchess."

Pauline turned away abruptly and entered the house.

Lally shrugged his shoulders. Let her go, he thought, to her undoing—what did it matter? But somehow he must get back to Eberbach and Gertruda.

A little breeze had come with the sunset and fluttered the prim white curtains of Die Platte.

Pauline's riding boots sounded loud on the stone staircase. She knew the house well. Often had she been one of a gay autumn party here. As an orphan ruler of great wealth some years out of guardianship, she had enjoyed great freedom.

Her love-affairs had been piquant but very discreet, and she had always intended to make a good match—had even dreamt of a foreign throne until prudence had assured her that, at eight-and-twenty, it would be wiser to profit by the infatuation of the Duke of Nassau—the best match in Germany.

And then it had all been lost, through her own weakness. She had not been able to prevent herself from falling in love with Lally

Duchene, a man different from any type she had hitherto met—a fine lover, bold and ardent, with the soft tongue of the Irishman and the grace of the Frenchman, and just that showiness, that *bravura* and *panache*, that she secretly admired, that her own formal life had always lacked.

She knew that these flamboyant qualities were considered the hallmarks of the adventurer that Lally—papal marquis, landless, almost penniless—really was, but she admired them.

Even now, much as she had grown to hate him, he could have won her over again without much trouble. She would rather have ridden away with him than have stayed behind to woo the Duke. Quickly she crossed the light landing under the branching antlers.

The door of the Duke's room was open. She entered. He sat at the harpsichord.

The lid was closed and sheets of pencilled paper were scattered on the ground; his head was bent and his hands idle.

There was something so forlorn in his attitude that her courage was renewed.

She dropped the long riding habit that she had held up above her spurs and flung out her hands. "Aurelio!"

Not until she uttered his name did he turn, though he must have heard her step in the empty house. He rose.

"Why did you leave me like that?" she asked boldly.

"Oh, Pauline," he answered, "if I could but be sure of you!"

Her heart beat more freely. He was not, then, wholly lost, and it was much easier to persuade him without the presence of Lally. She had been a fool to keep him before.

"Oh, my dear lord," she answered, speaking more naturally in her relief, "I am going away, but not like this. You must not, shall not, think of me as vile—"

"Never vile, Pauline."

"A liar—a—"

"Stop! You shall not name it!"

"You have named it, often enough, in your thoughts."

Pauline sat down on one of the hard chairs. She was very tired— near to fainting.

There was reason for it; after months of mental strain and distress she had done a thing requiring all her nerve and strength; risked much on a desperate move. The anguish shown in her weary face was not acting.

As she sat there, alone with the Duke in his house, she felt as if she was utterly lost and ruined; that in outraging convention she had outraged herself beyond hope of redemption. A sense that she was entirely at this young man's mercy overwhelmed her exhausted spirit. She thought of the long years ahead if he failed her, and her pride was overcome by fear.

She knew that all the world was against her, believed the worst of her, and would, unless this man saved her, conspire to hunt her into the abyss of lost creatures, and she had all the instincts of her class for honour and respect. She wanted to be, outwardly at least, spotless, admired.

He was standing near her, distracted, irresolute. She clasped her hands and looked up at him with all the weakness and abandon of a child.

"You *must* marry me," she said. "I had better be dead else! Do you not see that?"

Her emotion was genuine and moved him as no acting could have done. He saw her weakness, her little hands, her little neck and shoulders bowed, her face distorted and quivering.

He was instantly by her side.

"Why did you not tell me this before?" he asked. "Of course I will marry you, Pauline."

She was in his arms, sobbing. This was not the way she had meant and hoped to win him, but his words were as balm, and she was very tired. She would be the Duchess; no one need know by what means.

"Pauline, Pauline," he murmured, more moved by her appeal than he had been by any of her pride. He accused himself of selfishness in not having thought more of her point of view. He had been so absorbed in his own problem that he had not considered what her humiliation and ruin would be if he abandoned her. She was dependent on him for all that made life possible, and he, loving her, had hesitated, leaving her months in suspense.

So he blamed himself, forgetting the generosity with which he had spared her, and, even in the first horror of discovery, refusing to do more than postpone the marriage, removing Lally from Wiesbaden by the most diplomatic means in his power, sternly hushing up all scandalous hints—even from Sylvanus, the man who had first put him on the scent that had led to his grievous knowledge.

That, despite all his precautions, evil tongues had been attacking, with sharp success, the reputation of Pauline, was not remotely his fault.

But he was prepared to take the blame, and to thank God that reparation was in his power when he felt her thin arms round his neck and her tears on his cheek.

"You never loved me enough," she murmured.

"I could not have loved you more," he answered.

"You did not show it."

He held her tighter. Never before had she been in his arms; it was an extraordinary sensation to him to feel her light weight above his heart. All suspicions were immediately wiped out. He wondered that he could ever have had any. This was, must be, innocence that clung to him.

"I will marry you, Pauline," he whispered, and kissed her with less shyness than he had ever used.

"But only if you love me," she answered, struggling to regain her pride.

"I love you."

"And only if you believe me."

"Hush! I always believed you. But you, do you love me, Pauline?"

"I could not have come here to-day had I not—loved you—"

He quivered at that, and her courage increased with his passion. Disengaging herself from his embrace she returned to the buck-horn chair, and, putting her disarranged curls back with a trembling hand, elaborated her most plausible defence.

She did not attempt to excuse the wilful folly that had allowed her to coquette with Lally, but she explained it away as partly pique at the Duke's coldness, and partly a girl's stupid ignorance of the world. She had been used only to formal courtiers; Lally was a new type. She had never thought he would presume. At first he had amused, then frightened her—now she hated him.

There was so much in this that was true that she was able to say it with sincerity. It gave her pleasure to blacken Lally, both because she did blame him for her disaster and because he had ceased to love her. The Duke checked her with kisses. It was he who escorted her through the beech-forest to the hunting-box where the Baroness waited in grim suspense. Her fortunes also hung on this adventure.

The marriage was definitely arranged for the autumn; this was to be publicly proclaimed. The Duke, riding home in what should have been a lover's exultation, was swept, as by a cold wind, by a remembrance of how he had found them—Pauline and Lally—at night in the secret garden, and he shuddered to think of the pledge he had given.

CHAPTER XXI

There was little conversation between the two men that evening. The Duke announced that his marriage was to take place in the autumn, and in that all was said.

Lally knew well that he was not perfectly at ease in mind or spirit, and forebore to press the question of his own future, which was, to him, bounded by the wish to return to Eberbach.

When he rose the next morning the Duke had already left Die Platte.

Lally guessed that he had ridden through the forest to Pauline. It was a lovely day for an amorous meeting—summer flushing into autumn, the beginning of harvest.

He was playing with the idea of returning without permission to Eberbach when the Duke came back. Lally smiled. The lovers had not been long together.

The young Prince seemed dissatisfied. It seemed he had no intention of going to Wiesbaden until the heat was over, and no wish to stay at Die Platte, but had resolved to return to Eberbach and see to the improvements he had put in hand.

Pauline, Lally gathered, had been by no means pleased at this plan, and, on finding that she could not alter it, had resolved to herself visit the monastery, bringing with her the Baroness.

When Lally heard this two things were clear to him—first, that she was still not quite sure of the Duke, and second, that she was suspicious of, and wished to see for herself, the woman at Eberbach.

Both these things enraged Lally. He wanted Pauline well out of his way, safely Duchess of Nassau, and he fretted to think of the Duke and

206

Gertruda—that was an aspect of the matter that he did not at all care to consider. And it did not seem that the Duke was any better pleased. Plainly he did not want Pauline at Eberbach—considered her presence there distasteful, indecorous—yet did not know how to refuse.

Perhaps, deep in his heart, he chafed against a sense of pursuit, of capture. Pauline was making the very most of her renewed betrothal. Lally wondered if she was as wise as he had thought her to be.

The few days before the departure for the monastery were dull, inactive, full of tension and suspense, redeemed only by the glorious weather—the blue dawning and the gold setting that seemed to forbid any too deep tinge of apprehension or melancholy over the spirits. When the moment for leaving Die Platte came, the Duke announced his intention of going on ahead alone. Lally was to remain behind to escort the two ladies.

This decision seemed to Lally as extraordinary as vexatious. He could not understand if it was meant in scorn, in indifference, as a test, or as an expression of complete trust.

The Prince gave no hint of his feelings, but rode off in the early morning, quite alone. When Pauline arrived later and found that he had gone, leaving Lally as her escort, she made no disguise of her annoyance, the Baroness none of her dismay. Both the women interpreted the action as a worst insult.

"Of course," said the elder, "he does not believe a word of what any of us say."

"Well," answered Pauline with a look that made her seem a shrew, "he *must* marry me now."

The sun was already hot, and they went into the cool entrance-hall of Die Platte, where the shutters were closed, and Dietrich brought them Johannisberger and Rüdesheimer and light beer in leather mugs and green glasses, and spiced bread and cakes.

Pauline would have nothing. She leant back in the horn chair and dangled her plumed hat in a restless hand.

Her lovely face was haggard and slightly distorted. It was obvious that she had taken great care with her appearance. Her hair was waved and perfumed and curled on to her shoulders, confined by a knot of turquoise ribbon; her dark habit, cut in the fashion of a gentleman's coat, set off well her delicate figure; her feet looked tiny in the soft leather boots; her hands seemed minute when drawn out of the big leather gauntlets. Lally noted all these things, and wondered what whalebone and steel were needed to compress that frail waist. He was thinking of Gertruda, whose body ran straight from bust to thigh.

The Baroness drank, and sat and smiled at Lally.

She was a handsome woman, very vigorous, full of vitality, ambition, and gaiety. Though she lived and moved by a most rigid set of rules and conventions, she seemed to inwardly have no scruples or honour whatever. Men, at least, she considered lawful prey.

Lally knew that she would do anything to deceive, trap, or betray them, and never blush for it. For her a man's passions were a woman's opportunities.

To humour and fool her lover and come out of an intrigue with full pockets was, to the Baroness, what every woman should be able to do. She had small patience for those who were failures at this game, yet she made mistakes herself. One of them was in allowing herself to like and help Lally, who could never do anything for her, to the despite of the Duke, on whom her fortune depended.

Here her malicious humour, her dislike of the Prince, her love of an intrigue, had led her astray, and she had not reckoned on the fox-like cunning of Herr Sylvanus. She had not even known that he was her enemy—the enemy of Pauline, of Lally Duchene. Well, she had come badly to disaster and blamed no one but herself, and had fairly redeemed herself now.

She had stood by Pauline; prevented her from doing anything fool-ish; helped her to win the Duke again; inspired the daring voyage to Die Platte that had ended in his complete recapture, and never, never once fallen from the position she held in his eyes as a woman of high integrity and unblemished honour.

She had been amazed herself at the power which lay in that reputa-tion she had always been so sedulous to keep unspotted—her mere word was almost sufficient to rehabilitate Pauline.

Remembering some of the secret episodes of her own life, she was astonished at her luck and her cleverness. She had been married twice, and each of her husbands had believed her a good woman. That was no mean achievement.

She sat now, smiling over her wine at Lally, who knew her for what she was and whom she liked very much.

She bore him no malice whatever, and was really pleased to be in his company again. Lally liked her; she was dark in a warm fashion, rounded, handsomer than Pauline, and not so much older. The Margravine had never been the woman to tolerate a duenna, or to keep an elderly plain creature in her train, and though the Baroness often affected the dowager, she was in reality young in everything.

As a child she had known the Duke's father. His mother had petted her and her first husband had been his friend. She had lately made a great deal of this, and with good effect.

So they sat together, these three, all involved by one common action; fellow-conspirators, whether they would or not, all bound to deceive the same person for the same effect.

Lally disliked the position more than either of the women. He would not sit down, but stood against the door, booted and ready, playing with his whip.

"Are we to stay at Eberbach?" asked the Baroness, with a glance of amusement at his sullen face.

"I know nothing of these whims," he replied hotly. "There is no accommodation."

"I do not mean to stay," said Pauline. "But I mean to see this woman who attracts the Duke."

Lally wished she would not put things so crudely.

"You imagine this, Margravine," he protested. "You make trouble."

"And we have quite enough," said the Baroness. "Still, I myself am curious to see this girl."

Lally fretted under her calm, quizzing glance.

"She will startle you," he answered maliciously. "She has not the beauty that is fashionable in Wiesbaden."

The Baroness laughed; Lally's bad temper always amused her. She liked to see his handsome face flush, his too thick brows frown, his dark eyes flash.

"You are in love with her yourself!" she cried.

"Have done," cried Pauline, rising angrily. "If we are to reach Eberbach before night we must start."

Lally was glad to get away from Die Platte, yet he did not enjoy the ride through the forest between these two women, one mocking, one sullen; neither of them belonging to him or ever to belong to him; both in their hearts despising him, yet bound to him in this ugly common interest.

That he had once possessed Pauline seemed to make no difference; she was as alien as if their lips had never touched.

As they descended from the range of the Taunus and cleared the barren beech-forest his mood slightly changed. He could not resist the joyous influences of the scene.

The sharp mountain air became soft, and as they entered the Rhinegau and gained the fine, well-kept high-road, they were surrounded by a paradise of fertile abundance, riding through first vineyards, hop-gardens, then orchards of peaches, plums, nectarines, walnuts, pears, quinces, almonds, medlars, and figs growing in the most luxurious profusion; then again fields of flax and hemp and tobacco, Indian corn and clover, vegetables, and then all the different kinds of grain—wheat, barley, oats, and rye.

Lally felt a curious mental stimulus, a wave of excitement, at the sight of these fruits and crops ripening under the burning sun.

"It will be a beautiful harvest," he said. Pauline was not interested, but the Baroness enjoyed the prospect; she was apt to enjoy everything that came her way.

They took a meal at the first village they came to. The inn stood on the green, and there was a great plane-tree before it under which the tables were placed.

Here they ate their coarse meal, the children crowding round them and offering baskets of wild strawberries, raspberries, and whortleberries, and tight little bunches of forest flowers.

The experience was new to all of them, pleasant to Lally and the elder woman, but indifferent to Pauline, who resented being stared at, and drove away the children who pressed too near the trailing lengths of her riding skirt. When they rode on again the wood once more enclosed them.

Lally went a little ahead to discover the path, which was not too clear. Pauline began to complain of the fatigue and length of the journey, and of the fact that they had brought no guide.

It was indeed very hot, even in the forest; the close woven boughs of beech and elm seemed to hold in heat instead of coolness. There was hardly a breath of air.

They halted, dismounted, and tethered the horses. Lally laughed to see the beasts instantly cropping the tufts of rich grass.

"If we were peasants and were caught allowing our animals to feed thus it would cost us a term of years in Eberbach."

"It is the Duke's land," said Pauline indifferently, but the Baroness was astonished. She had never known, she said, of this severe penal code.

Lally took a paper from his pocket and showed her a list of offences and punishments that had come into his possession as commandant of Eberbach.

"These are the forest penalties, which are most sternly exacted."

The Baroness took the paper in her pretty hands, and glanced down the long list.

"For a load of dead wood, a fine of fifty-four keuzers; for a load of green grass, fifty; for a nest of singing-birds, five florins; for a nest of nightingales, fifteen. For a second offence the term is doubled; for a third imprisonment follows."

"Can you wonder," interrupted Lally, "at the abject poverty of these poor people, who are forbidden to pick up a few sticks to light their fires, a handful of grass or a few dead leaves for their animals?"

"Why may they not?" asked the Baroness. "I see the trees decaying in every direction."

"That is not considered. The dead leaves are supposed to manure the ground. I hope, Margravine"—he looked at Pauline—"that when you are Duchess of Nassau you will have these petty laws altered."

They were seated on the ground under a large beech-tree, and Pauline was leaning back against the smooth bole.

She did not answer.

"The children are punished also," continued Lally. "There are many little ones at Eberbach whose offence is no greater than that of tearing a few handfuls of green for their cow or cutting a switch for an ass."

"How is it that they are discovered in this loneliness?" asked the Baroness.

"The Duke's forest officers are very keen and strict," said Lally, "and the peasantry are very terrified of them. I myself have seen, in the hovels near Kiedrich, lack of fuel and grass and wild fruits when all are at the door for the picking up."

"Pauline, you must alter this," said the Baroness, and then she yawned.

She took from her pocket some of the blue Orleans plums they had bought at the inn and began to eat them. When they were finished she cast away the stones into the wild gooseberry bushes, arranged her cloak as a pillow, and instantly and naturally went to sleep.

She had been so full of vivacity, chatter, and gaiety that her sudden silence seemed strange, and the other two looked at each other in an embarrassment they had not felt till then. Pauline glanced scornfully at her friend, rose, and moved further away.

"Lest we disturb her," she said.

Lally followed and flung himself along the ground at her feet. He had gathered a handful of wild strawberries, and now separated the fragrant little fruits from the trails of hairy leaves and tiny white blossoms.

Pauline looked at him, at his graceful length, his vivid face, and strong hands playing with the strawberries.

"Do you not feel a fool?" she asked bitterly.

"I am in the position of a fool," he answered, but lightly.

"If the Duke knows," she amended.

"Oh, let that go," he answered. "The Duke! The Duke! Is he your god or mine?"

Most unexpectedly Pauline put her hands to her face and began to weep.

"Why am I so unfortunate? Most unfortunate!"

She looked pitiful, and Lally was moved towards her as the Duke had been when he had said, "Of course I will marry you, Pauline."

But there was nothing he could do.

She sobbed back her tears and pointed to her sleeping friend.

"Do you not think that she has been as wicked as I? Yet she has not paid."

"Oh, do not talk of wickedness," said Lally. With a smile he handed her the strawberries cupped in his palm. "Nor of paying. You will be happy yet."

"I am so tired," she murmured, pushing away the fruit. "I should like to lie down in the forest and never get up again."

Lally began to slowly eat the fruit himself. He looked at her anxiously.

Why would she make such a tragedy of it all? Why did she so greatly want to be Duchess of Nassau?

She was young, wealthy, pretty, free. It seemed stupid of her that she could not be content. What, after all, was this petty kingdom and this difficult, prudish young man?

"There is so much in the world, Pauline," he smiled.

"Not for a woman," she answered quickly, as if she was replying to an argument she had heard before.

"Oh, yes, for a woman." He was thinking of Gertruda; about her hair had been a perfume like that of the wild fruit trail he crushed in his hand. Pauline stirred, leant towards him; the sunlight slipped through the beech-boughs and lay on her throat and breast; her face was in transparent shadow.

"Kiss me, Lally."

He gave her a look that she did not care to meet, and then laughed. He had finished the strawberries, and threw away the flowers and leaves as he rose and moved slowly away.

CHAPTER XXII

They rode out of the forest through the harvest. It was very hot, yet, at least to Lally, there was a certain opulent luxury in the very blaze of the sun that drew out all the scents and flavours and colours of the fruits and flowers.

The crops were this year heavy, even for Nassau, where the light and poor-looking land is much more fertile than would be at first thought.

The bearded rye, oats, and wheat bent their heads with the weight of the load of grain they carried, and the harvesters, who were mainly women, had to lift up the corn before they could use their small light sickles.

These women, with their blue smocks and white kerchiefs protecting their heads, did not look up as the three travellers passed along the road that ran through their midst, either because they were too humble to even lift their eyes in the presence of the gentry or because they were too intent on the toil on which their very lives depended. Where the corn had been gathered and bound into sheaves and stacked, seven leaning together and a large one turned over all to form a thatch against possible rain, babies, watched by elder children, had been placed on some bright, clean, worn garment to sleep in the shade.

Each group working on its own patch of corn had one or more of these babies, fair, burnt golden-rose, half nude, sleeping in the hot shade of the wheat stacks, with their rounded limbs flung into adorable attitudes and their little faces placid in repose.

Lally marvelled at anything so lovely coming from such poverty. They would grow up to be peasants, rough and common, but at present they were beautiful. Lally thought of Gertruda with a sudden pang clutching at his heart.

He envied these wretched people the possession of these little children. He would like to have stolen two of these bold, strong, yet helpless creatures, and carry them away with him through the forest.

He glanced at Pauline, but she was looking straight before her. He remembered how she had repulsed the children in front of the inn. There seemed little that was soft and gentle about the Pauline of these days.

The Baroness, though a childless woman, noticed the babies, and praised them without constraint, but somehow her words rang false to Lally. He thought always of Gertruda; he would picture her lying on the stubble, with the gleanings in her hair and the babies climbing all over her, confident and joyous.

He thought also of the other woman—the prisoner in the cell next to Gertruda—and what the soldier had said of her silent anguish, "She is a mother."

Had she, then, been forced away from some of these delicious creatures? And who was looking after them?

Along the roads were little light waggons, adapted for going up and down hills, waiting to cart the harvest. These were drawn sometimes by oxen, sometimes by horses, but more often by little milch cows. As the travellers rode past they could smell in their breath the fragrant milk as the patient creatures, who were yoked two by two, their heads lashed to leathern cushions fastened to a pole, stood chewing the cud.

To Lally there was an enchantment over the whole scene. His own troubles and problems weighed lightly on him as he rode through the harvest land.

Nothing seemed to matter much as long as he was young. He looked at Pauline. The spurned kiss did not seem to rankle in her mind; she wore the same air of light bitterness, and her thoughts seemed fixed wholly on the Duke.

"Will you stay in Nassau when she is Duchess?" asked the Baroness, when Pauline chanced to ride ahead.

"No," said Lally.

He was sure of that, but what the future held he hardly cared; it seemed enough for him that he was returning to Eberbach.

As they passed again from the harvest lands into the forest he could not forbear telling the Baroness as much, and she looked at him with sharp curiosity.

"What, then, is the magic of this old monastery?" she asked.

"I do not know," smiled Lally. "None, perhaps, save that which belongs to any ancient building. There are many legends told of Eberbach."

"The Rhinegau seems full of legends," remarked the lady.

"It is. Strange how these simple people that you see so busy here with their kine and their harvest and their children should evolve this wild folk-lore. Though they all go so dutifully to church there are many of them still believe in Freia and Bacchus, the Nixie and the Lorelai, the gigantic monk who haunts the silver mines, and the dance of the Willis maidens."

He spoke with a certain eagerness, and the two women (Pauline rode alongside now on the wide forest path) regarded him keenly.

"You heard many of these fairy tales at Eberbach?" asked Pauline.

"All of them. What did one know of such things at Wiesbaden? Herr Sandemann, the pastor of the prison, can tell you some stories."

"A holy man too!" laughed the Baroness. "But recount us some."

Lally shook his head.

"The pastor will do it better."

"Are there fairies or phantoms at Eberbach?" asked Pauline.

Lally evaded this by a tone of lightness.

"The monastery itself is said to have been founded by a boar, who led St. Bernard to the spot, and this beast is supposed to have been a kind of devil or spirit that deceived the holy man, making him build what was really a temple for the pagan deities, where they revelled every harvest and held their orgies in the wine cellars and chapels."

"And the monks?" smiled Pauline.

"Oh, the monks were supposed to all be in on the secret, and to be seduced into following these strange gods."

"The place must be cursed, then," said the Baroness comfortably.

"The peasants say that it is still haunted, Baroness."

"By what?"

"Why, by Bacchus, Venus, Freia, as they call her, the boar—"

He suddenly stopped, as if he had just realised what he was saying. A most extraordinary sensation passed over him. He clutched his reins tight and stared about him.

"What is the matter?" asked both the women together.

He laughed, and stammered:

"Nothing—oh, nothing."

"You were talking of Venus and the boar," said Pauline.

"Ah yes, the crazy stories of the peasants," answered Lally quickly. "You must ask Herr Sandemann; he will amuse you. He has even a piece of the gallows-manikin."

"What is that?" asked the Baroness, still closely observing him.

"Have you not heard of the gallows-manikin?" asked Lally wildly, glancing round at the thick foliage of the forest that enclosed them on all sides. "It is a plant that grows at the foot of the gallows whereon has been hung one who is a thief by inheritance—that is, whose family for three generations have been thieves. It grows only when a drop of blood or sweat or a tear has fallen from the dying man. It is a hideous plant with broad, dark, rank leaves and a single flower of a poisonous yellow."

Pauline shuddered.

"Tell us of something else," she said. But Lally continued his narration in a loud and excited tone:

"The myth is this—that whoever possesses this manikin or mandrake shall never lack money, but it is very difficult to obtain. It must be taken up by the root, clean out of the soil, and as the spade strikes the earth the bitterest cries and groans are heard from the plant, and presently the yells of demons in chorus, and when at length the hand is stretched forth to seize the stem there is such shrieking, howling, clanking of chains, such thunder and lightning, such a letting loose of the fiends of hell, that the next morning the daring man's body is found mangled beneath the gallows-tree."

"How, then, is it," asked the Baroness, "that your pastor has a portion of this terrible plant?" And she regarded Lally uneasily.

"Well," said the young man, still with that air of unnatural and feverish excitement, "the story goes thus: the plant appears only on the first Friday of each month, and he who would pluck it sets out on the evening of that day, after fasting, and with his ears stuffed with wax. He also takes with him a jet black hound that has been kept without food for two days.

"At the hour of midnight he makes three crosses over the mandrake, then makes an exact circle round it and begins to dig for the roots.

"When these are laid bare he ties the tail of the hound to the top of the plant and flings a gobbet of meat away from the spot. The dog, springing after the food, drags the mandrake up by the root, but at the same moment is struck dead. The adventurer then seizes the plant, washes it in red wine, wraps it in a silken cloth, takes it home, and puts it in a strong chest with three locks.

"It must only be visited after every new moon; then it will answer one question or grant one request. If a piece of gold is placed beside it it will be found to be doubled in the morning. The life of the owner will be long and happy and his enemies will have no power over him."

"But your pastor—is he wealthy and fortunate?" asked Pauline.

"No, the mandrake is useless to him, because it belonged to his father and a youngest son can inherit it only on condition that he puts bread and money into his father's coffin, and Herr Sandemann's father dying at sea, this was impossible, so the mandrake has no power."

"You speak as if you believed what you said," murmured Pauline.

She did not like the wild aspect of Lally in the loneliness of the forest; she wished that they would come out into the open country again, but there was what seemed an endless vista of trees before them.

"There are many stories as strange," smiled Lally. "You have heard of the *Spiritus Familiaris*? It is a little devil like a spider or scorpion which is kept in a glass bottle, and whoever possesses him has all kinds of good luck, but he must go to hell finally unless he can find a purchaser for the *Spiritus* at a lower price than he himself paid for it. Nothing can save him who has paid for it with a heller, the lowest possible coin."

"Enough of these tales," interrupted Pauline, with an effort. "You frighten us with them here in the lonely forest."

Lally laughed, but his laughter did not seem natural. Since he had broken off his conversation in speaking of the wild boar of Eberbach there had been a great change in his demeanour. He himself did not know what was the matter with him, or why he had plunged into these wild narratives with a desperation as if he wished to keep his thoughts from something else.

Something else—but what?

He sought painfully in his mind for the cause of his sudden agitation; the connection between what he was saying and his vivid emotion.

For a second he had seen and known the whole thing clearly. Now it had gone again; he had missed the link, the connection; but that flash of insight had left him in a wild and distracted mood. The forest—perhaps the forest was affecting him.

Nothing to be seen, nothing to be heard, yet on every side a sense of the strange, of the unknown—a threat, an allurement, a menace, an enchantment.

He found himself peering from the saddle at the shadows behind the great trunks, staring up at the thick branches, glancing back at the deserted track through which they had come.

When they came to a large clearing or opening in the forest Pauline pointed out carriage tracks and footprints in the soft earth.

"Where did they come from or go to," she asked, "since they show neither behind nor in front, but only in this one place?"

Lally dismounted and examined the tracks.

They seemed to be the wheel-marks of some light vehicle, too elegant for a peasant's cart and not large enough for a carriage. They were crossed and recrossed by the imprint of a beautiful naked human foot and the marks of a small hoof. Lally obliterated both with his great riding boot.

"It is one of the keepers," he said as he remounted, "with a hand-cart collecting the dead leaves for autumn dressing of the vines."

They rode on. There came dimly to them the sound of the church bells summoning the harvesters home from their labours. Lally found himself praying:

"O Christ, save me. O God, have mercy on me!"

He put his hand to his forehead; it was wet with perspiration.

At last they cleared the forest, and saw immediately below them the monastery of Eberbach, illuminated by the setting sun, which hung just above the opposite ridge of hills and cast its last rays into the valley like drops of golden wine from a bowl. The mighty, lonely, towered building looked transfigured in this radiant light into something unearthly—terrible.

"It does not look as if it had been built by mortal hands," said Pauline.

As they came out from the last scattered trees this last light was over their faces. Pauline took her hat off, and looked again to Lally something like his lost love.

They rode down into the valley, and passed the gate with the three great statues.

A band of prisoners in the grey and orange uniform were returning from their work. Carts full of corn were passing up to the door of the great cathedral.

They met the pastor with a book in his hand—no folk-lore this time, Lally noticed, but a Lutheran prayer-book.

He stopped and looked up, startled at the grace and loveliness of the two women. Lally was already schooled in what he was to say.

"These are the two ladies, relations of Major Schomberg, who have come to visit the female prisoners. Will you look after them, Herr Pastor? I will see that one of the women is sent to wait on them."

Herr Sandemann bowed; he seemed ill at ease.

"Major Schomberg told me of this," he replied. "I have done what I could to furnish two of the rooms over the refectory."

"Anything will do for us," said Pauline hastily. "Where is Major Schomberg?"

"He is in the distillery, where he has been since his arrival."

"Alone?"

"With my assistant."

"Gertruda?" cried Lally.

"Yes."

"Take us," said Pauline, "to the distillery."

"Nay, ladies," replied the pastor hastily, "you must be fatigued. Let me take you to the chambers prepared for you."

He seemed in the greatest confusion and even distress, but Pauline took no notice of what was almost an appeal. She slipped down from her horse to the mounting block by the gate, and flung her reins to the old man.

"Take me," she commanded Lally, who had already dismounted.

The sun had sunk behind the hills now, and the valley was filled with translucent shadow. The radiance was withdrawn from the sky, which was pale as a wild hyacinth. The evening star glittered like a crystal above the dark line of the forest.

Neither of them spoke as they passed through the cloisters. Pauline glanced up at the carving of the boar's head as if she remembered Lally's story. At the door of the distillery they both paused.

Gertruda had lit a lamp, which she held up to place on a shelf; the Duke was leaning across a table looking at her; the air was heavy with crude perfume.

CHAPTER XXIII

The four looked at each other across the rich mingled light and shade.

Gertruda wore a loose dress of some coarse material, almost like sacking, that was fastened round the waist with a cord. Her feet were bare, and it looked as if she was arrayed in some travesty of a monk's robe. Her face, her hair, the curve of her limbs, the beauty of her feet and hands, made the austerity of her attire a mockery. As she set the lamp in its place a flood of light shone on her loose locks, detaching her head from the dusky background; for that second she seemed refulgent, like an image of gold and pearl.

Pauline looked at her, and the Duke looked at Pauline.

"I have made what arrangements I could for your comfort," he said, "but it is poor accommodation."

Pauline shook her head, as if she put aside all he would say.

"What are you doing here?" she asked. She looked round at the furnaces, retorts, pans, and piquettes. Oil of origeat or marjoram was being distilled; from this rose the powerful odour that filled the whole room.

Near Gertruda was a square frame with a glass bottom, covered with a thin coating of white grease, on which were thickly spread the buds and flowers of jasmine.

"I am preparing a perfume to be called Pauline," said the Duke, "but we have not all the ingredients. Anis, southernwood, and orange flowers we have, and I have sent for the Portugal water which contains bergamot and otto of rose, but we have not and cannot find calamus."

Pauline did not know what he was talking about; his seeming futility irritated her as it always irritated Lally.

She gazed at him with eyes that held a certain appeal. It seemed to her that he looked dazed and was talking wildly, as Lally had talked when he told the tale of the mandrake in the forest.

Then she looked beyond him to the strange woman whose calm face, like a splendid mask, was bending over the "enfleurage" frame.

She felt weak, foolish, wholly inadequate to any further effort; she wished that she had not come to Eberbach.

"Take me away," she said to Lally, and, turning, caught his arm.

For the first time since she had ridden up to Die Platte he felt a thrill of sympathy for her. He led her away, and the Duke was silent.

"This place is bewitched," said Pauline, as they came into the dark cloister garden. "That woman does not seem to me human."

Lally shuddered.

"You are tired; it is evening. Everything will seem different by daylight."

"The Duke must come away. Why should he linger here?"

"He is a fribble—a fool," said Lally bitterly. "Thinking always of his music or his essences."

"Something has changed him. He did not use to be so."

"It is that accursed jade then," cried Lally, beside himself.

"I knew it!" sobbed Pauline. "And you, too, you think of nothing else!"

"No! No!"

"Send her away then—give her her liberty—get her moved to another prison—anything!"

"You forget that the Duke is master," said Lally grimly.

"But you are nominally commandant here. You could send her away."

"Where could I send her in the Duke's domains where he could not find her?"

"You admit at least that he is infatuated with this wretch? You denied it."

"To-night has convinced me," answered Lally, "that you are right. But he is your promised husband, Pauline, and you must keep him to his word."

Pauline laughed wildly.

"That you may have this girl!"

"What does that matter to you," he asked roughly, "if it helps you to the throne?"

They parted at the door of the refectory. The Baroness was there waiting; she looked pale in the lamplight and seemed uneasy, as if upon her also had fallen some spell of fear or dread.

Lally left the two women in each other's arms and hastened back to the distillery.

The Duke, with his back to the door, was leaning across the table as he had been before, talking in low tones to the girl, who continued to strew jasmine reeds on the frame and did not appear to be answering.

"Major Schomberg," said Lally unsteadily, "it is past the hour for the prisoners to be locked in for the night."

The Duke looked round.

"Oh, yes, our work for to-day is finished," he said, without resentment of Lally's assumption of authority.

Gertruda cast the last handful of flowers on the frame and turned to put out the flame.

Lally found something sinister in this complete obedience.

"The Herr Pastor and I work later than this," she said, "but I think to-night the soldier was to come earlier for me because the Herr Pastor had to be away, preparing the chambers for the ladies."

"You can come with us," said the Duke. "I shall see you to-morrow. I have told Herr Sandemann that I shall be here again."

It was not the manner of one in his position to one in hers, yet it was void of feeling or even interest. Lally was puzzled.

"You can leave the furnace," he continued. "Herr Sandemann will return to see to that."

The lamp was extinguished, the door closed, and the strange trio left for the main building of the monastery. Before they reached it they met the soldier coming for Gertruda, and without any demur she left her two companions to go with him—seemed to vanish from them in the darkness without word or glance.

"You will find that you have one prisoner less," said the Duke. "I have released a woman—she who had the cell next to that of this girl."

Lally remembered—the woman with the little children.

"This girl told you of her?" he asked jealously.

"Yes."

"The forest laws of Your Highness are severe," said Lally. "I am glad that this poor creature is considered to have expiated the theft of a few blades of grass."

The Duke laughed. His manner seemed more than strange.

"Perhaps you will release Gertruda herself," remarked Lally bitterly.

"She is useful in the distillery," the Duke replied briefly; then he added, "A strange thing has happened while we were at Die Platte. The workmen who were digging for the outdoor baths have come upon an ancient temple."

Lally thought of the discovery of the golden chaplet which he had since so strangely lost.

"A temple to Mithras," continued the Duke, "Herr Sandemann assures me—Mithras, that mysterious deity worshipped secretly in so many different countries."

While the two young men were at supper the Duke talked of nothing but this discovery.

He had arrived too late to more than glance at the temple the workmen had unearthed, but he had been greatly impressed by this mysterious building, which was yet only partially cleared and not even completely dug out.

Seven steps led down into the body of the building, and as yet seven altars had been discovered beneath the earth and rubbish. The entrance was towards the south, and the temple about seventy feet in length and twenty-five in height, the walls being at least a foot in thickness.

"And who was Mithras?" asked Lally. He felt a distaste for the subject, yet a certain horrid interest in it.

The Duke reminded him that there was in the museum at Wiesbaden a statue of Mithras shown as a gigantic youth, kneeling on a vanquished bull and driving a knife into its side.

This certainly dated from the time when the capital of Nassau consisted only of the hot baths mentioned by Pliny, and one of the fifty forts built by Drusus for the defence of the Taunus mountains.

Lally remembered the statue. He had never taken any interest in the Roman antiquities discovered recently in and near Wiesbaden; these had always seemed to him utterly alien, lifeless, and belonging to an age entirely remote and dead.

But he was interested now in Mithras, and the Duke, who was a true scholar, well informed on all subjects, told him all there was known of the subject of this obscure deity, who certainly came originally from Persia and whose temples had been discovered from Hindustan, through France and Italy, to Germany.

What were the mysteries of Mithras no one now knew, but he was adored as the ruler over the sun, the giver of light, the original fire, his votaries being known as fire worshippers. His temples are generally built in inaccessible places—rocks or forests—often underground, and this was the second found in the Rhinegau.

"Strange that it should have been here, so near a Christian monastery," said Lally uneasily.

But the Duke would not admit this.

"It is a most beautiful and fertile valley, near timber and water," he said, "and secretly enclosed and sheltered, and so most likely to be chosen, and of course all trace of the temple had disappeared long before St. Bernard of Clairvaux founded Eberbach."

"But you know the story of the boar," persisted Lally. "He is supposed to have lured the saint into building Eberbach for the revels of heathen spirits, gods—beasts."

The Duke stared at him, half angrily.

"What are you talking of, Marquis? Do you compare this antiquarian discovery with the vulgar myths of the peasantry?"

"You do not think, then," said Lally slowly, "that there is something strange about Eberbach?"

The two men stared at each other across the candles on the supper-table.

The Duke had risen. Lally thought that he looked pale; his complexion was naturally colourless, but this seemed an unnatural pallor.

"Strange—about Eberbach?" he repeated. "What do you mean?"

"Oh, I do not know," replied Lally, with a desperate attempt to be serene and cool, "only it is old, and full of a strange atmosphere; and the finding of this temple—"

He set his face in his hands, his elbows on the table, in despair of making himself understood.

"You must come and see it to-morrow," said the Duke, walking about. "The bas reliefs on the main altar are wonderful."

"Pauline is here," said Lally desperately.

"Pauline?"

The Duke repeated the name as if it had no meaning.

"We are confused," said Lally. "We do not know what we are talking of, what we are doing; something *is* the matter with us. Herr Jesus! cannot we get the issue clear before us?"

"What issue?" asked the Duke obstinately and coldly.

"Pauline!"

"Well?"

"She cannot stay here."

"Let her go back to Wiesbaden," replied the Prince.

"But it is Pauline, the woman you are moving heaven and earth for; Pauline, the woman you are going to marry."

The Duke shivered.

"That window is set too wide and the night air is very cold," he said.

Lally rose and closed the casement. For his own part he felt hot; the sweat glistened by the edges of his thick hair.

"You are going to marry Pauline," he insisted.

"Yes, but what do you mean?"

"That she cannot stay here with us."

"Why did she come?"

"You know."

The Duke shook his head.

"I said I would marry her. I thought she was satisfied."

He did not speak in the least as if he was referring to the woman he adored. A frantic despair seized Lally.

"What are you going to do?" he said. "What kind of tangle have you got into? What do we mean, any of us?"

"I do not know," said the Duke, in a dazed fashion. He stopped and listened, as if waiting for some noise outside.

"I think you had better open the window again," he added.

Lally obeyed. The faint groans of the lunatics sounded in the silent summer night; the moon was at her full height along the valley.

"They know their goddess is at her full power," said the Duke.

He went to the window and looked out.

"Will you come to the point?" said Lally. "Pauline has come here to see that you keep your promise. Her position is desperate, impossible."

"Why, she can wait till the autumn," replied the Duke.

"Your indifference makes her think that you still doubt her."

"No, no," said the Prince, as if he brought his attention to the subject with an effort. "I have said I do not doubt her any longer." He sighed, and moved away from the window. "Good-night to you, Marquis," he added. "I will go to my room."

As he was leaving Lally made one more attempt to bring him to reason and some definite decision.

"How long do you mean to stay at Eberbach?" he asked.

"Until the harvest," said the Duke. "Again, good-night."

He was gone, and Lally left angry and distracted.

His first action was to close the window and draw violently across it the dull serge curtain, shutting out the moonlight. He then lit all the candles in the room and rang the bell that summoned Luy.

The soldier appeared at once.

He looked the same—neat and erect in his spotless uniform, well shaven and fresh—yet his peculiar ugliness had never before so much impressed Lally.

The small eyes, the pendulous cheeks, the thin nose and long teeth—all these points seemed to Lally to be accentuated, or was it only that he had not seen the man for some time and that his peculiar appearance came to him as something fresh?

"Everything has been quiet at Eberbach during my absence?"

"Absolutely, Herr Captain."

"And this temple—where is it?"

Luy grinned.

"Near the Steinberg, Herr Graf. The young Duke would have baths for the lunatics—open-air baths! And the workmen from Wiesbaden laid bare the entrance to the temple—a stone that was easily raised."

"I know. Have you been in?"

"Yes, Herr Captain. We all went in to see the altar."

"It has been cleared out very quickly."

"There was very little in it. It was hollow, like a cave or cellar, and there is a passage leading from it, Herr Graf, that leads to the monastery."

"What part?"

"The wine cellars."

"Then the monks knew of this buried temple?"

"Someone did."

Lally sprung up, in uncontrollable agitation.

"Will you come now and see the temple," asked Luy quietly, "while the place is empty?"

"No, *no*," said Lally violently.

The other began to laugh.

"This is not Walpurgis night! Why have you shut out the moonlight so carefully, Herr Graf?"

Lally looked at him, and sat down, and rose up again.

"There is no crucifix in Eberbach," he said. "Have you noticed that? They must all have been moved."

"By the Lutherans," answered Luy.

Lally abruptly dismissed him and bolted the door.

"To-morrow," he said to himself, "I will ask one of the carpenters to make me a crucifix."

CHAPTER XXIV

In the beautiful light of day Lally forgot about the crucifix. It came into his mind when he passed, on his usual tour of inspection, the room where the carpenters were at work, but the thought that had caused the desire seemed foolish in the daytime.

The Duke took him, while the morning was yet early, to see the newly discovered temple. The excavations were in a field just outside the walls of the Steinberg and near the apartments of the Duke and the chapel now used as a press house.

The sunlight, streaming down the seven steps, filled the long interior with a veiled gold light. Earth and rubbish lay about the bottom of the walls, and the whole was stained and damp; yet it did not, to Lally at least, look as if the place had been closed up for centuries. It was so near the surface, the stone that had closed the entrance had been so easily moved, that it was strange, he thought, that it had not been entirely choked and filled in with earth.

The Duke showed him the seven altars, all in perfect preservation, and adorned with bas reliefs illustrating the swift changes of the seasons and the slower changes of life—spring to winter, youth to age.

The main altar was a thing of great beauty, surmounted by the figure of Mithras in the person of a youth in a Persian dress, with long curls streaming from beneath his cap and the sun on his breast.

The carvings represented an infant holding up a lighted torch and an old man with one inverted.

The calm, beautiful features of the lad had a certain likeness to the sculptured Prince in the cathedral, to the living Duke—a common serenity and repose.

Lally did not like the place. The golden, dim light, the mystic statue, the seven altars on which had smoked who knew what sacrifices—it was all alien to him, almost hateful.

"The God of the morning—and of soldiers," said the young Duke.

"But we are Christians," answered Lally, with a certain violence. "It is not good to dwell on these pagan gods and pagan rites."

The Duke smiled. He had already displayed what the Lutherans considered a vexatious tolerance; Roman Catholic churches were permitted beside those of the national religion at Wiesbaden, and Lally could, had he wished, have practised his nominal faith freely.

The two young men ascended to the upper air.

No word had been spoken of Pauline; the Duke appeared to have forgotten her presence at Eberbach.

He talked of his proposed improvements of the prison, of his perfumery, and of the temple, but said nothing of the future, and Lally, in sheer uneasiness of spirit, could not mention Pauline's name.

After the mid-day meal Lally saw no more of the Duke. He was, Luy said, in the distillery, and so was Gertruda.

The pastor was with them, but the news was so unbearable to Lally that he at once set about inventing a pretext by which the Duke could be summoned away, yet was prevented, for Pauline met him in the orchard where he had heard Luy's report. (Luy, whom he had once suspected of spying on him, was now, at his instigation, spying on the Duke.)

He had not seen Pauline before that day. His greeting of her was impatient. She wore her riding habit, not having brought more than a hand valise to Eberbach, and this attire looked out of place.

So did her beauty; she required an artificial background. Standing beneath the laden fruit-trees that were now showering apples, pears, and quinces on to the grass, she looked insignificant.

But she looked also very feminine and forlorn, and after the first annoyance at the interruption to his own plans Lally felt a certain pity for this creature whom he had once loved.

"I must speak to you," she said, her pride all gone.

He took her into the cathedral, and they sat together on the marble step round the tomb of the Prince of Nassau.

The part of the church that had been boarded up to form a granary was now full of grain, and in among the tombs of the bishops were piles of roots being stored for the winter.

In the altar place stood baskets of fresh fruit waiting to be sorted and packed, while near the great open door were long boards of figs, plums, apples, and tomatoes, taken in from the sun, where they had been drying.

The air was sweet with the scents of these herbs and fruits, and with that of the stacks of hay that had been piled up over the tombs of the bishops of Mainz.

Here it was cool with a fragrant coolness. Even the sunshine that fell in squares, oblongs, and circles through the unglazed Gothic windows seemed tempered to a gentle mildness.

The two sat silent for a while, impressed and soothed by the strange atmosphere, half of the church, half of the fields.

Pauline pulled off her hat and laid her aching brow against the cold marble side of the tomb.

"What can I do?" asked Lally at length, sadly.

"I do not know," she answered simply, "but you seemed some sort of human ally."

He was touched by that, yet winced at the use of the word "human."

"What do you mean by 'human'?" he asked quickly.

She sat up, clasping her hands round her knees.

"There is something about this place not human. Have you not felt it? It is everywhere—and that girl! Is she not reputed a witch? Is not the monastery known to be haunted?"

"Pauline! You are overwrought. You have been listening to the idle tales of the pastor. I did also when I first came—horrible tales." He spoke eagerly. "In this old building they affect one, of course, and to you it must all seem so strange."

She shook her head.

"You are trying to convince yourself, Lally," she said.

It was incredible; he felt as if he could not believe the evidence of his own ears. Pauline of all people; Pauline, with the artificial training and background; Pauline, child of the court and city, in religion of the conventional Lutheran faith, slightly cynical, very worldly; Pauline to instantly absorb and believe these wild tales and dark superstitions.

"You must not think these things," he said, with great vehemence. "It will unnerve you—frighten you—"

"But the Duke," she interrupted, "do you not see that he is being drawn into these unholy things?"

"It is absurd," said Lally; "absurd."

"Do you deny that this girl fascinates him?"

"Even if it were so, does it prove her a witch?"

"Yes," said Pauline bitterly, "for he is not the man for light fancies, and when he came to Eberbach he was in love with me."

Lally knew that this was true.

"And you have only to glance at this girl to see that she is no common peasant; compare her with the other prisoners! But I believe that it is useless to talk of her to you, Lally; for you are under the same enchantment."

At this last word Lally started, and struck his shoulders against the corner of the tomb. He looked up and gazed at the calm profile of the sleeping knight.

"Yes, enchantment," repeated Pauline; "this place is full of it. That temple they have just discovered, do you like it? And the old cloisters and the cellars, and that chapel turned into a press house, and the apartments the Duke has—"

"You have seen them?"

"Yes, Herr Sandemann took us over all the building this morning. I hated it—and that boar's head everywhere."

"There is a silly tale about that—a monkish legend," said Lally hastily.

"I know. Lally, there was a small boar under my window last night. I have never known them to come so near a house before."

"Not at Die Platte or your hunting-box, because the undergrowth is so thick," said Lally quickly, "but here they can easily come in from the forest."

"Oh, Lally," she answered impatiently, "it is useless for you to argue—it is all wrong, wrong!"

"Go away then," he muttered uneasily. "Leave Eberbach."

"But I cannot."

"Why?"

"It would be to lose all hold on the Duke."

"Pauline, is that still everything to you—to retain your hold on the Duke?" asked Lally.

"Everything."

She faced him steadily, her tone as practical now as it had been fantastic a moment before.

"You must help me to get him away, Lally. I had him so securely! Now it is all lost again."

"You have his promise."

"He will never keep it. He has not been to see me to-day; instead he goes to that girl! Can I return to Wiesbaden or to the country leaving him here? What would be the use of talking of my marriage unless he was at my side? It would soon leak out that he was at Eberbach—and why."

"Well, well—"

"I must be Duchess of Nassau, Lally, and you must help me. You owe me that."

"I cannot fight the powers of evil for you," he answered. "You insist there is magic in this. How can I fight magic?"

"It must be done." She rose. "I am ruined else—ruined."

He took his head in his hands; he felt absolutely bewildered and totally at a loss.

On the one hand was Pauline, in a desperate situation, asking his help, claiming his support, grasping so eagerly for the throne of Nassau, panting after a loveless marriage, yet stating her belief in the world of phantasmagoria in which he had so long refused to put any credence. On the other hand was—what? This queer girl, the Duke, calm and sensitive, a thousand fancies and surmises—nothing else! His thoughts raced about in a world of confusions. The solitude of Die Platte, the ride through the forest, the children asleep under the corn sheaves, his own tale of the mandrake, the Duke and the girl in the distillery, the heavy odours of the new perfumes, Luy neat and respectful, the groups of prisoners, the shouts of the maniacs, and now himself and Pauline standing by the tombs, among the grain and hay and plucked fruit—all this was mingled in his brain into one racing confusion.

He did not even know his own wishes or desires beyond that hot, bitter feeling for Gertruda that he himself felt as deadly, and strove to keep in deep subjection.

Only one thing seemed clear—the figure of Pauline, with her firmly stated beliefs, her firmly expressed purpose, her resolute desires and determined plans.

She was watching him now, and seemed to guess at his confusions and hesitations.

"If you won't help me—" she said, and broke off with a gesture between contempt and despair and turned to the wide open door.

Lally sprang up.

"I will, I must help you, Pauline. I will go and find the Duke now. I will tell him this is impossible."

She looked at him as if measuring his strength or resolution.

"Tell him that if he wishes to stay in Eberbach he must marry me first."

"Marry you!"

"There is a pastor here; there are plenty of witnesses. The thing may be excused as romantic—a whim. I do not mind a reputation for being eccentric," she smiled bitterly, "and as Duchess of Nassau I will go back to Wiesbaden, or to Die Platte or Biterich."

Lally's mind leapt at this solution. Pauline would be satisfied; he would have made amends; all his responsibility towards her would cease. The Duke would not be able to ignore his wife as he ignored his betrothed, and he, Lally, would be free to pursue his own life unhindered, and in the background of his thoughts was always Gertruda.

"I will endeavour to persuade him," he said eagerly. "It is a simple way out of the problem."

Pauline eyed him scornfully, thinking, perhaps, of the days when he had loved her, and contrasting them with his present alacrity to throw her to another man.

"Tell the Duke," she said maliciously, "that if he marries me he may remain at Eberbach."

"Are you quite so cold-blooded?" asked Lally angrily.

Pauline laughed.

"Oh, you wanted your rival out of the way! But that is nothing to me. Once I am Duchess I do not care if I never see his face again."

She left him without another word or look, and Lally leant on the tomb and stared at the two beautiful marble faces of the Prince and his wife.

If the Duke married Pauline, and yet let her go while he remained in Eberbach, he, Lally, would be no better placed than he was now—at least, with regard to Gertruda.

How quick Pauline's wit had been to find a way out! Would not that same way do for him? If Herr Sandemann married Pauline and the Duke, might he not marry Lally and Gertruda? What did it matter who she was—her history, her reputation, her degradation as a prisoner—he wanted her, and he could see no way of securing her but by marriage. The Duke could not refuse her her freedom. They would go away together. Ecstasy touched him at the thought.

He had no family to hurt, no estates to think of; he was, if not an adventurer, at least a free lance. Why should he not do this thing?

It was the only way in which he could absolutely secure her—snatch her from the Duke, and other men.

Even if the Duke dismissed him from his service he could make a living somehow. He had a little money. If they lived as peasants in the wood, it might be—paradise.

Every pulse in his body clamoured with joy at these thoughts. He felt that he now held a trump card. Who could say anything against him now?

The girl must be flattered, pleased; it would be a joyful release for her. The Duke could not protest. For the wonder, scandal, amazement, he cared not at all.

The longer he considered this new idea, the more wonderful it seemed. He now admitted to himself that he loved the girl—furiously, desperately, to the absorption of all other emotions.

Once this feeling was admitted it overran all others. He left the church giddy, exalted, hot to put his plan into execution.

For a while he walked up and down the orchard, trying to steady himself to the triumphant calm he wished to present before the Duke. A soldier was in charge of a group of prisoners who were piling the apples into baskets. Lally did not seem to notice them. The soldier looked at him curiously.

And with reason. Lally's dark face was flushed, his showy eyes bloodshot, his lips quivering, the hand that played with the ends of his cravat was trembling.

A restless muttering came from the pavilion where the lunatics were confined; steady was the distant sound of spade and pickaxe as the workmen laboured at uncovering the temple of Mithras. The sun was declining, and when Lally lifted his eyes he could see that dark line of the wood, crowning the hills—this evening like a menace again, as if it was advancing, to blot out like an inrushing river the valley and all that it held.

Lally turned towards the cloisters. He would find them now, and take the girl away by virtue of a right that no one could gainsay.

Before he reached the distillery he met Herr Sandemann.

"Are they in the distillery?" asked Lally, as if there were no other two people in the world.

The pastor looked distressed, frightened; he seized Lally's arm in a nervous grasp.

"*They are in the wood,*" he said. "She took him up there hours ago."

CHAPTER XXV

"It is always like this as it nears harvest," muttered the pastor. "But this year it is more than it has ever been."

He sat with Lally in the old refectory which was used as a schoolroom. His camp bed was set down in one corner, for he had given up his two living-rooms to Pauline and her friend.

The brilliant evening had unaccountably clouded over; sullen black clouds hung over the forest, and the valley was like a pit of shadow. Not a star showed nor any gleam of moonshine. It was hot with a still and deadly heat.

Lally was sitting at one of the long, clean scrubbed wooden tables, his hand shading his eyes from the candle that burnt before him. He had come here for company, for something normal and sane there was about this dull, quiet man, for something comforting in his age and garb of religion.

In this part of the convent the atmosphere was different. It was steadying to look at the benches and tables, the shelves of books, the maps, and to think of the little children who worked and sang here, day by day.

The Duke and Gertruda were still out in the wood. "It is no use," added Herr Sandemann, "the place must be abandoned."

"What do you mean?" asked Lally, without looking up.

But the pastor was reluctant to explain.

"You must leave Eberbach," he said, "and take the two women with you."

"I am in command here," replied Lally sullenly. "As for the women, they are not my responsibility at all."

"Then I must do what I can for them," said the old man. "Take them away myself if need be."

Lally looked up now.

"Take them away?"

"Herr Graf, I do not know your story, nor that of this other young man and these two women, but I am aware there is some cloud or scandal, some unhappiness, which involves you all."

This seemed vexatious to Lally. He could not believe that the pastor was ignorant of what must be common talk in Eberbach.

"Our story has nothing to do with the matter in hand," he said impatiently.

"I know; it is enough that some trouble has brought you all—people who belong to another world—to Eberbach. If you do not care to confide in me—"

"I will tell you this much," said Lally suddenly; "that young man is the Duke, and that woman upstairs the Margravine, his betrothed wife."

"I had guessed so much from some words Luy let fall! And who are you, Herr Graf?"

"Oh, I am the *tertiam quid*," replied Lally bitterly. "*Arlequino* to His Highness's *panteleone*—what you will; the lover, the friend—the enemy!"

The pastor looked at him sternly, and Lally, recollecting himself, added more calmly:

"I paid more attention to the lady's beauty than the Prince cared for. The marriage was postponed, and I sent here in disgrace. His Highness follows me to have the matter out; the lady follows him to secure her jeopardised marriage—that is all."

"There is no need for any of you to stay in Eberbach."

"Why are you so anxious that we should leave?"

"The place is cursed."

"Ah, your mad superstitions again!" cried Lally violently. "It is cursed by the presence of this wanton who has beguiled a young fool to his undoing!"

"I think that she beguiled you, Herr Graf."

Lally had been prepared for this accusation; he repudiated it with vehemence.

"You cannot say that. I pursued her, brought her back, delivered her to the soldiers."

"Ah, Herr Graf," interrupted the pastor sadly, "you remember the night you lost the gold chaplet? Your good angel sent me to find you—outside this girl's cell, unconscious."

"*You* found me?" stammered Lally.

"I was visiting the sick woman who died that night; Luy was with me. Together we dragged you back to your rooms. Luy took the gold chaplet from you, by my desire."

"Why?"

"It is an unholy thing."

Lally pressed his open palm to his aching forehead.

"I swear before God that I have no recollection of that night beyond a confused memory of a dream!"

"It is that which makes it so terrible," said the pastor.

Lally could not, would not, understand. He put the thing from him with all the crude force and even violence of which his nature was capable; regarded it absolutely with shuddering horror and repulsion—and panic fear.

"There, you are frightened," added Herr Sandemann, looking intently at his face. "Leave Eberbach."

"No, no!"

"You stay only for your own destruction, Herr Graf."

Lally tried to clear away by a strong exercise of will the nightmare mists that were obscuring his reason; to fight off the heavy, deadly atmosphere that was terrifying all his senses.

"You talk foolishness," he said quickly, "great foolishness. Why, because it is a dark evening and this fool has been lured away by that jade—who must know, mind you, who he is, and be playing for high stakes—should he think of—of—"

"Is the Duke the kind of man to act like this? Was he not absorbed by another affection when he came to Eberbach?"

It was what Pauline had said. Lally moistened his lips.

"I do not know what we are talking about. I am waiting for the Duke to come back. I have something to say to him."

He tried to obstinately fix his mind on that—the fact of the mission Pauline had entrusted him with; the fact that he must induce the Duke to marry her at once.

Of his other project—the second marriage—he had not dared to speak or even think. It seemed now too wild, too utterly fantastic and impossible.

He went to the door and looked out. It was quite dark now, and the air heavy and of a hot sweetness, as if charged with some sickly poison.

"If a storm comes it will ruin the harvest," said Lally.

"The harvest is of little matter compared to—to—"

"What?" urged Lally.

"Other things—men's souls, for instance," said the pastor.

Lally grinned into the darkness.

"Souls are your business; you must talk of them, eh?"

Herr Sandemann's voice came clearly out of the large, dim-lit room.

"Are you a Romanist, Herr Graf?"

Lally shrugged.

"If not that, nothing else."

"I know you are without faith—that makes your danger the greater—but if you are a Romanist, you can have a crucifix in your room, and one on your person."

This was Lally's own thought. He was startled to hear it on the old man's lips.

"Why should I need a crucifix?" he asked defiantly. "What do you think, Herr Pastor, we need to defend ourselves against? Speak out; have you been dwelling on your tales of kobolds and nixies until you believe in them yourself?"

He came back into the room, secretly glad to arrest his gaze from the dense darkness of the night, and to look at the homely face of the old man in the friendly light of the candle.

He noticed, with a sense of horror, that the pastor had taken down his great Bible with the green markers and placed it on the table in front of him.

"It has been like this every autumn," said Herr Sandemann, "during the years I have been here; it must be the harvest that brings them. Often I have meant to leave them their stronghold, but there were the dull soldiers, the little children, the poor, innocent lunatics, the sad prisoners—these things seemed to hold me, and somehow we got through. But this year there is you and your meddling, and the girl. I must say at first I never suspected the girl."

As he spoke he fingered the book from which he had preached God's word every Sunday of his manhood.

Lally leant forward.

"She has never been here before?"

"Not in that form," answered the pastor.

Lally began to laugh.

"Why, what are you talking of? This is madness, is it not?"

246

"You won't understand," said the old man. "I can see that; you won't leave Eberbach."

"Tell me, why I am in more danger than the others?"

"Because you meddled—" The pastor broke off sharply and raised his head. "Shut the door. Why did you leave it open?"

"It is so hot," murmured Lally.

He went to the door, and, against his will, listened. Something was moving about outside—an animal, surely. Well, what more natural? A wild thing out of the wood. It seemed to be rubbing against the walls, snorting and grunting.

Lally was quite sure that it was the little dark boar that he had seen before. He waited, hoping that it might come into the dim stream of light that issued from the open door.

But though the noises continued nothing appeared, and at last, on a sudden impulse of terror and impatience, Lally plunged into the outer circle of darkness and clutched down where he thought the creature lurked.

He seized something rough, and at the same instant his fingers were pricked by a sharp bite.

He sprang back, caught at something else, rough—the same object or another—dragged it into the dim stream of light, found it was—Luy.

Lally gave a sigh of relief.

"There was some—animal there," he said. "Did you see it?"

The man's quiet voice was slightly muffled, for he was wiping his lips.

"It is very likely, Herr Graf," he answered. "They come up out of the forest. But I heard nothing for I have only just come up."

"Come in," said Lally.

They entered the refectory. The pastor was reading the Bible now and did not look up.

"Well, have they returned?" asked Lally impatiently.

"I cannot find them anywhere. But I did not ask too closely, as you told me to create no scandal, Herr Captain."

"Scandal!" cried Lally furiously. "There will be scandal enough before morning!"

He went up to the old man and shook him by the shoulder.

"What is to be done? The Duke is still abroad in the forest with that jade!"

As he spoke he saw Pauline in the inner doorway.

"I heard you," she said.

She came and stood the other side of the pastor, who looked up.

"What is to be done?" she asked.

The old man patted her hand kindly.

"You should be up in your room, away from all of this," he said. "You are quite safe there; the chapel is next to you."

"But the Duke—the Duke is still abroad with this girl?"

"We do not know," replied the pastor hastily, "we do not know."

She looked at Lally with a glance of piteous appeal that seemed to shrink from his flushed, dark aspect.

"I cannot stay upstairs. Caroline is asleep, but I cannot sleep; the air is so heavy, and the night so full of horrible noises."

"Those are the poor maniacs," said Lally hastily. "There is going to be a storm, and they feel it. It is always so."

"It is terrible."

She leant against the old man's chair and held her hand to her heart. Her beauty seemed quite gone; she was just a pale woman, only her hair falling over her shoulders remained bright.

Lally reflected, idly, that he had never seen it before without a trace of powder.

She looked at Luy, who remained erect and respectful, waiting his orders.

"You are quite, quite sure they have not returned?" Lally answered; he was vexed that she should know how he had taken this fellow into his confidence. "As far as he knows, no; but I am going now to look for myself."

"I will come with you."

"That is impossible!"

But Pauline was resolute.

"I *cannot* stay here. Whatever it is, I want to face it. You must let me. Herr Sandemann, you will come also?"

He rose at once.

"Certainly I will accompany you," he answered, and bade Luy fetch lanterns.

When the man had gone the pastor added:

"I am sorry that fellow knows so much."

"He has always known everything," replied Lally impatiently. "He is from Wiesbaden, and there was no concealing anything from him."

Pauline did not move. She wore a light cloak over her riding skirt and shirt, as the coat was too heavy for such a night; her cravat was loosened, and her whole attire arranged with careless indifference.

"We cannot leave the Baroness alone," she said. "Will this Luy stay here to watch—he seems a trustworthy if a surly fellow—or shall I wake her?"

"Wake her and bring her with us," said the pastor at once. "We shall need Luy with us."

As soon as Pauline had gone to fetch her friend Lally protested against this number of them going in search of the Duke. It made the thing, he said, almost absurd; he must insist upon going alone; and before Pauline could return or the pastor could stop him he had set out into the night, followed by Luy, with one of the lanterns.

"This is no work," he added, "for old men or women."

CHAPTER XXVI

The pastor hastened to the door and called after Lally:
"Take care of them, they are becoming very dangerous just now, and remember that they like human sacrifice."

Lally laughed in the darkness.

"What does he talk of—the fool—the old man?"

"His head is full of old stories, Herr Graf," replied Luy, "but it is also true, as I always told you, that Eberbach is haunted."

"You want me to think that for your own ends, Luy."

"You are very much mistaken, Herr Graf."

Lally answered recklessly.

"I think that you are a queer fellow; I think you are up to mischief. I do not believe in your hauntings. Who are they, these phantoms?"

"Did I say phantoms? Rather some immortals lingering from an older time and an older faith, robbed of nearly all their power now, yet not quite all, not quite—some remnant of the forces that overpowered St. Bernard of Clairvaux."

"Hush!" said Lally. "You talk nonsense. Do you think that I believe that Freia still wanders the wood, devouring the souls of men?"

"Who spoke of Freia?" demanded Luy quickly. Lally laughed again.

"Why, she was closed in her mountain long ago, was she not? I doubt if she could get out again—could she now, could she?"

"It is best not to speak of such things," replied Luy sullenly.

Lally stopped in his walk.

"I am quite sure that something bit me in the dark."

"It is very likely, Herr Graf. There are a lot of wild animals in the forest."

Lally gripped him in the darkness.

"And they come here? They come here?"

"You say that you have seen them."

"Yes, a little dark boar—by the gate. And what do you think I saw at the same time, Luy? I saw the blue drapery of the Madonna over the gate blown away, and her golden hair was crowned by flowers under her hood, and her bare body was circled by a girdle of stars. Hush! what was that?"

They stood together close in the darkness, listening to each other's breathing.

"It is the lunatics dancing in their chains—those in the pavilions. They smell the storm."

"Where are we?" asked Lally. "I have lost my way. All is alike dark, and your lantern gives such a dim light."

"The oil is low. We have passed the wall of the Steinberg and are by the press house. Do not you smell the nearly ripe grapes?"

Lally could discern no perfume. The air still seemed sweet with a sickly poison; it was difficult to breathe. The dim light of the dying lantern only showed a few feet of ground, then the long rays were utterly absorbed into the thick darkness.

"We must be near the temple," said Lally angrily. "Why did we come this way?"

"As good as another. How do we know where they are, Herr Graf?"

"Perhaps they have returned," said Lally wearily.

He felt suddenly tired of the search, as if his spirit and body had been beaten on by forces too powerful for him to resist.

He was drowsy, too, craving rest; all at once indifferent to the Duke, to Gertruda. He still gripped Luy by the arm; he thought that if he let go he would fall down.

"What can we do with a dying lantern?" he muttered. "Let us turn back, my head is aching. Let us turn back before the storm comes."

As he spoke a quick light glimmered ahead; a globe of fire, it seemed, more than a lamp or candle.

"The temple," said Lally. "It is in the direction of the temple. Someone went into the temple with a light."

But Luy said that he had seen nothing at all; if there was anything, it might easily have been a Heerwisch, which often appears before storms or where the ground has been disturbed.

"There is no Heerwisch here," said Lally violently. "He only haunts the marshes, like those on the Rhine reaches."

Luy began to laugh.

"I will soon see if it be he or no!"

And shaking himself free from Lally's clutch, he began to snap his fingers and sing:

> Heerwisch! ho! ho!
> Brenst wie haberstroh!
> Schlag mich blitzeblo!

"That is a song he hates," added Luy, "and if it is really he, he will flap in our faces and try to destroy us."

Lally put his hand to his sword, but nothing came out of the darkness save Luy's quiet voice.

"It is not he. It is true that he is found more often between Godorf and Rodenkirchen; there he plays some fine tricks! Have you heard how he ran off with Brother Sebastian from the Abbey of Kreutzberg? In the form of a lovely lady he was, tripping over the marshes. You may see them still on St. John's Eve, dancing over marsh and fen until the bosom of the Rhine swallows them up."

Heerwisch! ho! ho!
Brenst wie haberstroh!
Schlag mich blitzeblo!

Singing this with evident relish, Luy snapped his fingers into the darkness, ending with a low "Hullo!" or whistle. Lally checked him fiercely.

"Are we here to maunder over their fairy tales!"

Luy instantly became quiet.

"There is something that will interest you more than any Heerwisch,"
he said, and, raising his faint lantern, swung it in the direction of the
monastery.

Lally turned.

In one of the windows, quite near, a steady light tone, was burning.

"The Duke's apartment," added Luy.

"I will go," said Lally at once. "Perhaps, after all, he has returned,
the girl is in her cell, and we agitate ourselves for nothing."

Luy, who seemed to find his way as well as if it was broad daylight,
caught hold of Lally's hand and led him to the entrance to the Duke's
apartments, which stood open.

A dull light filled the wide stone stairs. Lally instantly entered, the
servant at his heels humming some words over in a low tone.

This irritated Lally. As he mounted the stairs (they seemed to-day end-
lessly long) he strained his ears to catch what the servant was muttering.

Dies iræ, dies illa
Solvet sæclum in favilla
Teste David cum Sibyllâ!

The words had some horrible meaning, Lally knew; they made him
shudder, but he could not place them.

Quantus tremor est faturus
Quando Judex est venturus
Cuncta stricte discussurus?

Lally turned round hotly; the impudent servant was muttering over the *Sequentia* from the Roman high mass for the dead. But no neat figure in the Nassau uniform was on the dim-lit stairs. Some shape there seemed to be, too tall for humanity and darkly hooded, but this proved to be but a shadow cast by one of the pilasters.

"Luy!" cried the young man.

There was no reply; only the mutter, in a ribald tone, came up the well of the stairway—came up with a hollow whistle from the darkness beneath:

Mors stupebit, et natura,
Cum resurget creatura
Judicanti responsura

"Luy! Luy!"

Liber scriptus proferetur
In quo totum continetur
Unde mundus judicetur!

Lally leant against the stone wall; from the shadows above him grinned the boar's head in stone.

"The place is bewitched," he muttered.

With an effort he made the sign of the cross and hastened on up the stairs. Luy's chant was lost in the distance, and he found the Duke's door open. From this came the faint glow that illuminated the stairway.

Lally looked in before entering. The broken spinet still occupied the centre of the room. On top of it were placed several candles. Between them and Lally stood a woman, with her back to the door. Pauline, he thought at once.

But where had she procured that rich silk dress, the colour of milk and a mignonette flower, and that coronal of gems so fine that they seemed a twist of twinkling stars?

The Duke was leaning over the spinet holding her hands, it seemed, and talking to her earnestly.

"I am glad that they are reconciled at last," thought Lally.

He entered.

A sudden gust of air from the open windows fluttered the candles almost to darkness; for an instant Lally could see nothing. When the candle flames straightened again Pauline had gone.

The Duke was alone. He was leaning over the spinet as if half asleep. Some sheets of music were in his hand. He looked up and smiled at Lally.

"I want to try my bouquet again," he said, "but the instrument is broken." And he struck one of the soundless keys.

"Where is Pauline?" asked Lally.

"Pauline?"

"Yes—she was here."

"Here? She is safe in her bed, I hope. What should she do here?"

Lally shuddered; if it was not Pauline, who, then, was it?

"I suppose Gertruda—" he faltered.

"Gertruda?" repeated the Duke, in a bewildered, sleepy voice.

"You went into the woods with her—where is she?"

"Into the woods? No further than the cloister garden, where we went to gather herbs. She is in her cell. We have finished the perfume. I have sent to Wiesbaden for some bottles of clouded glass—amber and rose."

Lally took him by the shoulders and shook him as one shakes a man drugged or wandering in his mind.

"Who was the woman with you just now? Where is she?"

"There was no one," repeated the Duke, without, however, showing any surprise. "I have been alone all the evening, thinking of my perfume, but I shall not call it Pauline."

"What, then?"

"Freia, I think, Freia."

"No," said Lally desperately. "Not that, not that. Do not say that name here or I shall think you bewitched and damned—as I am myself, as I am myself!"

The Duke smiled dreamily, and continued to move his fingers over the soundless keys.

Lally looked furtively and fearfully round the room.

It was so large that something—someone—might easily lurk in the shadows. The draperies had been left on the great bed, which stood in a dark alcove. Perhaps she was hiding there.

"Highness," cried Lally desperately, "will you come with me to Wiesbaden to-morrow? Help me to take away the women. Herr Sandemann advised it."

"I must stay for the harvest," said the Duke, unmoved, "but you need not tarry for me."

The curtains of the bed seemed to flutter. Lally could bear it no longer; he went to the alcove and dragged the tapestries apart.

Nothing within but the tattered coverlet and cushions.

The Duke took no notice of this action; he looked pale, and his lids kept dropping over his heavy eyes.

"I must not leave him," thought Lally. "No, I certainly must not leave him."

He went to the window that stood wide open with the curtains drawn, and stared into the blank darkness in the direction of the press house, the vineyard, and the temple of Mithras.

He thought of the Heerwisch and of Luy's derisive song; he wanted to lean out of the window and shout it, to see if the goblin would flap into the room on fiery wings and beat angrily in their faces.

Then he thought of Luy, lingering behind and muttering the awful words of the *Sequentia*.

"Oh, God," murmured the young man, "leave me my reason."

The air seemed sticky on his face; the oppression was unbearable, as if a cap of hot steel was pressing on his brows. Why did the storm linger?

There was no sound save the groans and cries of the lunatics in the distant pavilions. "Yet they are all abroad to-night," muttered Lally. "All of them."

He looked round over his shoulder at the Duke. That young man had fallen asleep on his outstretched arm, which was flung across the spinet. His long hair was scattered among the candlesticks.

Lally thought of his own sleep the night the pastor had found him outside Gertruda's cell.

He went out on to the stairs and listened. Above him the stone flights ran up into dense shadows; below the light fell far enough for Lally to discern the carving of the boar's head.

His mind was so full of strange images that he projected them on to this dim background, the statue in the temple of Mithras, the marble Duke in the cathedral, an old Bernardine chanting the solemn mass for the dead, Freia, the northern Venus, Bacchus himself, the boar of Eberbach, all the fantastical figures that crowded the wild legends of the Rhine.

Yet there was nothing, nothing there, only the empty stairs so faintly lit by candlelight; only the grotesque carving of the animal's head leering from the old Gothic design. And the woman in the peculiar coloured silk dress, with the wreath of stars—the woman who had seemed to be Pauline—leaning across the spinet and talking to the Duke in a low tone? She must have been a vision of his distraction. It was so likely; he had been almost beside himself with suspense and anxiety and the hideous night, and the impertinences of that ribald fellow Luy, with his Heerwisch and his Latin chants.

Lally was cooler now, able to judge and weigh; able to understand that nothing awful or tremendous had happened. It was even possible that the Duke had not gone to the woods at all. The pastor, in his over anxiety, might have made a mistake.

The coming of Pauline had agitated them all—yes, it was that. Pauline should never have come.

And then Lally, standing there on the old stone stairway that still seemed to retain the echoes of the feet that had once passed up and down it, remembered what Pauline had asked of him—the marriage, the instant marriage, as the price of her return to Wiesbaden.

How grotesque that, somehow, seemed now, as grotesque almost as his own chimera of an idea—the wild idea of marrying Gertruda. He returned to the room. It was cooler now, and a few stars showed in the rifts of the black clouds.

This gave Lally great comfort. He put out the candles that were guttering over the Duke's hair and arm, and, folding his cloak as a pillow, he lay down to sleep, or to watch, beside the spinet.

CHAPTER XXVII

With the dawn Lally was back in his room. He did not want to face the waking of the Duke, whom he had left still asleep across the spinet.

There had been no storm. The black night clouds had rolled away as silently as they had come.

The day was again fresh and beautiful and free from spectres; the air was redolent of woodland scents and the perfumes of the gathered harvest that all day long was being brought for storage into the monastery.

Lally laughed at his own imaginings. He mockingly rated Luy, who, quiet and trim, prepared his chocolate, on his behaviour of last night.

"Why did you not follow me, as I bid you? Instead, rascal that you are, you stay behind, muttering blasphemies. Where did you learn the *Sequentia*?"

"The *Sequentia*, Herr Graf?" asked Luy blankly.

"Yes—what you were chanting last night."

Luy stood arrested, holding the chocolate pot.

"Ah, that was the monk then. That was why I could not come up—a monk passed me on the stairs, chanting. He must have been ten feet high."

Lally laughed angrily.

"So your wits, too, are wandering. There were shadows on the stairs—a great many of them. Did you not notice them? But there was nothing else—nothing else!"

Luy, however, remained unshaken in his tale.

He had seen, he declared, a huge monk, who ascended the stairs close behind Lally, and who had pushed him down, muttering the while what seemed awful words in a foreign tongue.

"It was you," persisted Lally angrily. "Do you think that I do not know your voice?"

But Luy protested that he did not know Latin, or, indeed, any of the offices of the Church of Rome. And this, Lally had to admit to himself, seemed reasonable enough.

Where and how could such as Luy have learnt the words of the *Sequentia*?

He himself had but seldom heard them. They brought memories of terrible masses for the souls of dead friends, heard as a youth at that Romist Church in Wiesbaden that he had so soon ceased to attend.

Yet if it was not Luy, who then? The door was opened on hideous possibilities—those possibilities that he wished least to entertain.

This made him still further angry, and he vented his wrath on Luy.

"Perhaps you will say," he sneered, "that you did not sing a song in patois in the gardens?"

"Ah, the Heerwisch!" said Luy. "The Heerwisch is a different thing."

He poured out the chocolate, and Lally was silent.

His resolution to leave Eberbach had faded with his terrors of the night. Desirable and beautiful lay the valley, the vineyards, orchards, fields, and gardens; intoxicating were the scents of summer; the opulence of fruit and flowers delighted the senses, the steady radiance of the sun was like God's benison of the earth.

Lally thought of Wiesbaden with distaste and of Pauline with renewed vexation. Her tragic figure spoilt the scene.

That morning he did not see the Duke, nor did he go near the distillery. No comment was made to him about any prisoners being missing last night, so he concluded that Herr Sandemann had spoken wildly, and that the girl had returned to her cell at the usual time.

Pauline and the Baroness he could not avoid; they wandered about the grounds of Eberbach arm in arm, two dreary figures to his thinking, for even the Baroness had lost her gaiety, and seemed ill at ease and suspicious.

Pauline was cold with Lally, and now and then, when she found him alone, broke out into sudden railing. He had betrayed her, she declared, by not speaking to the Duke on her behalf, and she questioned him indignantly about his adventures of the preceding night.

"Did you not find that jade with the Duke?" she cried. Lally was able to stoutly deny this, but Pauline remained scornfully unconvinced.

She was sure that the witch-like girl had ensnared both the men who had been the lovers of Pauline.

Lally, weary of it all, could only advise again that she returned to her hunting-box near Die Platte, or to Wiesbaden.

"What is the use?" she answered desperately. "I am ruined, anyhow."

Here the Baroness, whom he had hitherto considered his friend, turned on him with bitter fierceness.

"Yes, she is ruined. It was always a folly, this coming to Die Platte and then to Eberbach. Of course, it is known now all over Nassau. I hope you are pleased with your work, Marquis."

Lally looked at her in despair. The three stood in the orchard, which seemed to overflow with fruit, for the trees were still heavily laden, yet piled-up baskets of apples, pears, and quinces stood everywhere, and the grass was covered with the windfalls and careless castings aside of the fruit gatherers.

The three had to speak in low tones because of these who, in their orange and grey garb, moved about their task under the stolid supervision of an armed soldier. Beneath the thick clustering branches of the fruit-trees the sky showed a perfect blue; in the shadows the fruit-strewn grass looked gold, in the light emerald.

"Speak to the Duke yourself, Pauline," said Lally. The woman's grievance seemed so worldly, so trivial, here.

"If I cannot even come into his presence!" she objected hysterically. "Where is he now? Nowhere I can go!"

The Baroness supported her.

"Do you think we can force into his apartments or into the laboratories, where he is with that girl?"

Lally's thick brows swept together into a dangerous frown.

"Why do you goad me?" he muttered. "What do you think I can do?"

"You owe me something," she said angrily.

Lally turned away impatiently, but the Baroness took him by the sleeve.

"Do you not see," she whispered desperately, "that Pauline is ruined unless she leaves here Duchess of Nassau?"

Lally shook off the woman's fingers.

"Unfortunately it is not in my power to make her Duchess of Nassau!" he answered.

And with that he left them to cry out against his brutality.

Yet he was resolved to make an attempt to keep his word, and silence and satisfy this pitiful woman.

He went to find Herr Sandemann, and had to wait in the refectory while the pastor's class finished their singing.

The sight of all these children, many of whom wore wreaths of fresh green round their heads and carried small boughs in their hands while they stood in rows and sang one of Luther's hymns, pleased and soothed Lally.

These classes were the holiest, most innocent things he had seen since he came to Eberbach—nay, since he last stood, a child himself, in a church, or played, with his hands full of flowers, round his mother's skirts.

When the children had all trooped out Lally still sat in his corner, his elbows on the end of the long table and tears in his heavy eyes.

"What did you want with me, Herr Captain?" asked the old man gravely as he went along the benches, collecting and putting away the prayer and hymn-books.

"I've told you everything," said Lally half sullenly, "and now I want your help."

"Yes, Herr Graf?"

"Persuade this young man—persuade the Duke to marry the Margravine. She is a desperate, she says a ruined, woman. I must in some way make amends."

"Amends?" asked the pastor sharply. "Amends for what? You assured me that there was no wrong."

"Old man," interrupted Lally fiercely, "do not seek to probe into what you cannot understand. Enough that this woman is the Duke's affianced bride; that she has followed him here, and that it is for her honour that he wed her at once. Go to him and tell him so; marry them within the day, if you can."

"I marry them?"

The pastor stood staring, holding the pile of small worn books against his breast.

"Aye, marry them," returned Lally impatiently. "What does it matter who marries them as long as she is satisfied and leaves Eberbach?"

"Why do you want her to leave Eberbach, Herr Captain?"

"I tell you the woman is plaguing me. She will be Duchess; she has set her heart on that."

Herr Sandemann interrupted him.

"I will take no share in this business. I will not meddle."

Lally rose.

"Old man," he cried furiously, "do you mean that if they come to you you will not marry them?"

"If the Duke comes to me I might, but for you and the lady—I feel that there is some unworthy intrigue."

Lally left the refectory an angry man; there was now nothing left for him to do but to get the Duke to see his responsibility towards Pauline; to, in some way, take her off his, Lally's, mind and conscience.

He waited, hoping that the Prince would appear at the mid-day meal that they usually shared together in Lally's rooms, but he did not, and Lally had to eat alone, waited on by Luy.

As before, he was forced to make a confidant of the servant; as before, Luy proved himself efficient and reliable.

He had, somehow, during the morning gathered information as to the Duke's movements.

He had visited the temple of Mithras and the vineyard, now so near the full bloom of the grape, then, in company with an old peasant employed in the Steinberg, he had inspected the cellars. In no way had his behaviour been remarkable, nor had he, as far as Luy knew, been near the laboratories.

"He will go there now," said Lally. He wondered why the Duke had not come to the mid-day meal.

Luy said that it was likely that he had had the whim, which he had taken before, to dine with the little garrison, or even with the prisoners or lunatics in the great kitchen.

Lally, who wished, above all things, for a clear head, touched no wine, and as soon as his meal was finished went to the old distillery.

As he paused on the threshold of the open door he saw that the Duke was not there.

Gertruda sat alone by the rose-shielded window, her lap piled with grapes, from which she was slowly eating.

Against his own wish—for he had resolved at all costs to avoid this woman—Lally entered.

She looked up. Her unsmiling face reminded him of the mysterious statue in the ancient temple, calm, blank of emotion, yet conveying a curious menace. Her faded blue linen dress, girdled with leather, was stained by drops of perfume and the juice of fruit; her feet were bare; on one arm she wore a bracelet formed of two rows of immense pearls.

Lally pointed to it at once.

"Where did you obtain so fine a jewel?" he asked jealously.

"Your friend found it in the cellars," she answered, "and gave it to me."

"So you have seen him this morning after all?"

"Yes."

Lally went up to her and seized the warm, soft arm, round which the jewel pressed. The pearls were of extraordinary size and rich with a thousand colours.

"Fresh-water pearls from the Rhine," said Gertruda.

"There are no pearls in the Rhine," answered Lally briefly.

"Perhaps there were where these were found." And she smiled a little.

"Discovered in the cellar!" exclaimed Lally, still holding the beautiful arm.

The bracelet was discoloured with earth and lees of wine, like the chaplet that had been found in the corridor outside her cell.

"Did you go into the woods yesterday?" asked Lally.

The girl rose. The heavy loops of her hair fell from the horn pins, and the long locks slipped to her waist.

"Where were you, Lally Duchene?" she asked; and she was still smiling.

He stood silent, sullen and alert.

"You are afraid of me?" she asked.

He flung away her hand with an angry gesture.

"I am not afraid of you, but I know that you are a witch. Listen. Do you think that I have not seen your devilments, your enchantments, your black arts? I am not fooled by them, nor beguiled. I do not know why you stay here, nor if your powers are insufficient to procure your liberty, but I know you are a witch, who in ruder times would have been drowned or burnt."

He spoke roughly, persuading himself by his own speech. Yes, this was the solution of everything—the girl was a witch, an adept in those unholy arts in which he had hitherto misbelieved; yet he had often been assured that they were extensively practised among the peasantry of the Rhinegau. He felt a relief at having come to this conclusion, for it excluded other and more terrible possibilities.

Gertruda seemed neither surprised nor angry; she turned over the bunches of grapes, which were of varying sizes and colours.

"Where is that wretched young man?" asked Lally. "What have you done with him, eh?"

"The Duke has gone into the wood," she answered, "to find the wild strawberries that have so sweet a flavour. There may be a few left, though it is so late."

"You fool me," said Lally. "And does he allow you to call him so—the Duke?"

"Aurelio Johann of Nassau," she smiled. "I knew him from the first."

"It is strange," sneered Lally, "that he has not given you your liberty."

"I wish," she answered, "to stay in Eberbach at least till the harvest."

Lally turned aside at that word, which he had come to regard as one of ill omen, he knew not why.

He leant against the flat window-frame. The air, heavy with the rich odours of aromatics, was beginning to make his head ache.

"It will be an early harvest this year," added the girl. "The grapes are so soon ripe that they will not be able to wait, as usual, for the first frost."

"Why are you not also in the woods?" asked Lally. She pointed to the furnace.

"I must watch the essences," she said. "Will you watch with me, Lally Duchene?"

But he, with a great effort of will, turned aside, and in silence passed into the hot cloister garden, where the herbs were withering in the sun.

CHAPTER XXVIII

As Gertruda had said, the vintage was very early that year—early, that is, for the Rhinegau, where it is sometimes as late as November, and nearly always after the first frost. But this spring and summer had been so fiercely hot that the grapes were ripe to bursting by early September, and the harvest could no longer be delayed. Lally felt in a vague and uneasy fashion as if this harvest was the climax of a great drama, unseen, only half guessed at, in which forces beyond even the comprehension of a mortal were involved. The glorious days seemed heavy with menace; the purple nights heavy with portents.

Yet nothing happened.

The routine of the prison went on as it had gone on, year after year. The prisoners and the lunatics toiled at their appointed labours; the little garrison performed their daily round of monotonous duties; the farmer who rented the Steinberg made his usual preparations to reap the fruit of his three seasons' work; the little band of workmen from Wiesbaden employed themselves in excavating the temple, and in laying the ground plans for the new swimming baths.

Even the presence of the Duke and Pauline did not disturb the regular round of these peaceful, regulated, and unceasing labours. The first fitted into his place as an officer sent to supervise the improvements to be made in the old monastery, and the two women lodging with the pastor came to be considered as indifferent details of a busy whole, either, as some gave out, relations of Herr Sandemann, or, as others said, ladies from Wiesbaden sent to inquire into the conditions under which the female prisoners lived.

The behaviour of the Baroness helped this supposition. She had lost her good humour and her gaiety but not her energy and tact; she went about among the women, made friends with them, helped them in their work, and even sympathised with their complaints as to the harshness of the Duke's forest laws under which most of them were suffering.

Pauline moped and sulked. She would not speak to Lally, and even seemed to avoid the Duke, but she would by no means return to Wiesbaden.

The Duke, on his side, did not seem to greatly trouble about her presence. He had smiled aside Lally's suggestion of an immediate marriage, and went his way, calm, reserved, absorbed—in what?

Lally could not discover.

Of only one thing was he sure—that was that the Duke's heart and mind were no longer occupied by the problem of Pauline as they had been when he first came to Eberbach.

Lally was certain that Pauline's truth or falsehood, the question of which had so convulsed the soul of her betrothed husband, was now not occupying him at all.

He had said that he trusted her word and that he would marry her in the autumn, but Lally believed that this was all vague to him; that he did not think of Pauline as his future wife, and that she did not occupy his thoughts much under any aspect. If she had, how was it possible for him to allow her to remain at Eberbach in this unhappy position? How was it possible for anyone of his sensitive, chivalrous temperament to permit her, even if he had ceased to care for her, to linger here under these circumstances?

This Lally could not understand. The Duke was like a man bemused or dazed, going through his days evenly and quietly, without thought for the morrow. Lally wished to accuse the black arts of Gertruda of having bewitched the young man, but he could not, for all his own and Luy's spying, discover that these two were much together, or that they had a great interest in each other.

The Duke did not spend more than an hour or so every day in the distillery, and then Herr Sandemann was generally present, and there was no sign that he met Gertruda on any other occasion.

Lally's own jealous eyes saw her locked into her cell every evening and generally saw the Duke into his own lonely apartments.

And then, when the harvest began, the laboratories were closed, and the girl went, with all the others, to work in the vineyard.

Lally himself avoided the girl with a secret terror and an inward wild longing. If he by chance passed her he scowled, and if possible flung her some sneer or rough reproof.

Often he would contrive occasion to speak to her that he might say something harsh or contemptuous.

She appeared never to resent this, but sometimes she would turn her full eyes on him with a look so passionless it was like the gaze of the blind, and then he would turn away muttering, shivering in his soul.

Once curiosity urged him to again enter the temple, now nearly completely cleared of rubbish and washed by the light of day.

The sightless eyes of the mysterious statue turned on him just such a look, and Lally crept away.

The Duke, on the other hand, went often to the temple, and seemed to like to stare at the young man with the curls and Persian cap, whose god-like figure was to Lally so awesome and even horrible.

It was Mithras, the Duke declared, the deity of the sun, of youth and warriors, and he delved deep into the history of this mysterious Eastern religion. He ransacked the pastor's library, and books were sent from Wiesbaden. Herr Sandemann protested against a research that seemed to him heathenish, if not blasphemous, but the Duke went his way. He was not affected by the pastor, by Lally, or by Pauline, nor even, it seemed, by Gertruda; yet in something he remained entirely absorbed.

Lally was caught up in the strong wheel of circumstance and sent round and round the routine of days that he began to dread and fear. There seemed no escape and no hope. He would have given much to have got away from the scornful reproach of Pauline's silence, from the spectacle of the Duke's ghastly calm, from the pastor's gloomy hints and fearful suggestions, from the queer, watchful eyes of Luy, and the moans of the maniacs in the pavilions—and the nights, heavy with mysterious portents—of what?

For still nothing happened, and, as Lally asked himself with a shudder, what should happen? What could possibly happen?

The Riesling grapes had now become of a rose-red colour; the stalks were drying, and some bunches beginning to shrivel and drop to the ground; the harvest could no longer be delayed.

"This year they will be late," said the pastor, and for all Lally's pressing he would not explain himself further.

Then one morning he said:

"They have come."

Lally looked round the white sun-filled refectory. The books and the benches were alike put away, for the children were helping in the harvest and did not come to lessons now; only the big Bible remained on a stand of black oak.

"Who have come?" asked Lally impatiently.

"Go to the Steinberg," said the old man, "and you will see them."

He seemed very ill at ease and put his hand continually on the Bible, as if he did not feel safe far from the holy volume.

"He loses his wits," thought Lally, "with much reading and brooding over wild legends."

Yet it was with a flutter of inward dread that he made his way through the glare of the mid-day sun to the Steinberg. But nothing strange was happening. The farmer, standing in the shade of one of the high slate and timber walls, was allotting work to a number of peasants who had come especially for the harvest.

A certain number of prisoners was among them, but not many, as they were mostly employed in the inferior vineyards in the valley, leaving the Steinberg to the more skilled workers.

Lally, half blinded by the sun, went to one of the little pavilions that adorned the great vineyard and watched idly the even rows of rosy grapes hanging among the golden-brown leaves.

An old vine-dresser, complacently observing the result of his long labours, was also sheltering in the pavilion, and Lally, from sheer weariness of spirit, began to talk to him.

"It will be a magnificent harvest, eh?"

"Yes, Herr Graf, but better if we could have waited for the first frost. Never have I known the harvest before October, but this year the grapes would not have kept a moment longer. They will soon be overripe as it is!"

With a chuckle he added: "I thought that they would be late this year!"

Lally started.

"Who are they?"

"Why, the foreigners who come to help in the vintage."

"Are they foreigners?"

"Well, they come from a long way off and they speak a strange language among themselves," replied the old peasant vaguely, "and they seem to know a good deal about foreign countries."

Lally smiled, with a certain sense of relief.

"They come from another part of Nassau and speak another dialect, I suppose," he said. "Probably they go all over Germany, or do they always come here?"

"Some of them always; they have never missed a year since I can remember. But then, isn't this the best vineyard in Germany—better than Rüdesheim or Johannisberg, Marcobrunner or Ellfeld, where they still grow the vine in *stock*?"

"Yes, yes," said Lally impatiently, "but who are these people? And why do they wander about instead of working in their native places like others?"

"I cannot tell you that, Herr Graf. It is enough that they are good workers and can tell you fine tales. There is nothing that they do not know about vines—about the Lieste vineyard, where they grow the Hermitage grape to make the wine that goes into the cellars of the castle of Wartzburg in Franconia, where there are tuns so high one must use a ladder of twenty-four steps to reach the top; and the Champagne, where good King Probus began making wine—the 'stopper jumper' or 'devil's wine.'"

Lally rose, hastily interrupting.

"You talk nonsense, old man; I think that you are doited."

The peasant laughed quietly to himself. Lally thought now that he had a peculiar and unpleasant face. "I will talk with these people myself."

With this Lally left the shade of the pavilion, and, following one of the carriage roads that intersected the vineyard, made his way to the group standing in the narrow shade of the roofed wall.

He was greeted by respectful salutations from all, and the farmer would have stopped his instructions in deference to the commandant of Kloster Eberbach, but Lally bade him proceed, and, leaning against the wall, observed the new-comers. He counted eight of them mingled with the prisoners and the peasants always employed on the farm. They were all so young that the vine-dresser's tale was proved absurd; it was impossible that he could have seen them year after year.

There were six men and two women, all wearing the blue smocks and leather belts of Nassau. The women had the usual white kerchiefs folded over their heads.

Save that they were all more than usual handsome, robust, tall, fair, and fresh-coloured, Lally could see nothing unusual about them. Fine types and a heavy type of animal beauty was not rare among the peasantry of the Rhinegau. This favoured spot, like a bay in the mountain, bounded by the Rhine and the Taunus, and so overflowing with fruitfulness as to have been called the Garden of Bacchus—these were fitting inhabitants of such a country. Lally admired them, yet found something repellant in their size, their strength, and their calm.

He remarked with anger that the girl Gertruda was among them. She was of the same type and bearing, and seemed to be conversing with them in their own dialect.

Lally was vexed that she should have been allowed the privilege of working in the Steinberg, one usually accorded only to those prisoners whose sentences were light and offences slight.

He went over to her, looking an incongruous figure in his uniform, with his sword and powder.

"Do you know these strangers?" he asked her rudely.

"Yes, I know them."

"What district do they come from?"

"All from the Rhinegau, but they have travelled."

He now perceived that two of the men had a shaggy, wild appearance and an aspect serene but ferocious, while the others were youths of a more noble aspect, flushed and handsome.

The women were like Gertruda, heavy-browed, wide-eyed, large limbed, with that animal look Lally had so often noticed among the peasantry who toiled in the earth and were untouched by any breath of any town.

Everyone was now supplied with scissors and knives and little baskets, and to every six labourers was allotted a collector, who carried a quantity of empty baskets. Those vintagers who were new to the work were told to cut out of every bunch thick stalks, tendrils, unripe and decayed berries, and to proceed as fast as possible with their labours.

Lally walked beside Gertruda as she stepped between the rows of vines; the other side of her walked one of the young peasant strangers. He and the girl were almost of a height, and their stride swung well together. Lally felt incongruous, alien, but he kept his place.

The perfume of the grapes, overripe and bursting; the sight of them, rose-red, bunch after bunch on the well pruned vines, from which all superfluous wood and foliage had been cut away; the unshaded azure of the sky, which danced with points of light; this press of people, burnt and coloured by the sun, their healthy flesh scantily covered, the sweet odours of the open air coming from their skin, their hair, their breath—all these things began to affect the senses of Lally. A feeling of giddiness possessed him; purple of fruit and sky, rose of fruit and flesh, gold of hair and sun, all mingled together in a whirl of piercing colour that made him giddy. He had to put his hand to his eyes.

"The sun makes you dizzy," said Gertruda. "If one is not used to it one cannot support the vintage time."

Lally gave her a savage look; but he did indeed feel that he must at once leave the vineyard.

As he turned away all the vintagers were laughing together, and it seemed to Lally that they were laughing mockingly at him.

CHAPTER XXIX

Lally, like everyone else save Pauline, spent his day in the vineyard. It seemed, indeed, impossible to keep away from the place where all life and interest was now concentrating. The excitement over the good harvest was contagious; without doubt the vintage was magnificent. This year there would be no need to make the wine palatable by the addition of sugar or to put chalk into the cask; the wines of the Steinberg would, this autumn, compare with any from Walluf to Lorch, and even probably be better than those from the Rüdesheimer Berg and the Johannisberg; nay, better than the best that could be produced from any of the terraces of the whole chain of the Taunus hills.

The austere, or first gathering, had been splendid.

To make the choicest or Cabinet wines—those that were sold in bottle only under the seal of the Prince—the best bunches of grapes were plucked by the vintagers, all faulty fruit removed from them, and delivered to the collectors, who went over them again before throwing from the baskets into the first press, a small perforated tub which rested on two boards placed across a larger one. In the first tub a young boy stood treading the grapes with bare feet, so that all passed through the holes into the larger cask before.

As there were not sufficient of these presses for the splendid abundance of the harvest, several casks of a different kind were being used in which the women, with bare arms stained to the elbow, beat the grapes to a pulp with heavy pieces of wood.

The grapes, whether pulped by hands or feet, were then poured into wooden tubs strapped on to the backs of men, who carried them to the rows of carts that stood waiting on the carriage way harnessed to stout little ponies or to oxen.

These carts consisted of huge casks on wheels, with a funnel at the top, which were at once driven to the press house. The juice, skins, and stalks were then poured through an opening at the end of the cask into tubs, which were immediately carried to the press reserved for the Cabinet wines.

These men were operating the presses—gently at first, to prevent the overflowing of the abundant juice; afterwards so vigorously that they sweated at their task, and the pure juice, free now from skin and stalk, ran in a thick yellow stream out of the two holes in the press into a small vat beneath, and then directly into pipes that ran into the tuns in the vaults beneath, which had been prepared by washings with hot water and afterwards with sulphur.

Lally tasted this raw wine, and found it of a sweet and pleasant flavour; a cloying, over-luscious liquor.

Perhaps, he thought, this was the old nectar of the gods.

After the presses had been screwed down for about three hours these were loosened, and Lally watched the murk or hard residue of the grapes being removed in the compact shape of the press.

The centre of this, which had received the greater pressure, was cast outside into the sun, where it was soon covered by large pale wasps. The more juicy outside pieces were replaced under the press, after being broken up in small morsels. The resultant wine was, however, of a very inferior quality, and was kept apart.

After the vintage of the Cabinet wines the gathering of the second quality began, and after that the rest of the vineyard was gone over for the common kinds of wine.

By this time three or four days had passed, and the Cabinet wines had begun to ferment in the cask, to the great pleasure of the vintagers, who told Lally that if fermentation did not fully take place at harvest time it would begin again in June and the wine take much longer to ripen.

They also explained that this white wine must ferment after being separated from the skin and stalks in case it received a pinkish colour, much disliked in Rhine wine. On the other hand, the red wine must ferment with the stalks and skins for over a week, so that both colour and bitter flavour is extracted. This was told to Lally by one of the handsome young peasant strangers. All these new-comers seemed to be experts on the subject of viticulture. Lally was amazed at the extent of their knowledge and the skill and swiftness of their work; they seemed tireless, and the farmer declared that they were worth all the other labourers put together.

Gertruda worked with them, and Lally, half-sullen, jealous, reluctant, could not keep away.

All his leisure was spent with this group of vintagers; sometimes he shared their meals of bread and fruit eaten in the shadow of the roofed wall. They slept on the ground outside the press house, sheltered only by the trees that shaded the vaults where the Cabinet wines were kept. Lally wondered how they could endure to see Gertruda taken, as soon as twilight fell, back to her cell.

Now and then the Duke came and looked at the vintage. He never stayed long, and took no notice whatever of Gertruda. He hardly ever spoke to Lally, who believed that he passed his time between the temple and his room, where a new harpsichord from Wiesbaden now occupied the place of the broken, ancient instrument.

He had also sent to Die Platte for his floral clock and had finished painting that. The perfume that was to have been called "Pauline" was also complete and put up in long necked white glass bottles, but the Duke persisted in calling this bouquet "Freia"; the name of the northern Venus particularly attracted him, he declared.

These details Lally learned from Luy, who also brought him reports of Pauline. She was ill, the servant said; but Lally did not greatly care; since the harvest began he had never been near the refectory, nor seen Herr Sandemann. The days passed like an enchantment. They seemed to Lally to be drenched in sun and wine, colour and perfume—the colour of the ripe, crushed fruit, the perfume of the harvest.

The rosy, purple stain of the grape was everywhere—on the bare limbs of the vintagers, trodden into the warm earth, on the walls and floors of the press houses, on the casks and carts and baskets, on the late vivid-coloured wild flowers that grew outside the wall of the Steinberg.

Lally did not see much of Gertruda; she kept with the two women strangers; but in the men he found good companions.

As they worked or as they rested over their meals they told him tales and legends, and gave him accounts of the different vineyards of the world. The youngest and handsomest, a youth whose heavy beauty seemed to increase daily, and who owned the strange name of Gereon (after, he said, the basilica of that name, in which are laid the bones of a hundred saints, slain by order of Diocletian and Maximin), spoke more than the others of the vine and its glory.

He told Lally of the great scorching arid desert, extending from Coquimbo, in Chili, to Payter, in Peru, where were the towns of Rica and Matilla, whose vineyards, in this rainless land, are irrigated by the melting of the snows on the Cordilleras; of Teneriffe, or Vidonia, in the Canary Islands, from which came the ancient sack; of the luxurious vines that covered the bleak mountains of Madeira; of the coarse, sweet wines of Hungary, Tokay, Meneses, St. Gyorgy, and Oden, the rare wines of Russia, Massandra, Aidani, and Aloupka, from the Crimea. The vineyards of Sicily, Italy, and Greece were also well known to this young man, and he spoke of the vine-covered islands of the Archipelago as if they were his home. Particularly did he dwell on the luscious taste of *commander* from Cyprus and Napoli de Malvasia, and the beauties of the little Isle of Santorin, green with vines from one end to the other.

These ancient Greek wines, the very names of which were unknown to Lally, seemed to the young peasant of far more importance than the modern wines of France, Spain, and Portugal, but when pressed as to the sources of his information he became silent and even restive.

His companion, the other young peasant, spoke of the wine of Boudistan and Chan-si from China, the wine of Faristan, Armenia, Erivan, Nak Adgeny from Persia, Jannina from Turkey, the Asian wine of Laos, and other wines that it was impossible that he could ever have tasted.

But he was quiet in his ways, and spoke very little.

The four older men, on the other hand, spoke more of Germany, particularly of the Rhinegau and the Rhine, of which they seemed to know more than Lally had ever found out from the books of Herr Sandemann.

The eldest, a heavy-shouldered fellow whose locks were bleached to a fairness that had almost a greenish tint, spoke of the days when there were no cathedrals in Germany, but when the gods were worshipped in grove and thicket. These altars, he added, were overthrown by the monks and saints, but they had never been able to entirely destroy the gods themselves nor the myriads of spirits who attended them. Ghosts and nymphs and penates, kobolds and fairies, water spirits and wood spirits, devils and wild hunters had never been exorcised from the banks of the Rhine. Lally, absorbed, listened to tales of the fiery chariot of Main; of the phantom of Nicias Varus at Niers; of the wild hunter and his hell-hounds who haunted the Odenwold and Rodenstein, and his hideous host who possessed the Berstrasse. This man, who was called by his companions Hoddeken, which Lally guessed to be a vulgar dialect name, was full of such wild and ghastly stories and of others that Lally dimly remembered to have heard before, such as the river fight of Westhofen, with its prelude; St. George's Day, when the cathedral and palace of Cologne were sacked by the mob, who betook themselves to the bishop's cellars and there were either suffocated by the fumes of the strong wines or drowned by the overflowing of the butts which they had broken open.

The fourth peasant, who was known by his surname of Vatermann, and was of a more gloomy and taciturn character, sometimes told Lally tales of the Rhine, the Undine, the nixie, the water wolf, the Lorelai, and the wonderful halls of pearl and crystal beneath the waters of the Rhine.

He knew also of the romances of the *Nibelungenlied*, of Siegfried working under Mime, at Xanten, and the marvellous hoard lost for ever beneath the waves of the river. In these stories he was joined by the fifth peasant, whom he spoke of as his brother. This was a man of much the same appearance as himself named Ursel, but if he was so called from that village or no Lally could not discover. The last stranger, Willigis, seemed a whimsical fellow, and related many stories—which appeared to give him great delight—of the tricks played by gnomes, goblins, and pixies on human beings.

Lally, listening all day in the wine-scented atmosphere to these tales, thought less and less of Pauline and the Duke; less and less of past or future.

One evening, returning in the hot and purple dusk from the vineyard, he met the pastor, who appeared to be in search of him.

Lally stared as if he had seen a stranger; indeed, for the moment he did not realise who this sombre old man was.

Herr Sandemann took him by the arm and led him into the shadow of the cloister garden.

"You have been avoiding me, Herr Graf."

"I have not thought of you," answered Lally simply. "I have been occupied by the harvest."

"Aye, aye," groaned the pastor. "Tell me, what do they call themselves this year?"

"Who?"

"They—they!"

Lally smiled at the old man's foolishness.

"You mean the peasants who come to work at the vintage? I do not know the names of all of them—one is Gereon, one Vatermann, one Ursel, one Willigis. I do not think that I have heard the names of the others."

The pastor was clinging tight to Lally's arm. The young man felt him shudder.

"And you are so simple that you do not understand, Herr Graf? Is it possible?" asked the pastor anxiously. "Cannot you see what is disguised behind these foolish names. Do you not see that you are not dealing with human beings at all?"

Lally laughed loud in the darkness.

"You have indeed lived too long alone with your old books, Herr Sandemann, when you see in these poor peasants evil spirits."

"Did I say evil spirits? Perhaps rather gods."

"What gods?" whispered Lally.

"I dare not name them."

"But I do," said Lally in the same tone. "Bacchus, Mithras, Freia—" He caught himself up with another laugh. "What madness we talk!"

"As well say," returned the pastor, "that the others are Heerwisch, the Kobold, the water-wolf—the Rhine himself, eh? As well say that, Herr Graf?"

"Say what you like," said Lally desperately. "I am not bemused nor enchanted—no; and all your ugly stories do not frighten me—no, not at all!"

"The Duke—" began the pastor.

"What of him?" interrupted Lally sharply. "He is occupied with his music and his flowers."

"In the daytime—yes. But at night—the nights!"

"The nights!" cried Lally.

"You sleep at night—now?"

"I sleep, more or less."

"Do you think that you can sleep when the festival begins? Do you think that the Duke sleeps now? Every night he is out. Where do you think he goes?"

"I do not believe it," answered Lally roughly. "Luy would have told me. I have set Luy to spy on the Duke."

"Luy!" cried the pastor. "Why, Luy is one of them!"

Lally shook himself free from the old man's clinging grasp, and hurried, muttering to himself, into the monastery.

CHAPTER XXX

The harvest was nearly over, and at the same time the bottling of other years' vintage almost complete. The wine brokers and private buyers from all parts of Nassau were beginning to arrive for the annual auction of wines. These were accommodated in the farm and the monastery. Their presence lent an ordinary, cheerful aspect to the place, and broke up the busy monotony of the days.

Lally resented them; they seemed like the figures of flesh and blood obtruding into the drowsy mysteries of a dream; but everyone else at Eberbach seemed to welcome them. The farmer entertained them handsomely, and every day ended in feasting, in drinking, in laughing and dancing.

Lally kept away from their rejoicing, maliciously glad that Gertruda could not take part in them. Every violet dusk saw her locked in her cell.

The Duke also avoided the vineyard and the press houses; he was afraid, he said, that one of these strangers, some of whom came from Wiesbaden, might recognise him. Lally thought that he must be infatuated, not to realise that his presence at Eberbach must be known now all over Nassau, despite the cleverness of Herr Sylvanus. Nay, Lally did not doubt that the presence, not only of the Duke, but of the Margravine Pauline, was equally noised abroad. Yet, as far as Lally knew, none of these new-comers gossiped about these matters; all were absorbed in the harvest, the wine.

The burning splendour of the sun lent a species of intoxication to the quietest movements of the day. The perfume of the wine was abroad like a tangible thing, sometimes with the mignonette-like odour of the vine blossoms, sometimes with the rich aroma of the matured grape.

As the harvest approached the end everyone worked with redoubled energy; there were the last gleanings of the inferior vines to be picked and pressed, the wines of last year to be racked, the wines that had lain two or three seasons in cask to be bottled and sold, the vineyard to receive the first dressing ready for next year.

The stranger peasants of whom the pastor had spoken so grotesquely were always in the centre of this busy life, and Lally saw less of them, though whenever he went into the vineyard, finding his way among empty casks, carts, baskets, pails, and drying murk, his glance always sought out the wine-stained, sunburned, rosy-flushed figures.

Once, when he heard them talking among themselves of moving on early so that they might be in time for a later vintage somewhere else, he experienced a feeling of sudden homesickness, as if it would be unbearable for these people to go and leave him behind.

And he thought, with a sharp pang, what would Eberbach be like when the harvest was over?

These were strange days for Lally; neither the past nor the future seemed to hold any meaning, and the present was like a dream in which emotion is fantastically heightened and action nullified.

He had no more desire to rouse himself from this mood than the drugged man to escape from his drowsy sleep. The only two people who could bring him into touch with reality—Pauline and the Duke—he avoided.

The doctor, Herr Lindpainter, was one of those who came to Eberbach for the harvest. For some time Lally avoided meeting him, but at length they found themselves face to face beneath the hot walls of the Steinberg.

The doctor looked at Lally very queerly and told him bluntly that he appeared ill.

Lally, who had never felt better in his life, laughed.

He was conscious that he had neglected his dress of late. His uniform was untidy, his hair unpowdered; he was lean and sunburnt too, he knew, and that something too flamboyant, too coarsely handsome, in his appearance that he had been so careful to subdue at Wiesbaden was now very noticeable. The eyes were too splendid, the brows too heavy, the hair too thick—but ill? No, he was not ill.

The doctor asked him if his appointment at Eberbach was a permanent one, and when Lally merely laughed Herr Lindpainter turned away, shaking his head.

It was that day that Lally, returning from the open-air vaults where the Cabinet wines were being sold, met Pauline, who came across his vision like a creature from some other world.

She took him by his unwilling arm and led him to the clean, white refectory that seemed to be still full of the sweet echoes of children's voices. The benches and books were still packed away, and even the great Bible had gone from its place.

The windows were wide open on the blue and the green and the sun, and by one of them sat the Baroness. Lally felt uneasy in the presence of these two women, and even bewildered, like one suddenly forced to drink water after feasting on luscious wine.

Both of them wore what rough cotton dresses they had been able to procure at Eberbach and had lost all trace of the great lady. Pauline looked faded; the colour seemed to have gone even from her hair; her eyes were reddened and her mouth drooping.

The Baroness kept her eyes down and did not greet Lally in any way.

Lally nearly wrenched away from Pauline and left both of these sad figures. Why should he remain? There was Luy waiting with his dinner, and afterwards singing and laughter in the vineyard, and Gertruda, wine-stained, sun-kissed.

But Pauline clung to him, and sullenly he remained.

"You want to rail at me," he said, frowning.

"The pastor has gone," answered Pauline.

"Gone?"

"To Mainz. He would not stay another night."

"He had no right to go without permission," said Lally angrily.

"What did he care for that? He said that the place was cursed and that he could not, for his soul's sake, remain."

"The man was crazy and has affected you, foolish women that you are!"

"It is you who are bewitched, Marquis," said the Baroness, looking up at last.

"So this mad old man made you believe that! He was crazy, with his legends and his books!"

"It is you who are crazy," answered the older woman steadily.

"If you think that," said Lally fiercely, "why did you not leave Eberbach with the old man?"

"I would have gone, but Pauline would stay, and I could not leave her."

"I wanted to save you and Aurelio," said Pauline, in a terrified voice, "but I fear that I am not strong enough. I have been a wicked woman."

Lally had never heard her talk in this fashion before.

He sat down on the one bench remaining out and took his chin in his hand, while he glanced sullenly from one woman to another. They were both on his hands now that Herr Sandemann had fled. He cursed the foolish old man.

"I have tried to pray," continued Pauline, "but who am I to be listened to? The little chapel upstairs is a holy place—the only one in Eberbach—the only safe refuge against—them."

"Stop," said Lally harshly. "You talk sheer madness!"

He bit his lip in great agitation. He hated the room—the wide-open windows, the great wash of light that penetrated to every corner, so that there was no seclusion or privacy; yes, this, the very thing that he had once liked about the refectory—this white simplicity—now annoyed him.

He endeavoured to shake off this impression—to exercise a conscious will and energy. He looked at the two women and tried to recapture something of the feeling he had entertained towards them in Wiesbaden.

"Let us try to get this clear," he said heavily. "What are we talking of? What are we afraid of?"

"It is better not to put it into words," answered the Baroness quickly, "better not to talk about it."

But Lally insisted; he had this great desire to make matters, as he said, clear.

"You are here to marry the Duke," he began in laboured fashion.

"No, no," interrupted Pauline, with an accent of distaste. "I do not think of that any more. Do not misunderstand me—"

"You do not think of that any more?" he cried, in amaze.

"Everything is so different. It is enough if one can save one's soul alive. The Duke will never belong to mortal woman."

"Tell me exactly what you mean," said Lally.

"Have you not noticed the Duke?"

"Yes—he does nothing, nothing!"

"How do you know?"

"I have taken means to find out."

"You spy on him?"

"Not that. But Luy watches him."

"Luy! Luy!" cried both the women together.

Lally glanced from one to the other with a fearful sharpness. Again he repeated stupidly:

"What do you mean?"

"Why," whispered Pauline, "Luy is—"

"Don't say it," cried the Baroness.

But Lally knew; he had known for a long time; but he would not admit his knowledge—not for a second, a breath of time.

With all the willpower of which he was yet capable he cast from him and rejected what would, if accepted, plunge him into a depth of horror, an abyss of dread, more vast than eternity, and peopled by terrors more awful than the worst panic imaginings of humanity.

He felt now a coldness down his spine and round his jaw, and knew that his teeth shook together a little.

"The Duke," he said quickly, "is always in his room. You remember that night when you were frightened? Well, I stayed with him; till the dawn he slept across the harpsichord."

"His body was there, yes," said Pauline, "but they have confused his soul out of his body. He is with them—every night."

"Who told you?" asked Lally.

"I know, and so would you, were you not also under the enchantment. And when the harvest is over and they go away?"

"When the harvest is over," repeated Lally. "Yes, what then?"

For a moment he seemed to glimpse her meaning, to see it in a clear and rational light then it was lost again. The supernatural had now become to him the natural. He could not easily return to this plane on which the two women moved. Even the shock that their words about Luy had given him had passed away; he only felt a desire to return to the vineyard—an impatience of this sad, mundane company.

"Why do you look at me so compassionately?" he asked harshly. "I do not understand what you talk about. I am due back at the vineyard."

"Could you," asked Pauline, "come upstairs and pray with me? You are a Romanist. Do you think to ever take a crucifix with you?"

Lally remembered that this thought had once come to him; now it seemed utterly ridiculous.

"Who is to look after us now?" continued Pauline. "Herr Sandemann has taken the Bible with him."

"I will send sentries—a guard," said Lally hastily.

"These heavy soldiers, who are sensible of nothing, are no protection," answered the Baroness sharply.

"Well, then, return to Wiesbaden," cried Lally, and abruptly left the whitewashed room.

When he was once more outside in the burning sunshine he stopped, with the air of one dazed coming to himself, and looked round.

Everything was there; everything was the same, still, peaceable—the splendid building, the orchards, the valley, the sun—the sun.

There was no need to think of those two women; nay, it was impossible to think of them; they seemed of no importance whatever.

As he passed through the cloisters he looked up at the carving of the boar's head.

Of course he had known for a long time—but did it make any difference to anything? None whatever!

CHAPTER XXXI

The merchants, the wine brokers, and most of the vintagers had gone; the presses were empty and the casks full. Only the wood and the leaves remained in the vineyard, and these were brown and dry. Round the press houses and the roofed walls of the Steinberg the murk and dregs lay decaying in the sun, swarmed over by pale wasps and peculiar little flies.

The last handful of grain had been gathered from the fields, the last apple plucked from the orchards. The music of the merry-makers was stilled, for the peasants had turned to other labours of the year only a few remained to watch the fermenting of the new wine in the cellars.

The harvest was complete.

Only the sunshine remained unchanged, unclouded, undiminished, only taking on daily the deeper hue that paints the luscious tints of autumn. If it had not been for the heavy dews drought might have been feared; as it was the leaves and grass dried before their season. Where the hay had been cut for the second time the fields were like burnt gold, and the woods had taken on fiery and metallic colours—scarlet, crimson, and red yellow.

Only the strange peasants lingered, despite their talk of leaving early in order to go to some other vintage.

They had now no definite work to do. They had taken their fee and accomplished their labours, but they remained at Eberbach as if for their own pleasure. They spent a great deal of their time in the wood; Lally knew that. He was tempted to follow them, but he never did. He had not been into the wood since a day that he did not allow his memory to dwell on.

And he was well assured that the Duke did not leave Eberbach.

These young men still avoided each other, and the women lived alone in the rooms above the refectory; but on the second day after the departure of the pastor Lally, with a greater effort of will than he had for some time made, and with this problem of Pauline beating in his heavy head, sought out the Duke in the evening, when the great heat was over.

The Duke was seated at the harpsichord playing over old airs; he had the manner of one waiting. The room was most quiet, as if filled with the very essence of sleep.

The Duke looked completely pale, thinner, too, Lally thought, even ill, yet even more than usually serene and aloof. He smiled at Lally and ceased his playing.

He had put aside the heavy braided coat, and his slender figure was covered to the waist by the thin lawn shirt; only his cravat was loose, leaving his throat bare between the frills. His hair was unpowdered and falling free. He seemed very young—a boy.

He looked at Lally without malice or surprise.

"The splendour of the harvest has fatigued you," he said.

"Do I also look weary?" asked Lally, conscious of some haggard looks.

"There has been almost too much sun, too rich a vintage," replied the Duke. "The whole world seems stained with wine and to smell of ripe fruit. Every night I dream of apples tumbling into bins and grapes crushed into the press."

"You dream of nights?" questioned Lally, leaning over the harpsichord.

"I dream, yes, but it is difficult to know which are the dreams. The woods are so full of curious things."

"The woods!" cried Lally sharply. "But you do not go into the woods; you are here all day. I know that."

"All day," repeated the Duke vaguely.

"And at night you dream—you have just said so." The Duke's fingers strayed over the keyboard.

"The harvest is over now," continued Lally, with an accent of fear, "and you are free to return to Wiesbaden, Highness."

"The boar," said the Duke, "comes to-night with all his troop."

"The boar!" cried Lally, with wild laughter. "What fairy tale is this?"

"I mean the boar of Eberbach, who persuaded St. Bernard to build this place and who has never left it, hardly for a day, since, save to go into the woods where the gods dwell. They always come for the harvest, and when they go they take someone with them."

Lally laughed again; it had a mournful sound in the quiet chamber.

"You babble, poor youth!" he said.

"Are you afraid?" asked the Duke serenely.

Lally lowered his voice.

"Are not you?"

"Why should I be? It is more wonderful than anything I ever dreamed of."

"It is a dream."

"A dream?"

"A dream."

The Duke sighed. A little breeze rippled in through the open window and faintly stirred the heavy curtains of the massive bed. At the faint stir this made Lally quickly turn his head and gave the corner a fearful glance.

"Listen," he said thickly, "there is Pauline. We must think of Pauline. Herr Sandemann has gone, and she is left to our charge."

"Pauline?" repeated the Duke vaguely. He was different now indeed to the anguished young man of the interview in the press house, whose whole soul had seemed to hang on this one name—Pauline!

"You should have married her," continued Lally heavily, "but now the pastor is not here."

"Has he taken the Bible?" interrupted the Duke, with sudden sharpness.

He leant forward across the harpsichord; the light was beginning to fade, and his sudden animation gave his face a sharp, foxy look.

"What do you know about the Bible?" demanded Lally, moving back.

"Luy told me."

"You have been seeing Luy?"

"Isn't he—"

Lally interrupted.

"You must not talk of it, or think of it. Herr Jesus! we must leave Eberbach."

The Duke shivered.

"For me it is too late. I would rather go with them."

"Speak reason—speak words of good omen," cried Lally. "Will you wait to be lured to those places that are neither heaven nor hell nor earth, to wander as the victims of the Willis, the nixie, or the Heerwisch?"

The Duke did not reply; it seemed as if he had not heard Lally's words. The twilight was closing in and it seemed that, after the heat of the day, the chamber was suddenly chill. Lally felt his body relax, his senses dull; only by a great effort, like that by which a man swooning under a drug will keep his senses for a little while by fixing them on some tangible object, did he keep his mind on Pauline—Pauline.

"She is going to be your wife," he said, "your wife."

The Duke repeated "Wife?" as if the word was unfamiliar to him. Lally thought that many of the terms and symbols used by humanity were becoming strange to him now.

"I speak of Pauline," added Lally, but wearily. He felt how useless it all was; also, what a matter of indifference. A great star had appeared in the square of pellucid sky framed by the window. Looking at that like a crystal twinkling with many colours, Lally felt that nothing mattered.

"Well, good-night," he said.

He glanced towards the bed, now almost obscured by the shadows that began to deepen in the corners. Surely a foot and ankle gleamed, like silver under water, through the transparent shade, as if someone lying carelessly asleep there, had thrust out a delicate limb beneath the folds of the faded damask.

"She is here," whispered Lally, and the Duke looked up with an air of expectancy. The wind blew with a stronger gust, stirring the curtain with a quick movement, and the foot was gone.

"My fancy," muttered Lally, "and the shadows. Good-night, again."

He sighed, hesitated, then, still striving to hold to that tangible image of Pauline, he added:

"Shall we not all go to Wiesbaden to-morrow? Yes, if we are wise."

"There is no such thing as wisdom," answered the Duke. "We are all fools."

And he looked away from Lally and out of the window at the star which seemed to be larger and swinging nearer, like a lamp in a trembling hand, and his face showed a gentle impatience for the other man's presence—indeed, for all the things of this world.

Lally left with a sudden quickening of his pace. He remembered with a curious thrill of panic that it would soon be dark and that he did not want to be out after night had fallen.

A strong, colourless light still held as he passed the vineyard, which lay stripped and bare, brown and dry; the air, however, was still full of the savour of the wine.

At the door of the press house stood two of the strangers—he whose name Lally did not know and the other who called himself Gereon.

These two youths, serene and beautiful in the half-light, with bare arms and feet splashed with grape-juice, glanced at Lally with a calm more menacing than any threat. He hurried on.

As he passed the great gate of the Steinberg two of the other peasants, Hoddeken and Vatermann, came out from the vineyard, carrying on their shoulders the long trail of a dead vine which had been violently uprooted.

They directly crossed Lally's path, and he could not choose but speak.

"A dead vine! That is a rare thing for the Steinberg!"

"It had been ailing for some time; indeed, it never flourished," replied the peasant, Vatermann, "and now it is dead: dead! See!"

He thrust into Lally's hand a branch of the vine, which crackled into dust between his fingers.

"This is not a Riesling? I remember it—the great vine in the corner. It was pointed out to me for some reason, I forget what."

"It was the plant the monks used for the sacramental wine," replied the peasant, and he and his companion went on with their dead burden.

Lally hurried away. He looked up at the star, and the sight of it seemed to reassure him. The woods were still just visible against the light violet of the sky. In this dusk their hot and vivid autumn colours were hidden; they appeared dark as when Lally had first seen them, and seemed to have again the fantastic shape of a beast crouching to spring into the valley below.

Lally hastened through the cloister garden. The flowers were all fallen and the herbs all plucked. He lingered by the door of the laboratory; it was quiet and very desolate; the red roses were withered from the window, and only the bare thorns and dead leaves laced across the casement. The odour of musk, tonquin, and neroli still clung to the threshold.

Lally hurried on his way. As he passed the boar's head he saw that it was hung with a garland of autumn berries. Everything was so still that he paused to listen.

Not a sound from the prisoners, the maniacs, the soldiers; no one seemed abroad.

He went to his room and called for Luy. There was no answer, nor had he really expected one.

He lit the lantern and all the candles that he could find, and then hesitated, peering about the room and down the corridor.

Nothing.

He crossed himself from some long-dormant instinct and left the room, taking with him the lantern.

With a nervous step he hastened to the women's quarters, where Gertruda was imprisoned. The lamps were lit as usual and everything seemed in order.

Of late Lally had ordered a guard to be set here at night. He saw the man now, prone on the floor, heavily asleep. Lally did not wake him.

Proceeding cautiously down the long corridor, he paused before the door of Gertruda's cell.

It was wide open. He could see the little square of window that just framed the great star.

He looked in; she was not there; the cell was redolent of the scent of rose and grape and lily, and quite empty. It seemed to him that a white bird fluttered somewhere out of the reach of the lantern beams, but he was not sure.

He went back to his room, cautiously, softly; he did not reason or wonder. Feeling deeply drowsy, he went to sleep flung across his bed in his uniform, but he remembered to unbuckle his sword and put the hilt of it near his hand—it was the only cross he had.

CHAPTER XXXII

Lally woke and lay still, gazing into the darkness. He knew at once that during his sleep everything had changed; that what they had all been waiting for had come.

Just as some dweller on a marshy coast, who daily sees the ocean and knows the peril of it, yet never thinks of it, wakes some night to hear the waves lapping against his window and knows that he is doomed; just as a sick man, lulled by the length of a tedious illness into thinking no more of death, all at once finds the moment come in which he must die, so did Lally, who had long known of the mysteries and awful forces that surrounded him, know that now the hour had come when they were unbound from whatever restraint had held them, and upon him.

Something was pouring into the old building through every window and every door; something was filling it from cellar to roof—something that filled him with panic fear, and yet was alluring him, calling him.

He put his hands to his face and felt the cold sweat there; his soul fumbled for some assistance.

"Christ—Jesus," he said.

He listened.

There were voices everywhere, and the sound of feet and hoofs, and winged things continually passed the bed; sometimes so heavily that Lally was shaken, sometimes so lightly that he felt a mere quiver of movement.

And yet there was nothing there; his outer senses knew nothing save darkness and silence. He flung out his hands and circled empty space, though fingertips and sweeping hair touched his face.

He put his feet to the ground, grasped his sword, and called his servant; but he knew quite well that there would be no answer; knew that he should never see Luy again.

They were crowding, pressing all about him; hurrying, they seemed to him; yet as he made his way from the bed to the door nothing impeded him—the room seemed empty.

The corridor was full of them. *They* had invaded and overwhelmed the whole building; *they* were in complete possession now, without disguise or subterfuge. Lally moved slowly, grasping his sword, fumbling in the darkness. He wondered why he had been enabled to break the enchantment that held all the others asleep. Without conscious volition he went downstairs and out into the orchard.

There were a few stars abroad, but the night was cloudy and dark—seemed too full of dark yet stifling vapours, like the emanations of a marsh. A low wisp of fire flickered here and there among the orchard trees. "Heerwisch," thought Lally.

A shrill, thin piping, like the voice of a single reed, pierced the darkness; it appeared to come from the direction of the vineyard.

Lally shivered to hear this unearthly note, more ancient than music, more enduring than humanity, that rose and fell with a passionless menace. Lally looked up at the stars; these also seemed far away and unfriendly, and he to be adrift in an alien world.

There were so many of them—in the dry grass, lurking under the stripped trees—that he did not dare proceed, but stood with his back against the building, as if that afforded him some protection.

He thought of the vineyard and the temple near by, and the Duke in his lonely apartment, and Gertruda's cell, with the door standing ajar and the great star looking in through the tiny square of the window.

The piping shrank to a low whimpering, like something tired of waiting for its prey. Lally turned in the direction of the vineyard.

Then he paused, hesitating.

Surely the piping came from the wood, not the vineyard. Wherever it was he must follow it. Was it not a call to the altar of Bacchus or Mithras, where he should once more find Freia and the boar?

The trail of frail light glanced across his path. Lally began to follow it; the Heerwisch would be the guide to where the pipe played.

He went quickly after the dancing globe of frail fire that now kept deliberately in his path. The night was warmer and heavily scented with the perfume of the grape; he felt that they were all urging him on to follow the will o' the wisp.

Then someone caught hold of him, flung arms round his waist and held him still; he knew at once the touch of common humanity.

"Who are you—abroad to-night?" he asked hoarsely.

"Pauline," came the woman's voice, "Pauline."

He had forgotten Pauline; the name sounded unfamiliar; he was annoyed that she prevented his following the will o' the wisp.

"Listen," he said. "I must go up to the woods. Do you understand? The Heerwisch is guiding me."

"I see nothing," she answered quickly, "yet certainly there is something evil abroad to-night. That is why I came to find you."

"Do you not hear the piping?" asked Lally.

"No; there is only an awful stillness."

"*Do you not feel them—everywhere*, Pauline?"

"Yes, but you will not go with them; you will stay with me."

She put her arms along his shoulders now and drew his head down until his cheek touched hers. This gave him a curious sensation; the light of Heerwisch grew dimmer, and the call of the pipe fainter. The touch of her warm humanity gave him a certain strength. He breathed more freely; the air seemed less oppressive. He could just see the shape and substance of her as she leant against him.

"It is the Duke you should have gone to find," he said.

"I only care for you," replied Pauline; "the only man I could save to-night was my lover. You were once—and never another. That is something between us. There is no love now, I know—"

He interrupted.

"Oh, Pauline, Pauline! What has happened? I think we have all been wicked! Pauline, I am lost now. I must go with them; there is no hope. I think they make a sacrifice in the woods. They will slay me across Freia's knees, and the boar will lap my blood. This will crown the vintage of the gods."

"You are distraught with these strange happenings," said Pauline, and he felt her tears on his face. "Come with me to the little chapel."

But he struggled with her, knowing he must follow the piping and the dancing light. Pauline was strong and held him tightly. His sword fell down between them; Lally felt weak and faint; he was conscious that something—an animal—was leaping up at him, snapping at his hand, at his throat; that the red eyes of Luy were looking at him out of the visage of a boar; that the white form of Gertruda, showing at the flowing open of the Madonna's blue robe, was before him, and that she beckoned him with star wreathed head—and yet, all the while, he knew that the human woman held him fast.

A great wind blew, and he lost sense of time and space; a vast eternity, in which a lifetime seemed but a twinkling, enveloped him. He felt his feet on the edge of plumbless abysses, measureless skies above him. Nothing mattered but sleep.

He was thus far on the paths that humanity dreads to even dream of when the woman, who must have surely loved him, staved his steps, so that he became conscious, though with agony, of her fleshly presence, of her hard grip of him and her tears, and so with deep pangs of spirit shuddered back to the earth, and found himself standing there with her in the withered orchard beneath the broken clouds that showed the stars.

And nothing had happened.

There was only Pauline, weeping to be comforted, a woman, poor creature, after all.

"*They have gone,*" said Lally.

They said no more, for both were very weary. He led her to the refectory through a world that began to glimmer with the soft fires of the dawn, and though neither had thought much of these things before, they spent the short time till daylight in the Lutheran chapel, where the Baroness already kept vigil on her knees.

With the stir of life in Eberbach came the news both expected. The strange vintagers had gone, and the girl Gertruda, and Luy—and the Duke.

This last the searchers found, but not alive, and scarcely in human shape. His fate was clear; he had ventured into the forest after dusk and been slain and mangled by a wild boar. Lally saw that the poor remains were honoured by burial beside that other Prince of Nassau in the cathedral church, but he dare say no Christian rites over the grave. Shaken free of these poor bones and flesh, the young man wandered in some region of which it was best not to think.

It was certain that he would return for the next vintage in the train of the old gods, following Freia and Luy the boar—nay, it was likely that he was here now, somewhere, and would never again leave Eberbach. But Lally and Pauline returned to the world, loving each other at last in a kind and human fashion.

For more Tales of the Weird titles
visit the British Library Shop (shop.bl.uk)

We welcome any suggestions, corrections or feedback you may have,
and will aim to respond to all items addressed to the following:

The Editor (Tales of the Weird), British Library Publishing,
The British Library, 96 Euston Road, London NW1 2DB

We also welcome enquiries through our Twitter account, @BL_Publishing.